Careful What You Wish For

A NOVEL

Myrlin A. Hermes

SIMON & SCHUSTER

SIMON & SCHUSTER
Rockefeller Center
1230 Avenue of the Americas
New York, NY 10020

SIMON & SCHUSTER and colophon are registered
trademarks of Simon & Schuster Inc.
Designed by Barbara M. Bachman
Manufactured in the United States of America

1   3   5   7   9   10   8   6   4   2

Library of Congress Cataloging-in-Publication Data
Hermes, Myrlin A. (Myrlin Ambrosia)
Careful what you wish for : a novel / Myrlin A. Hermes
p. ; cm.
I. Title.
PS3558.E6863C37   1999
813'.54—dc21   98-44503
CIP
ISBN 0-684-84932-1

For my mother

Acknowledgments

THIS BOOK WOULD NEVER HAVE COME INTO BEING without the guidance and help, at various stages, from Tom Gillchrist and Laurie Chittenden, and from Laurie Liss, who took a chance on me and kept my feet on the ground. Thanks also to my family, both blood and *hanai* and to all of my unrelated sisters. And for reminding me of passion in writing and life, I owe Ozi an unpayable debt.

*A*bove the tiny whistle-stop station that marks the town of Liberty, a bubble of memory hovers, repeating through the years; a woman steps down from the train onto the wooden platform. There is a screech of wheels behind her as the train pulls away, sliding south like a river or a snake through the grass, abandoning her to the town. She does not look back, but her fear and hope are so palpable and true that the sound of her heartbeat crystallizes in the crisp early-morning air, preserving the emotion perfectly, keeping the moment in case it is needed again. Nothing is ever lost in Liberty, not even time.

She carries a piece of paper like a passport, clutched so tightly in her fist that her knuckles have turned white, though it could be just an illusion—the way the morning light hits the fear radiating from her skin. She will show it as explanation to anyone who questions her right to be here. She reads the paper again, but most of the words are meaningless by now and do nothing to calm her. Only one word sparks her mind—Liberty. She folds the paper back into her hand and continues through the tall, damp grass, toward the town.

The sun is rising quickly now, and her shadow stretches out before her. She hurries, but she will not overtake it. She is walking into the future. She is walking into the past.

1963. Gossip travels more slowly through Liberty these days. Time was, it flew from person to person, carried on the threads that linked each soul invisibly, invincibly to a dozen others. Everyone was related somehow—by blood or marriage or the sort of deep friendship or enmity that grows to be stronger than blood or marriage, and news didn't even need to be spoken aloud, but traveled along those ties that wove the town together like a fine piece of handmade lace.

They did not need to be told the history of the town; it was inborn, rarely spoken, though sometimes a stranger passing through would ask how the town got its name. When in 1872 a lady carpetbagger stepped off the train, she spoke of the irony of slavery in a place called Liberty. The crowd stared at her blankly. They'd forgotten that the word had any meaning other than the two thousand acres of farmland and thin strip of road that made up the town.

The carpetbagger, Helena Blackmar, had come to ensure that voting rights were upheld, only to find that in this tiny, remote town, the slaves hadn't even been told they were free. A crack of frustration crept into her voice, and she waved the paper in her hand like a flag while her young son dug a toe into the dirt. "This is a copy of the fifteenth amendment to the Constitution," she said. "Do you understand what that means?"

The people shrugged and remained silent. You couldn't reason with a woman like that. She finally shut her mouth and stared at them until the veins popped out purple against her pale city skin.

"Who is in charge here, anyway?"

Finally, a question they could answer. Someone pointed the way, and, with her son in tow, Mrs. Blackmar marched up the steps of the tall white plantation house and demanded to speak to Jean Cardon.

Jean Cardon had been a French nobleman in times that, whatever their other numerous characteristics, were particularly unkind to the French nobility. Lord only knows why he fled to America instead of the Caribbean, where some people at least spoke his language, but given how quickly his neighbors came to despise him without understanding what he said, perhaps it was just as well that he didn't settle someplace where every one of his insults was understood to the letter. His harshness had served him well; his escape from France had been less a matter of cunning or luck than one of cruelty. He did not try to save family or friends, did not look back as he booked his passage under an assumed name, his grandmother's jewels sewn into the lining of his opera cloak. The man who sold him two dozen strong, tame slaves paled when the foreign gentleman pulled out a knife and slit open his coat, letting rubies flow like blood.

Did Cardon name his plantation Liberté as a sarcastic tribute to the revolutionaries who had driven him from his home? Or was he thanking God for his own freedom, his escape? No one but his slaves on Liberté ever came close enough to find out. There was no chance that the small farmers whose tiny plots of land clustered around his fields would pronounce the name correctly; they called it Liberty, and hated it so much they were willing, when the carpetbagger turned up, to give up the one or two slaves who worked beside them in their fields, if it meant getting rid of *him* as well.

No one knew what he said to Mrs. Blackmar or she to him, but his slaves continued to appear before dawn in his fields and work until long after dusk. Helena Blackmar bought for cheap a parcel of land too ravaged by Johnson grass to be any use for farm or pasture. She hired men to build a house across the lake from Cardon's tall plantation house, where she could watch the lights come on in the evening and sometimes see shadows flickering against the windows.

Helena grew herbs in her garden, made flowers spring up in soil that had choked everything but weeds. Across the lake, Cardon sickened.

"Your mother's a witch," the boys in the school yard taunted Henry Blackmar as they shoved him against a tree, punching his face, his stomach. He touched his throbbing nose and felt something warm and sticky.

"She's not a witch," he said, crumpled against the roots, but his bloody hand went to his father's cross hanging around his neck.

Cardon died, leaving no descendants unless you counted a dozen mulatto bastards, which no one did. The farmers cast suspicious eyes at the Blackmar house, but quietly split Cardon's land among themselves and freed his slaves and hunting dogs. The plantation house fell into decay until it was bought and turned into a hotel and then (when it was found that no one would pay money just to sleep in Liberty) a brothel. But by 1963, even the brothel was dying down, the aging whores as familiar and predictable to the men as their own wives.

Down ten miles of rough roads was Bradford, a mill town. It had a movie theater and high school and a drugstore with a soda fountain. The folks in Liberty thought of Bradford as urban. It was the only city that many of them had ever seen, and though in the back of their minds there was an awareness of places like New York and Boston and Paris, heaven had always seemed much clearer and more attainable.

In 1963 those cities didn't seem so far away, though. More and more young people were moving away, and stories once known innately now needed to be spoken aloud. The woman slapping whitewash onto the railings of her porch could feel it. She had given birth to five children, and except for the oldest in the cemetery behind the church and the youngest lying on her stomach in the backyard, every single one of them was gone, married away or off to college and never come back except to visit. And even the youngest was dreaming of escape from Liberty. Who could blame them? The fabric of the town was unraveling.

The arrival of someone new could still be felt in the air, though, a slight disturbance as the town tried to decide where the newcomer belonged. The woman on the porch felt the ripples even before she heard the whistle blowing at the station that afternoon, and in the dripping whitewash there was an expectancy, a question that once would have been answered almost before it had had a chance to form in her mind. As it was, she didn't know until she saw the figure with her own eyes (in trousers, and her hair cut short as a boy's, but the pride in her walk unmistakable, even after thirteen years), and she had no one to tell until her husband came home for supper.

"Eleanor's back in town."

He looked up, his eyebrows rising in surprise. "You mean John Cline's wife?"

Even the daughter pricked her ears up then. She had only been a baby when it happened, but everyone knew the story of John Cline's wife—how her husband had taken up with a colored girl half his age and flaunted her before his wife and the whole town—but no one except John and the undertaker knew whether it was true that Eleanor had killed the girl, or the girl had killed her, or both of them had taken up and run off together like some women do. They just knew that one morning they were both gone, and John, behind the counter of the General Store as usual, was so stony-eyed and quiet no one dared risk a question.

The woman nodded. "Eleanor," she said again. She didn't say *the Blackmar girl, the last to be born with that name in Liberty.* She set the casserole dish on the table. "I expect she's in town for the funeral. She had a piece of paper looked like a telegram."

"The son got in yesterday, didn't he?" He reached to take his wife and daughter's hands for grace. With the other children gone, it was a stretch to keep their elbows from grazing the silverware. "I wonder if he's going to sell the house. It's good land, by the lake, but that place has been falling apart for years. Maybe I should talk to him about it."

"You never know." She was lost in fragments of memory. The heat of that summer, thirteen years ago. The thick scent of honeysuckle. The sound of Eleanor's laugh. "You never know," she said again, softer this time. She took her husband's hand and they bowed their heads to God.

One

1949. Summertime in Liberty was heavy that year. Heat weighed down the humid air, turning the scent of sweet gum and honeysuckle cloying and sickly. Men wiped sweat from their faces with soggy handkerchiefs and accepted glasses of cold milk from their wives and wondered when it was that the sourwood leaves had turned waxy as corpses laid out for viewing in church. And the wives leaned against the doorways and looked at their husbands and wondered, as they sipped their coffee (hot to make the air feel cooler), where the cool, carefree summers of their girlhoods had gone, and why August had turned the cold, sweet memory of July's watermelons into something sticky and thick and sluggish as blood.

Only the children didn't feel the heaviness. Boys stripped off their shirts and plunged right into the lake behind what was still called the Blackmar place, though Henry Blackmar had been dead going on fifteen years. Girls swam there, too, in old house-dresses or their brothers' shorts. And their mothers cast their eyes in the direction of the house and thought of their daughters there and drew breath through their teeth, though the Blackmar scandals, it seemed, had died along with the Blackmar name at the marriage of Henry's granddaughter, Eleanor. But no one forgot Henry's daughter Evalie, the wild one, or that her daughter, Eleanor, had no father. And now that her boy was thirteen, Eleanor had that hungry look of a woman married too long to the wrong man. Something about the Blackmar house told them that scandal never truly died, it only died down, and so the women watched the house on the hill and waited.

*S*weat bloomed on Eleanor's forehead as she took the pie out of the oven. It was too hot for pie, too hot even to think about heating up the oven, but every afternoon for fifteen years she'd made sure there was a picture-perfect pie cooling on her windowsill. Even Wednesdays, when the Sewing Circle's evening meeting gave many women a welcome excuse to serve a light supper. Even on wash days, when bacon and eggs or Sunday leftovers were the customary fare served by other women without a maid or older daughter to help them run the sheets through the wringer and hang them up to dry. Leftovers were the wages of exhaustion, and even the better-off women of the Sewing Circle, women whose fingers had not been spread too wide by driving a plow to thread a needle Wednesday nights, let it be known that some nights any dessert to be gotten would be of one's own getting, thank you very much.

But Eleanor took care to serve a full, hot supper every night, and if John did not notice that the pie placed before him was always oven fresh any more than he noticed the perpetual spotlessness of his floors, Eleanor never said a word. The women had noticed her devotion and had granted Eleanor a kind of provisional absolution.

John appeared in the doorway and wordlessly handed her the empty water glass. Beads of condensation slid down the side of the glass as she refilled it with ice water and handed it back to him, her actions and his as smooth as machinery, no need even to meet one another's eyes.

He drank the water in great gulps. "Hot as hell in here," he said.

"I just took the pie out, and the biscuits won't take but a minute. With the oven off, it'll cool down."

"What kind tonight?"

"Cherry." She made a well in the biscuit flour and poured the milk. He was still leaning against the door frame. Why hadn't he gone? Had she said something wrong?

"Apple's my favorite," he said.

"Sometimes a change is nice."

He shrugged. "For breakfast the next morning . . . ," he mumbled, his voice trailing off.

She looked up from her dough. "What?" He shook his head. "Tell Adam to get washed up for supper," she said.

It was too hot to be hungry for steak and Eleanor had burned the biscuits as well. They were not inedible or even burned particularly badly, but there was a definite edge of black on their smooth, golden-brown bottoms, and she apologized with her eyes as she served. She did not know if John had noticed; he was always filled with wide, sweeping silences, and it was hard to tell which were specific and which were merely general. Adam, too, was silent. After meticulously scraping off every trace of the black from his biscuit, Adam ate slowly, his eyes closed and moving slightly under the lids.

"Open your eyes, honey," Eleanor said gently. "What are you doing like that at the table?"

He looked up at her. His eyes were gray, long-lashed, and too serious for a thirteen-year-old. "Rereading *Great Expectations*," he said in his soft, even voice. "It's a good book, but I didn't like the end."

"I got you that subscription to *Boy's Life*," John muttered. "Why don't you ever read that if you don't like the books you've got?"

Eleanor glanced over at John, and he met her eye. "What?" he said.

A fight hung in the air, suspended somewhere in the thickness of the heat. You only had to turn your head to catch it. Like a storm, she thought. She would keep perfectly still. "Nothing," she said. She smoothed her napkin over her lap.

"Another shipment was left off in Bradford today," he said. "*By mistake*, they keep telling me. I'll have to go pick it up on Monday morning."

Eleanor nodded. "I'll mind the store."

He stared at her, a square of meat suspended on his fork. "If I'm going into town *someone's* got to be at the store. Did you think someone else was going to volunteer?"

She looked down. "I'm sorry. Of course . . ." So it was going to be one of *those* days. Some days, weeks, nothing she did was right, so the only solution was to be as close to nothing as possible until it passed.

He shook his head and chewed on his steak. "And another thing. I won't be home for supper Wednesday night. Card game."

"But . . . my meeting," she said. He was not looking at her, concentrating instead on spearing his green beans. She spoke more forcefully. "The Sewing Circle meets on Wednesday nights. Who will be here to watch Adam?"

John's head snapped up from his plate, darting from his wife to his quiet, dark son. "Adam can take care of himself. Can't you, boy?"

Adam put a single green bean in his mouth. He looked at his father in silence for a moment before shrugging his shoulders in noncommittal agreement. He cut a thin slice from his steak, revealing the meat's pink core.

John laughed. "That's my boy!"

"Mother?" Adam sat, awaiting her approval.

"Why don't you call me Mama, darling?" she reminded gently, sugaring her voice. Adam was thirteen now, at an age when most boys would be just dropping the pet names, their last vestiges of baby talk. Jane Aston had been in tears only last month because her twelve-year-old daughter had started calling her "Ma" instead of "Mommy," and Eleanor, whose son had not called her anything but "Mother" since he was two years old, had felt a slight twinge. It was not regret, exactly; she regarded the playful, physical relationships between other women and their children with something that should have been envy, but was, in fact, a mild curiosity—like an anthropologist might feel, studying with interest but without emotion how these people raised their young.

He rolled his eyes. "Mama," he said.

"I'll ask around after church tomorrow to see if someone can come stay with you," she said. John looked up and met her eye. "Your father shouldn't be gambling, anyway," she whispered.

John stood up so suddenly his chair clattered to the floor. "And you shouldn't be spending time with those gossipy bitches," he said. "I'll do whatever I damn well please with my evenings. Don't I spend every day at the store?"

Her throat was too tight to answer. She nodded.

"Do you think I enjoy it? Do you think I get up in the morning and go over there because I want to? Or because I don't have a choice, huh? What do you think?"

He was waiting for her to answer. She wouldn't, though. She stared at the table, and eventually felt his eyes move off her.

"I'm done with dinner. I'm going out." His voice was soft but his feet were heavy and the front door slammed behind him.

Eleanor sat a minute in silence, trying not to let out the tears that were threatening. It was normal, just one of those days when he was impossible. For days, weeks even, everything would be fine, undisturbed. Some days without warning he would sweep through the house casting off sparks of affection like candies at Christmastime, and her heart would leap to catch them, though her body knew better.

Adam was watching her. She cleared her throat. "I guess your father's had a hard day," she said brightly. "Do you want dessert?"

"I'm not hungry."

Eleanor nodded. Her stomach had drawn in on itself, tight as pursed lips. "Go play, then," she said. He nodded, and walked solemnly upstairs.

She had never seen him actually play in his life. Even as a young child, five, six years old, he would sit at the kitchen table with his crayons, coloring with a studious, worried expression on his face, as if the wax never came out *quite* the right color. When he was older, he would send away for model kits from the catalogs John kept in the store for special orders and spend hours in his room with a knife and glue, cutting things apart and putting them back together again, not pieces anymore, but something whole. It amazed her what he could do with bits of wood.

There was something about him, though, that wasn't quite right. His teachers noticed it; their reports all agreed he was bright, but "odd." But what could she do? He was bright, polite, behaved himself. She kept him fed and clothed and made sure he did his homework. What more could she do? She loved her son, but ever since he had stopped being a baby and become a person, he had been a stranger, a visitor who had come out of her body to watch her from a distance, with suspicion.

It had been different when he was an infant. Adam had been born with wisps of blond hair and eyes that were blue for so long some thought they would stay that way. Women had cooed at the baby in his crib, then looked at John's dark hair and almost black eyes and given Eleanor meaningful, knowing smiles.

The women's secret looks made John angry, and Eleanor would catch him sometimes staring at the baby, frowning. She knew what he was wondering, but neither of them dared bring up the subject. For him to do so would be an accusation, for her an admission, and neither one was prepared to break the silence that way. He finally sidled up to her one evening as she was bathing Adam in the sink. He put his arm around her and fingered the wisps on Adam's head. "Any of your people got blond hair?" he asked casually.

It was a little cruelty. Not the accusation—she had been prepared for that—but the way he was trying to be kind. The Blackmars were dark-haired; he was asking about her father. A flash of memory burned Eleanor's mind—thirteen years old, and a blond head comes through her window, a man who at thirty still has the shadow of his boy-self, the sound of his feet alighting on the windowsill merely a long-delayed echo.

Are you my father? She steps toward him, into the shadow. A hand reaches for her, slides into the crevice between her hair and neck.

Oh God, you're just like Evalie. Had he spoken, or had she heard it with her secret ears, the ones that heard what grown-ups said but not aloud, the ones that frightened them? The difference hardly mattered now, because she had screamed at what she had heard or *heard*, and whether it was the scream or the blast from grandfather's shotgun she never knew, but one of them had deafened her secret ears forever.

The baby cried out, and Eleanor let go of the wrist she had grasped without thinking. White marks from her fingers slowly faded into his damp pink skin. She felt John tense behind her, still waiting for her to speak. He was asking her to remember, to allow that memory in with the others, ones that could be spoken. She fingered the chain at her neck and Jesus danced with his cross.

"No," she said finally. John shook his head and pulled away. Something closed, and she instantly stopped minding the way he looked at her, eyes hooded with disappointment at what they saw.

Instead, she spent more time with the baby. She told him stories of her lonely childhood in a house everyone said was haunted, told him how even now memory clung to everything in the house, how she was afraid to look too long at anything for fear that she would be rooted to the spot, paralyzed by generations of grief. She folded sheets and stacked dishes carefully, touching them, noticing them as little as possible. The shatter of china could loose shards of history. Only Adam was new, was safe. He was hers.

She did not coo baby syllables at him but instead held long conversations, pausing to imagine his answers. She was falling in love with him with a closeness, a completeness she had never felt with her husband. She loved their time alone, knew no better than to love even the sleeplessness of the late-night, early-morning feedings. The exhaustion was like a drunkenness that left everything hazy, dreamlike. He would wake her with his rising, floating cries, and she would leave her bed and creep down the hall to offer her bared breast. She stood there, cradling him in her arms and feeling the pull of his mouth send shivers through her nipple as she watched the stars fade and the sky turn her favorite colors in the world.

John began staying out late, and as often as not, when he came home, he slept on the cot in the spare room downstairs. The first few times he'd mumbled the next morning about not wanting to disturb her, but when he saw that she did not care, had not even questioned with her eyes about where he'd been, he fell into silence again.

One morning she looked up from nursing to find John standing in the doorway, watching them. She started, pulling Adam's mouth from her nipple as though she'd been caught in something furtive. He moved toward her, and she set the baby down in his crib. There were tears in his eyes, and she thought he was going to kiss her; instead, he reached for her breast, closing his teeth around her milky nipple. She tried to pull away and he grasped her tighter. She smelled whiskey, felt a day's rough growth of beard.

His hand never leaving her breast, he steered her firmly to their bed where he took her, his mouth moving jealously from one nipple to the next as if angry that he could not have both at once. The sex was their first since the baby's birth, and Eleanor bit her lip in pain as he entered her, but she kept silent. As if by agreement, neither spoke a word.

It was over quickly. When John was snoring, his face half-buried in the pillow beside her, she slipped from the bed and crept to the baby's room. She sat for a long time leaning against the crib, tears running in long streaks down her face, arms drawn around her sticky thighs.

Eventually, the baby woke, fussy. She offered him one tender nipple, but in his mouth she felt a sharp pain. She gasped and pulled him away from her breast, and running a finger along his gumline, she felt the beginnings of a tooth.

"That means it's time to wean them," the reverend's wife had said, and the others had nodded their heads in silent agreement. Almost immediately, Adam began to change. The blond baby-wisps that had barely grown since his birth gradually fell out and were replaced by thick, dark curls. The blue faded until his eyes were left a serious greenish-gray.

By the time he was a year old, the whispers and sidelong looks had been replaced by loud remarks of how "he barely looks like Eleanor at all," so strongly did the Cline baby take after his fa-ther's side. Everyone seemed slightly embarrassed by their previ-ous suspicions; the reverend's wife even asked Eleanor to join her weekly Sewing Circle. Eleanor gratefully accepted, and so she be-came the first Blackmar woman to sit at Mrs. Fay's family quilt-ing frame since her great-grandmother Helena had sewn sloppy stitches and spoken with more passion than was seemly for a woman with that many eyes on her. But Eleanor kept quiet and murmured at the gossip and laughed at the jokes, and everyone called her Mrs. Cline, as if the Blackmar blood had been forgot-ten at last.

John relaxed then, too, and he began bringing the baby in his basket to the store. He set him up with the merchandise on the counter, where he would announce loudly to everyone who came in "Have you met my boy, Adam? Yessir, this is my son. Helping me mind the store he is today." He also began spending more evenings at home and sleeping in Eleanor's bed, but in the months of their silent separation, a wall had been built up between them, seamless and unscalable.

$\mathcal{D}$ay in Liberty is determined not by clocks or the sun but by the birds. Dawn is when the cock crows, even if the paleness in the east is fainter than moonlight and the sleepy cows must be milked by the twinkling of the stars. Lamps wink on in kitchens as the stars fade from the sky; breakfast is yellow light and rose-gold clouds and songbirds—robins in the spring, the speckled cry of chickadees on winter mornings as the hands come in from milking to be unstiffened by the stove. By the time the sun has peeked over the distant hills, the birds are pecking at the freshly sown fields for seeds or diving to snatch the insects out of the crops. There is no place for beauty—whether they eat crops or the insects that eat the crops is what separates the good birds from the bad, and boys (and a few incorrigible girls) learn early on which ones they may kill with their stones.

Sometimes a woman, her heart softened by a prosperous year or a new baby, will take pity on the cardinals and the blue jays. She secretly considers them the most beautiful and bold of all the birds, and she will throw them the leftover biscuit crumbs from breakfast. They descend in swarms of color, all squabble and shriek, then rise again as the sun clears the tops of the farthest trees. When they can see their shadows, morning is over, and day has begun.

The sun was rising in the sky when Eleanor stepped down from the cab of the truck. She turned to wave goodbye, but John was already pulling down the road, disappearing in a crunch of gravel and a cloud of dust. She fit her key into the lock, feeling as always a little thrill as the door swung open to reveal the dark shelves and shadows of the store. It was not novelty; she had wandered through the labyrinth of shelves, running hands over the bags of flour and bolts of cloth since she was a child and her grandfather had stood behind the impossibly tall counter in front. Sometimes the old man would watch her fingering the cloth, memorizing the feel of cotton gauze, of gingham, of heavenly velvet, until she could tell them apart with just the brush of a fingertip. When he smiled, she knew she could approach and perhaps ask, in her softest Sunday-school voice, for a piece of licorice.

"That's your favorite?" he would say, reaching into one of the glass jars on the counter. "Evalie always loved the rock candy." His voice would waver a little and his eyes go slick, like glass. "And peppermint. At Christmastime, the peppermints."

Eleanor would suck on the licorice, and if she held perfectly still, out of the corner of her eye she could see Evalie. She was always Eleanor's age—at six carrying a doll almost as large as she was, at eight wearing an old-fashioned dress the same rose color as her flushed cheeks, ribbons sliding out of her tousled hair as she breezed through the store, grabbing handfuls of whatever she wanted out of the jars. Sometimes she would notice Eleanor and frown quizzically as she sucked on a peppermint stick or popped five caramels into her mouth at once, but whenever Eleanor looked at her straight on, she disappeared. Eleanor never told anyone—her grandfather grew sad at the mention of Evalie, and anyone else would have slapped her for telling tales.

Evalie had been a specter of her childhood; as soon as Eleanor was old enough to stand behind the counter and make change and reach into whichever jars she pleased, the girl had disappeared, and so had Eleanor's taste for sweets. Now when Eleanor tended store for John, as she did perhaps a half-dozen times a year, she barely glanced at the candy jars. She would bring her knitting along to work on while she stood behind the counter, setting it aside to pencil down how many bags of sugar or yards of cloth were sold. She liked working in the store, and everyone always seemed pleased and surprised, though not to any extremes, to see her there.

"Well, if it isn't Miz Cline! What, is John out East again?" John went to Boston every year on a shopping trip for the store, causing among the women in the town a seasonal mumble of pity for Eleanor, who had never been fifty miles from Liberty and could at least have been invited along for a vacation, they said, shaking their heads at the blind selfishness of men.

"No," she said, "just Bradford. A shipment was left off there by mistake."

He shook his head. "Ha, that's what they tell you. Probably just didn't want to take the time, come the extra ten miles off the highway. Make you go get it yourself, like your time's any less valuable than theirs." It was Bill Johnston, buying coffee beans and baking powder. His wife had died four years ago and since then nothing had been cooked in his house but coffee and biscuits. He ate supper nightly with one of his two married daughters, let the dust gather on the furniture, and stubbornly refused all suggestions that he remarry.

"Well, perhaps." Eleanor counted the change into the palm of his hand.

"That's just the way it is nowadays. Well, see you at church on Sunday, Miz Cline."

A woman had come in while Eleanor was totaling the sale. She was sitting on the floor in front of the shelf of men's leather boots, turning them over to size them against her feet. Her back was toward Eleanor, but something about her hair, loose and curly and coppery brown, seemed familiar. Eleanor's memory was stubborn; it was not until she saw the small wicker suitcase on the floor beside the girl that she remembered where she'd seen that hair before.

It had been—what, three, four months ago? She remembered the blanket she had been working on, yellow with a blue stripe. When had she finished it? Days were so alike—time could only be measured in seasons, in knitting, in marriages and births, in deaths and how long the grief remained afterward. The girl who had come into the store that day had seemed sophisticated, urbane, not at all the sort to be sitting on the floor to try on men's shoes. She had been dressed in a neat dove gray traveling suit, and her curly copper hair had been done up under a fine hat in a violet velvet that was dangerously close to being outright purple. She was not from around here, that was certain. Something in her profile, too, had seemed odd, foreign in a way Eleanor could not quite place. Was she from Europe? Italian, maybe, or Greek? Eleanor was not quite sure she would even be able to tell the difference. A picture drifted across her mind of some sultry seaside where the people were dark and passionate. It was a scene that served her imagination equally well for either country.

Eleanor had ached to engage her in conversation, but the girl carefully avoided her eyes, browsing the aisles slowly, picking up a can to look at the label, running her fingers over the merchandise with a vague, uncurious leisure. Eleanor recognized the look, knew that if the girl bought anything at all, it would be something small and unnecessary. She would barely notice herself what her hand grasped—she would be purchasing her few minutes in the store.

"Can I help you find anything?" Eleanor asked.

The girl looked up, startled by the voice. Eleanor had been unprepared for her eyes. Haunted, cat-yellow, and red-rimmed, they were the eyes of someone lost, desperate. Eleanor had seen that look on girls driven almost to madness by unrequited love, but in their eyes, there was always a glimmer of hope, the knowledge that one word or even a smile from him could transform their wretchedness into unimaginable glory. Behind this girl's eyes, there was only emptiness. She moved like someone uncomfortable in her own body, with the coltish awkwardness of a thirteen-year-old, though she looked to be at least five years older than that. She unfolded a piece of paper crumpled in her hand. "I just arrived on the train today," she said. Her voice was hesitant, but melodic, educated with a slight New England accent. "I'm supposed to be . . . visiting someone, but I seem to be lost. Can you help me?"

The paper had an address written on it. Feminine handwriting, but bold and unhesitating. Eleanor examined it carefully.

"Across the railroad tracks, 'bout half a mile."

The young woman had nodded and began a smile, but before she could finish it, she was gone, closing the door so softly that the bell didn't even jingle behind her.

The girl sitting now on her floor had none of the hesitant awkwardness of that woman of three or four months ago, but Eleanor did not doubt that it was she. Strangers were rare enough in Liberty. Oh certainly, people came to visit—relatives would gather for birthdays or special occasions, and sometimes a town boy would bring his bride back from whatever distant county he'd courted her. But those people weren't strangers, not really. They were family, and they slipped into life in Liberty as easily as if places had been saved for them.

"May I help you?"

She turned, and when Eleanor saw the yellow eyes, it erased any shade of doubt she'd had that it was the same girl who had come in before. Her skin was a couple of shades darker, true, but nothing that the sun couldn't have done, and its color made sense of the "foreignness" Eleanor had seen in her face—the slight curve in the nose, the shadow at the lip. A colored girl. Eleanor started, embarrassed not to have seen it before. Of course, the address written on that scrap of paper had been in the colored part of town. She just hadn't thought about it, too startled by those eyes to think of such things. She flushed, wondering if the girl had been able to tell by the tone in her voice that Eleanor had thought she was white.

But in the next instant, Eleanor wasn't sure that she wasn't, that the Negro features in the girl's face hadn't been just a trick of the light. She had selected the boots she wanted and was smiling at Eleanor as she strode toward the counter.

"These," she said. She picked up a small bottle of caramel-colored perfume. "And this. And some cloth. I'll need to make some clothes." She was wearing a pair of long purple pants (*Pants?* thought Eleanor, *in the middle of town and at this time in the afternoon?*) and a silk blouse with tails hanging loose around her hips. She did not wear a bra, and Eleanor could clearly see the dark circles of her nipples through the white silk. She tried not to stare as she led the girl to the bolts of cloth at the back of the store.

"This makes lovely *dresses*," she said, unwinding a light cotton floral print, but the girl was fingering a bolt of wine-red velvet.

"This one is beautiful. How much is this?"

"That?" Eleanor touched the velvet. "That one's mainly used for upholstery, around here. Or sometimes someone requests it as a coffin lining." There wasn't much call for red velvet clothing in Liberty—too fine for everyday wear, too indulgent for church.

Eleanor didn't even know why John kept it in stock, though nearly every woman in town paused to stroke it longingly before picking out their yards of practical gingham.

"I'll take six yards," she said. Eleanor began to unroll and measure the cloth, but the girl was already looking through the other bolts. "And this, I'll want some of this."

Eleanor took the black silk out of her hands. "Where did you get this?" she whispered. She hadn't seen it in years, had sworn that the remnants of black cloth had disappeared into thin air. And now this girl had pulled from air and memory the silk, left over from the mourning dresses. She had almost forgotten. The dresses had instantly gone limp in the damp air as the clouds gathered for the legendary twenty-eight days of rain that followed her grandfather's funeral.

The memory came down on her suddenly, like the heavy clouds. Her grandmother had not shivered at all as she stood in front of her husband's grave. Others had shifted on their feet, stealing glances at the widow or the sky. Women saw the extravagance of silk mourning dresses, when few of them had had a new dress in years, and if so, homemade, pieced together from the cloth of last year's fashions. Alice Blackmar had spared no expense in creating for herself a gown that, except for its color, would have been more appropriate for a young debutante than a widow. The décolletage was embarrassingly low for a woman nearing seventy, and her wrinkling cleavage, tightly corseted into existence, mocked the small gold cross that hung between her breasts.

Eleanor's dress had been a copy of her grandmother's, as simple as she could persuade the old woman to make it. It was not the style of the dress that shamed her, or even the material, as expensive and impractical as it was, but the newness. It was the newness that turned the simple dress gaudy and narrowed eyes as they briefly touched on her.

The silk had held on to the memory, and Eleanor felt it all again, the shame as her grief was drowned out by embarrassment, her hot cheeks and the sting of the first cold droplets of a torrential downpour that was to last for weeks. She felt ill. "You don't want this," she said. "There isn't even enough left here for a proper dress."

"I'll make something with it." The girl touched the silk. "And look at how it takes to body heat. I feel like it belongs to me." She looked up and Eleanor saw that her eyes were still sharp, not with loss anymore but with a kind of high light, an intense freedom. Her skin looked new—unwrinkled, and flushed and glowing, as if underneath there were not flesh and bone but instead a film of gold. She radiated light; the silk, aged into a pattern of fine spiderweb lines, absorbed it, drew it in until it became invisible, until the wearer seemed more naked than if wearing nothing at all. It did belong to her.

"I'll wrap it up," Eleanor said.

"It's beautiful." The girl leaned in close to stroke the cloth. She smelled sweet, like violets and vanilla and rosemary. How could one imagine covering a scent like that with perfume? Eleanor wrapped the silk and placed it in the bag, nestling the small, caramel-colored bottle. The velvet went on top, covering the whole package like a shroud.

"Do you want it delivered, or will you take it with you?"

The girl looked surprised. "Oh, could I get it delivered? I walked here and it's a ways back." She took the pen Eleanor offered and wrote, in clear, bold handwriting *Natalie Joseph, The Victoria Hotel, Liberty.*

The whorehouse? Of course—what other kind of woman would wear purple slacks and no brassiere out shopping in the middle of the afternoon? Eleanor pulled her mouth into a small smile of distaste. The girl laughed at the look. "Oh, I'm just a boarder," she said, and again Eleanor was unsure that she had not misjudged her. She sounded more refined than Francine Cartwright, who had been to a girls' college in Philadelphia. She handed Eleanor a crisp twenty-dollar bill, and as Eleanor was counting out the change the door banged shut. Eleanor called out to stop her, but the girl was gone. She slipped the change into an envelope and nestled it in between folds of velvet. She picked up the piece of paper the girl had left. Natalie Joseph—was that the name of a white woman, or colored? She remembered the purple pants, and though the color had meant nothing to her before, she could see it flooding in, permeating her future, if only with the knowledge that nothing she ever wore was quite so bright. The smell of vanilla and violets hung in the air. It was sweet, and it made Eleanor's mouth water for things she'd almost forgotten the taste of—fresh summer plums and cherries, caramels and chocolate. She slowly lifted the lid of one of the jars, her hand trembling against the possibility that nothing might ever be as sweet as she had once remembered it. It happened; colors dulled, tastes, too, and after the girls with the red-rimmed eyes gave up their dreams and settled down with boys they'd known all their lives, never again was there such passion in every instant as in the torment of those terrible years. Life just faded, like laundry hanging on the line. The heavy dark smell of the licorice mixed in the air with the light, sweet violet scent. She could not bear to think that it might not taste as strong, that the licorice might have faded away along with everything else. Quietly, lovingly, she replaced the lid.

*F*or twenty-five years the Liberty Ladies' Sewing Circle had been run with unquestionable authority by Bonnie Fay. She was the wife of Reverend Fay, and therefore her judgment of who was decent was privileged with authority. Every Wednesday night without fail she would gather together those women who met her standards, marinate them well with her heavily spiked punch, and allow them to simmer around the quilting frame in the heat of her parlor. To be asked to join her "little group" was such a high honor that no one mentioned the faint but noisome odor that filled the entire house. It smelled like mold and mothballs, bitter almonds and something burned, with the slightest hint of rotting meat, and though Mrs. Fay's housekeeping was of course impeccable, people wondered privately (for no one would speak of it, even in whispers, even among themselves) whether a skunk or a muskrat hadn't died somewhere behind the walls.

Perhaps it was the smell that attracted the crows (and the occasional buzzard) that could be seen at all hours circling in the air or perching on the roof, their excrement making black dots on the perpetually fresh white paint. No matter what poisons or traps Mrs. Fay set out, they came at all hours of the day, and when the ladies came for the sewing circle, the birds watched them crookedly, almost with suspicion.

Still, once a week the ladies sat around the quilting frame, breathing through their mouths against the stench and ignoring the caws filtering in through the frilly curtains. Reputations had been made and lost in Bonnie Fay's parlor, and if the effort of not noticing the unmentionable while whispering the unspeakable

meant that very little actual *sewing* was done, well, certain sacri-
fices were necessary.

Eleanor was late but in no great hurry, stopping before the hall
mirror to smooth back her hair before gathering up her things
into her little sewing basket. John seemed happier than he had in
years, whistling as he dressed in the morning and even slipping up
behind her to kiss the back of her neck as she put on her hat. His
sudden warmth was cause for worry or cheer; she decided on
cheer, and she swung her arms as she walked, enjoying the
rhythm created by the crunch of her feet on the gravel road and
the jingle of the keys hanging from the basket's wicker handle.
She walked briskly, smiling at the feel of the early-evening air, the
sunset shining bright gold through all the dust. She hoped there
would be something to laugh about tonight, a funny story or a
piece of news to send thrills of shock up her spine.

Sometimes the gossip was barely worth a sigh and a shake of
the head, such as for Theresa Chadwick, who had let her children
run wild and dirty for so long that it was no longer news. Or perhaps murmured pity for a woman whose husband had lost his
shoes playing poker and come home drunk and barefoot. Sometimes, though, the news would be real scandal. The best nights
were those when she had something to tell. She would recount
what she had heard or seen at the store or after church, lowering
her voice to a whisper, raising her eyebrow in just the right way to
give an insinuation of wickedness to even the most innocent event
as the other women watched her, nodding with rapt admiration.
If only she had something to tell tonight.

The sun had just disappeared from view when she reached
Reverend Fay's, but the sky was still light. Mosquito time, she'd
called it as a child, and sure enough in minutes she was swatting
away the horrid little insects. The crows were settling into the
cherry tree in front of the Fays' house, and she could see the
lights shining through the parlor window, the shadows of figures
on the drapes. She was late—they had already spent their settling
minutes and were listening to someone tell what she knew.
Eleanor's knock would interrupt a story. She hesitated. She hated
coming in in the middle of a story, the way everyone turned to
look at her with the slightest glitter of annoyance in their eyes.

And when it was over, she never quite understood the point, having missed the beginning, and she hated having to ask someone to fill her in.

It was all right, she thought—she could apologize. "Just so much to get done," she would say, "and you know how John just *has* to have his pie." She could see already how they would nod in sympathy. She wouldn't mention leaving Adam alone in the house.

Mrs. Fay seemed surprised to see her at the door. "Oh, Eleanor," she said. "I didn't think you were coming tonight."

Eleanor laughed a little. "Of course I'm coming," she said. "I'm not *that* late, am I?" Eleanor's words echoed in her mind— had they been all right? Something was lurking behind Mrs. Fay's smile.

"No, of course not. Look, everyone," she called, "Eleanor's here after all."

A few smiles and hellos rose from the ladies, but most of them seemed intent on their sewing. Mrs. Greene began explaining a complicated stitch to Francine Cartwright and quiet conversations seemed to grow up around theirs. Eleanor leaned over to Carrie Hawthorne. "What did I miss?" she whispered.

Carrie shrugged and patted her hair into place. "Oh . . . this and that. Nothing much, I suppose." Mrs. Fay offered Eleanor some lemonade.

"Thank you," she said. A few eyes glanced up at her. "I *do* apologize for being late, but you know how John must have his pie."

A giggle escaped from Jane Aston, silenced by a sharp look from Mrs. Fay. "Oh, it's nothing," Jane said. "Just remembering something someone said to me earlier."

"A joke?" said Eleanor. "Tell us."

"I'm sure it was nothing," Mrs. Fay interrupted. "Jane always gets worked up over nothing." A silence fell over the room. Eleanor couldn't shake the feeling that it was somehow her fault.

"The strangest girl came into the store the other day," she said, "with the funniest yellow eyes. She wanted to make a dress out of the upholstery velvet, can you believe it?" She laughed, and a murmur of polite titters circulated the room and then died.

Everyone was staring at her. Carrie smiled weakly. "I guess it wasn't all that funny . . . just odd, is all." Eleanor forced a smile and concentrated on the needle and thread in her hand, and talk began again, softly around her.

Eleanor's cheeks were burning. What had she done? Fifteen years of blameless married life and now she felt like a child again, as if everything she did was somehow wrong, made wrong by the very fact that she was the one doing it. She felt the familiar tightness in her throat. No, oh no. Not here, not now. But the tears were already blurring her eyes. She could not have threaded the needle if she'd wanted to.

"Excuse me," she mumbled, hurrying from the room. Someone called for her to wait, but she didn't turn back to see who it was.

The air on the porch felt cool against her hot face. Her tears spilled over onto her cheeks and she dried them immediately with her sleeve. She had to pull herself together, think about something else so that the tears would stop coming. She would die if she had to go back in there with red-rimmed eyes. She sat down on the porch swing, listening to it creak under her weight. She rocked softly. The sound was comforting, somehow. Odd, she thought, with the gingerbread perfection of the Fays' house and yard that they couldn't bother to oil a squeaky hinge. Maybe they never sat out on the porch.

A crow lit on the porch railing and regarded her with one intelligent eye, then the other. It was so like a cat that Eleanor had an urge to reach out and pet it. In the reflection in its blue-black eye, she saw her great-grandmother Helena Blackmar walking away from the first sewing circle, her razor-sharp posture cutting through the whispers and the whisperers like a boat parting the reflection of clouds on the surface of the lake. The crow blinked, and Helena was gone. It cawed loudly and flew away, and she noticed that the porch was sprinkled with glossy black feathers. *Of course*, she thought, *probably common as leaves in autumn around here*. She picked one up, spinning it between her fingers. She would keep it, to remind herself of what this place really was. When she got home, she would tuck it into the stocking in her drawer where she kept the pretty stones she found and her pennies and nickels of saved pin money. Since she was a little girl, her grandmother had shown her how to skimp in ways that wouldn't be noticed, exaggerate the household budget and save the extra "because you never know when a woman might need to have money of her own." It was habit, now, to hide away anything beautiful or valuable she found.

She took a deep breath. She was feeling better now, though she didn't know whether to return to the parlor or merely walk away. The thought of either made her want to cry again. She didn't know what any of them thought of her, she realized. She considered them her closest friends, had traded stories and yarn with them for years, but no one ever invited her over for coffee in the afternoon, or called with an impetuous plan to ignore the housework for a day and go into Bradford to catch a matinee at the movie theater. They knew she was busy—perhaps that was it. They knew that she never skimped on suppers for her family or put her own pleasures before her responsibilities. Everyone respected her for it—but did anyone actually *like* her?

She remembered Rebecca Cummings. Not how she had looked when Eleanor had seen her down by the creek with Leonard Samms (mouth parted in delight as he kissed her neck, head thrown back so that her hair fell over her shoulders like a girl's). Not the hush of knitting needles being stilled, breath held, as the ladies listened to Eleanor's description of Mrs. Cummings's fingers on Leonard's cheek. Even Bonnie Fay had stopped refilling lemonade and praising quilt squares long enough to hear the story.

What Eleanor remembered, listening to the creak of the porch swing and the cawing of the crows was the set of Rebecca's mouth when Mrs. Fay had approached her after church one Sunday and told her, smiling smugly, that her contributions to the Liberty Ladies' Sewing Circle would no longer be needed. Eleanor had stopped talking to the reverend to listen.

"We only have so much room in the parlor, you know," Mrs. Fay had said, "and I'm sure you're"—her mouth twisted into a smirk—"busy . . . with other things."

Rebecca's husband, James, a stocky, robust farmer, appeared before she could reply. "C'mon," he said. She hesitated, trying to speak, and he locked a hand around her arm, his fingers fitting neatly into the yellow marks of bruises, and led her away. Eleanor tried to remember whether, on the days she ran the store, she had ever seen him buying a bit of ribbon or candy or selecting one of the perfumes for a birthday or anniversary, as some husbands did. She couldn't recall.

"Hello." Anna Mackay's face was peeking out the door. She sat down beside Eleanor. "Are you all right?"

It would be useless to try to pretend that she was. "I don't know," Eleanor said. The tears came up again and she didn't try to force them down. "What have I done? What is it?"

"Oh no, honey," Anna said, "it's not you." A frown passed over Anna's face. She patted Eleanor's hand softly, as if she were comforting one of her daughters. Anna always seemed so gentle and delicate that it was hard to imagine her raising six children, especially since she was only two years older than Eleanor. "But I don't approve of what they're doing, either. It stinks in there in more ways than one."

Eleanor couldn't believe Anna had actually come out and said it. She blinked. "It does, doesn't it?" she blurted. She laughed through her tears. "It *stinks!*"

Anna laughed, too. "So you see—it's not your fault." She grew serious again and took Eleanor's hand. "But I think at least that you ought to know."

"Know what?"

So Anna told her. And Eleanor's tears did not come back.

It was, in the end, the smell that made Eleanor say it. That is at least what she believed later, what she tried to explain. It was not a smell she could identify, not the stink of Mrs. Fay's house, not the sharp, flowery alcohol scent that clung to John's pillow in the morning with the feathers and the odor of his sweat. That was a woman's perfume, yes, but there was something underneath it, a disturbing, strangely familiar sweet smell that seemed to go with the light in his eyes and lightness in his step. She raised the pillow to her face to find it, caught a hint of it on his breath as he kissed her goodbye, but never could find quite enough to identify the source. It hovered on the edges of her breathing, elusive and faint.

So she waited. All day she had been waiting, watching. When the light coming through the windows turned from yellow to orange and cast shadows that stretched halfway across the room, she went into the cellar and returned with an apron filled with potatoes. She had taken a chicken out of the icebox earlier and now she disjointed it. She dipped the pieces one by one in milk, then dredged them in flour and arranged them on a plate. When the sun was so bright and orange in the kitchen window she had to lower the blinds, she stopped working and listened. For a few minutes, there was only the noise of birds making their sunset calls. Then she heard the porch step creak, and the sound of the door banging shut, and boots against floorboards. Eleanor did not need to turn around to know exactly where he was standing.

John was hanging up his hat, his fingers trembling, restless. "I'm not going to be home for supper tonight," he said at once. Eleanor wiped her hands on her apron, leaving white flour streaks there.

He unbuttoned his shirt as he began up the stairs. "I have to go back to the store, go over some orders," he said. "There was a mix-up last time." She continued to stare at him, trying her best to seem angry in a quiet way. "I'll probably be home late." In a few minutes, she could hear water running in the shower.

When she went into the bedroom, he was polishing his shoes with an old rag. His hair was damp, and he smelled good, like soap. He went to the strongbox where he kept his money and took out two ten-dollar bills. On the dressing table was a small bottle filled with a yellow-brown liquid.

"What's that?" she asked. He turned around with a question on his face. She held out the bottle.

"Oh," he said, "cologne. A new shipment came into the store today, and I brought some home." He smiled, and a dimple appeared in his cheek. "Thought you might like me to smell nice, for a change."

She watched him as he buttoned up his collar, then went to the mirror to knot his tie. He was humming something to himself.

"Is that what you were wearing last night?" she asked.

"Hm?" He didn't turn around, but moved so he could see her behind him in the mirror.

"The cologne," she said. "Were you wearing it yesterday? I thought I smelled something strange . . . like perfume." It was a chance, one she was giving to him and to herself. She held her breath.

"No," he said, speaking as if to a small child. "I just told you, it came in today." As if to prove his point, he broke the seal on the bottle of cologne and slapped it onto his cheeks. She watched them redden.

"What I'm trying to say," she said, "is that I know. I know you've been seeing someone else, keeping her in a room in the Victoria Hotel." The words came out like a waterfall, like a scream she had not even known would erupt from her mouth. Her heartbeat thundered through her body and she was almost blind with the shock of what she had dared to say.

John was frozen for a minute, staring at her. He went to the bottle of scotch. She watched as he poured the alcohol into the glass. It was the same color as the cologne, and she imagined him drinking the scent, the smell permeating his body so that every day, his urine, his sweat, his tears would remind them both of this moment. He sat down on the bed.

There was a silence. She was thinking, *He will lie, say that the smell on him last night was his own when I knew from the moment I smelled it and even before then, what it was. He will lie and he will think that I do not know, that other women know nothing or have told me nothing. And when he lies I will smile and keep it woman knowledge because, wall or no wall, he loved me enough to lie.* She waited for his rage to erupt, for the glass to shatter on the floor, spilling alcohol everywhere as he thundered his righteous anger at the accusation, making her cower and cry and apologize for listening to women's talk. She waited.

"I'm drowning, Eleanor," was what he finally said. "I'm standing in my grave and every year someone throws another shovel of shit in and I'm drowning in it." He drank the scotch down in one motion. He was not meeting her eye. "I need her," he said. His voice shook. "I didn't plan this. For fifteen years nothing in my life has surprised me, and now she has. I'll do anything to keep her. If you don't want me to come home tonight, I'll pack my things."

He fell silent, waiting for her answer. With his hair damp and hanging in his face, he looked younger, almost as impossibly young as they had been when they married, and the meaning of his words hit her at the same time as the pungent, musky scent of the cologne. There was an instant, only one, of stabbing pain as she realized he had not played his part. He had not lied to save their love because there was no love to save. The cologne made her feel light-headed; she almost laughed.

"Those bills are for her, aren't they?" Eleanor said. "You bring her money." A crazy idea came into her head. Crazy, but when he hadn't lied a chink had been made in the wall and the air that flowed through had been sharp and sweet. She was floating outside of her body. It was something, someone else who said it.

"If you're going to be paying for her anyway," she heard this voice say, "you might as well bring her to live here where she can help with Adam and the house."

Later, she would wonder what had made her say it. People,

women mostly, would ask her *Why?* and she would be left with no answer that she could give them, and hardly one that she understood herself. *It was the smell* was all that she could say, laughing like a madwoman. The flowery, fruity, alcoholic smell, the smell of freedom.

John stared at her, dazed by her words, still not fully recovered from his own. Then he began to laugh. It was a sobering noise, and as Eleanor listened, she realized that she could not tell if it was a laugh of relief or derision or insanity. He went downstairs and she followed a few steps behind, afraid of what might happen next. They had both jumped from their scripts and were rushing wildly forward into a vast, invisible future. John paused at the front door and turned to her, the expression in his eyes hidden by the shadow of his hat. "Good night, Eleanor," he said, with a smile as genuine as she'd ever seen.

At first, she thought he would not come back at all. Something in the way he had put on his hat, the way the door closed behind him had seemed to her like the ending of a book, the cover closing over characters whose stories, if not their lives, were over. John had put on his hat and, with twenty dollars for a whore in his pocket, had walked out the front door, and Eleanor knew that whether or not John stepped through that door again, her husband was gone forever.

She was surprised by how badly the thought frightened her. In the one giddying moment, she had felt free, and the thought of losing John had seemed as irrelevant as it was inevitable. When he left, he had taken away the heady alcohol scent, and it sobered her. Fear hit her then, suddenly. What had she done? It had not been Eleanor who had said that—no, not at all. Who had that woman been?

She moved distractedly from one room to the next touching familiar things with fingers that felt thickly gloved. She sat down in the parlor, curling up like a child in her grandfather's old leather chair. It was where she had always gone when she needed to think, but it was bad for crying; tears just rolled off the soft leather. Through her tears, the parlor was a swirl of hazy colors. It was like her wedding day, the way everything had seemed so unreal, obscured through the veil. It had been hot, and she was light-headed from the corset her grandmother had pulled tighter and tighter. She had felt dizzy, and wanted to lie down, but a hand gripped her arm and steered her into the church. Grandfather was dead, so John's father had led her down the aisle, past the rows and rows of faces. "I should have known," she cried softly to herself. "Even then." Even young and stupid and blinded by love, "I should have known."

The wedding ceremony itself had been a blur. She'd felt afterward that it was the sort of event for which one's memory works backward—it had been clear and deep in her fantasies and dreams, but afterward, the memory was vague, shadowy figures moving, in her sight, but just outside of focus. She'd been left feeling unsure that anything had really happened at all, like at any moment she might suddenly realize that it had been the memory of a dream that made John Cline's face seem familiar.

John had taken the train to Liberty every other Sunday since their engagement had been announced, and as they sat in the parlor together, she poured tea and lemonade, imagining herself as his wife. She listened to the stories he told about himself when he felt like talking. When he didn't, she sat watching him silently as he read or went over his papers, the expression on his face dictating how she felt at every moment. It felt odd, being engaged on top of mourning, but when the twenty-eight-day rain after Grandfather's funeral stopped as suddenly as it had come, she took it as a sign, silently counting the days until John's return.

She was constantly terrified that he would fall out of love with her, become disenchanted and suddenly call off the wedding. Sometimes he would catch a later train than he had said he would, and she would be left standing at the depot of their tiny station, waiting as the train passed her by in a rush of wind and color and noise. The first time, she had thought he wasn't coming at all. She had gone home in tears and spent the next two hours in her room, sobbing. When he arrived at last, the face in her mirror was so blotchy with crying that she refused to see him. She had expected him to protest, but he left, and she felt hollow for the next two weeks, snapping at her grandmother as they sewed in the parlor, altering the old lace wedding dress.

Holding John's attention while listening, rapt, to his stories (never mentioning when she heard them a second, or even a third time) was exhausting, and while the thought of being Mrs. John Cline, a respectable woman married to a man who looked more like Clark Gable every day, set her heart pounding, his visits wore her out. Was it any wonder that by the wedding day she could barely feel at all?

The crowds of people in her house for the wedding reception made her nervous. The entire town had turned out, and those who could not be held by the house spilled into the garden in the back. The house was alive, and it throbbed, the noise pounding through it like a headache.

She drifted through the garden, the crowd parting to let her pass, touching her arm and murmuring the same things she'd heard in the reception line. The blessings and compliments embarrassed her. She answered with vague thanks, and after a while she was careful to keep her eyes unfocused, darting her head about above the crowd as if she were looking for someone, to avoid meeting anyone's eyes.

She had intended only to find some shade outside, and a place where the tiny gulps of air she could manage with the corset could at least be fresh, unclouded with the human odors of perspiration and perfume, but the garden was, if anything, more crowded than the house. John was standing near the side of the house, talking with his father and his brother. She was glad he did not see her; she loved being able to watch him, unobserved, without worrying about how she appeared in his eyes. *I'm married,* she thought, *I am a married woman.* It filled her with joy and frightened her, and she wondered, staring at John as he scowled darkly at his father, whether he was the sort of man it might be better to love at a distance.

It was John's older brother, Edward, who met her eye and smiled. She had been surprised when, coming down the aisle of the church, she had found that the best man was quite harmless-looking, with his shock of red hair perched at the top of a noticeably tall and skinny frame. Still, remembering what John had told her of his stupid, irresponsible brother, undeserving of his lion's share of their father's attention and pride, she returned Edward's grin with a cool nod. She slipped as casually as possible through the garden to the place past the trees where the land turned wild.

As the voices of the wedding reception fell away behind her, she felt careless. She let go of the heavy skirts and let the dress brush against the ground, snagging in the blackberry bushes. She didn't care—she would never wear it again. And though it had been her grandmother's, she vowed then that she would not pack it away in mothballs for some daughter or granddaughter to be corseted into and led, half blind and dizzy with June's heat, to a hazy altar.

The blackberries were at their peak, and the fruit left dark red spots staining the skirt as the thorns tore the lace of her dress. She reached down to pick a handful of berries, and that was when she realized she had lost her taste for sweet things. She noticed the sting of the scratches covering her hands, tearing at her legs. She turned to go back to the party.

"Hi there." John's brother had followed her, and was picking blackberries with gentle, thin fingers.

She said hello. She couldn't manage anything else. In the sun, Edward's hair was a fascinating bright golden orange, richer and brighter than anything that passed for red hair in Liberty. He offered her a handful of berries. She thought it would be rude not to accept and so she ate them, staring at him all the while.

"I can't believe John's actually settling down," he said, "especially in a little town like this. You must be some girl." He looked at her sideways, so that a curl of his hair fell over his eye, and she couldn't help smiling, though she remembered what John had said about his brother's charm, how he used it to turn people, especially women, to his favor.

"Do you plan on marrying, Mr. Cline?" she asked, coolly, she thought, despite a slight catch in her voice. He ran his hand through his hair and flushed slightly.

"We've been waiting to make a formal announcement. Dad's suggestion. Mamie—my fiancée—she's . . ." He hesitated. "Well, she's a fine girl," he said gently, "but I expect John's told you about her."

"I see." She felt a twinge of jealousy, which she immediately pushed away. It was silly, but after John's description of his brother, she had been expecting to have to fend off advances and was almost disappointed that he was such a gentleman. She realized she was staring. She could feel her face grow hot, and she turned away so he wouldn't see her blush.

"I'm sorry," he said, "have I said something to offend you?"

"No, no," she said, "I was just . . . wondering where you got your red hair."

He ran his fingers through his hair again. "Oh, that," he said. "My mother was a redhead. They all say that I take after her."

"And do you?" She needed to move. She walked with no particular aim, and Edward followed alongside.

"I don't know," he said, shrugging. "I never knew her. She died a few days after I was born."

"Oh. So did mine." She never consciously decided to lead Edward down the path to the lake. She paused, turning back to see John still engaged in his conversation. From outside the garden, the party seemed very small and far away. They picked their way through the roots and weeds down to the lake. It was that sliver of the year during which the plants flourished, between the last frost and the withering summer heat, and watching her step took most of her concentration. She was turning over his words in her mind, though. "But what about John? Isn't he younger?" she said.

He looked confused. "My father's second wife," he said. "John and I are half-brothers. He didn't tell you?" He brushed the dirt from a rock and sat down, gazing over the water. She stood behind him, watching the sky perfectly reflected, complete with razor-sharp copies of the trees at the water's edge.

"It's odd," she said. "I expected that you would look more like your father, seeing as you two are so close." It was just conversation. She was really wondering what else John hadn't told her. It was foolish to think that, though. If John had never even known Edward's mother, of course he would think of him as a full brother.

"Oh no. John is the one who's most like Dad." He turned around to her and smiled that dazzling smile. "Maybe that's why they never have gotten along. They're too much alike. They each remind the other of what he most dislikes about himself." He stood up and tried, mostly unsuccessfully, to brush the dirt from his trousers. "I'm glad he's found you," he said. "Now we can stop worrying about him." He started up the dirt path. "We—I—do love him, you know," he added, before she could ask *Worrying about what?*

She felt guilty and flushed for no reason at all when she returned to the wedding party. John was gone. She searched through the crowd of faces so familiar they were invisible. That was why she had fallen in love with him, she realized much later, much, much too late. It was not that he was handsome, though he was, or so confident he'd said *You're going to marry me*, predicting their marriage, their very lives after five minutes in her parlor, but for the fact that he had his own face, a face that was not one she'd seen in church or Grandfather's store every day for all of her life. He was a person, and not merely a color woven into the tapestry of the town, so integral to it that one does not even notice the color itself, but only the role it plays in the picture.

A tiny grain of fear implanted itself in her throat. Had he gone? She threw open the doors upstairs and found the rooms still and silent, the guest bedroom downstairs empty and undisturbed. Rumor had it that one of the Blackmar women—some great aunt, or distant cousin, she tried to remember which—had been left on her wedding day. Of course, her suitor had disappeared *before* the wedding. For the first time she realized that being respectably married didn't protect her from scandal. If anything, it raised the stakes of what she had to lose.

When she found him, he was leaning against the south wall of the house, holding a flower in his hand and pulling off the petals one by one. A little scattering of naked stems and daisy petals clustered around his black patent-leather shoes. Her heart pounded, filling with joy at having found him, infinitely grateful that he was there.

"Oh, there you are," she said, reaching out a hand to lay on his arm. She needed to touch him, to reassure herself that he was real, really there. For once, she did not think about how she appeared, she was so glad to see him standing there. "I've been looking for you."

"Really?" It was not the way he pulled away that made her feel like she had been kicked in the stomach. It was not even the coldness in his voice, or the eyebrow he raised in disbelief. It was the look on his face, utterly without warmth, his eyes glinting with rage. John's rage was not the manic, scattered kind that stormed around yelling and breaking things. It was as controlled and sharp as a razor blade, and it stopped her outpouring of joy and love as surely as a stone wall, turning it in on itself so it needled a hole in her stomach, directly below the heart.

Her eyes instantly filled with tears. "What have I done?" He did not look at her, and continued to pull the petals from the daisy in the interested but unconcerned manner that suddenly reminded her of grammar-school boys pulling the wings from flies.

"I saw you," he said. He tossed the broken daisy stem on the dirt and stared at her. For the first time she noticed just how torn and bedraggled the hem of her wedding gown had become in the mud on the banks of the lake.

"You saw what?" she said. "I don't understand. What did I do?"

"I saw you talking with Ed," he said. "Down by the lake. I saw the two of you."

"What?" The tears were coming on top of one another now, racing down her face to make spots on her bodice and arms, folded to her chest as if she could by force of will keep his eyes from dissecting her.

"It's all right if you want him," he said. "I don't care. But you have no right to humiliate me in front of my guests."

"You don't care?" she said.

He continued. "Just tell me one thing. As you were disappearing with my brother, I thought I saw you turn back to me for a moment and smile. Was I correct in thinking that?" He paused and stared at her for his answer.

"Smile? Nothing happened, John. We talked about you. He told me about his fianc—"

"Did you or did you not smile at me?"

"I. . . I don't know. Perhaps. Yes. No, I don't know. What am I supposed to say?" She searched in John's face for some sign. What was wrong, she thought, in smiling at your husband? But in the shadow that crossed his face when she said yes, there was a triumph, as if her confession proved something cruel and sordid. Had she smiled? She could not even remember. Perhaps she had looked back.

"I'm sorry," she said. "I'm sorry. It won't happen again." His face relaxed a bit, and she ventured a small smile, gazing up at him through wet eyelashes. "I love you?" she tried.

He laid a hand on her shoulder, drawing her into his embrace. "Just remember that you're my wife now, and your reputation reflects on me as well."

"I know."

"I've heard things, since I've been here, about your family. Your mother." He kissed the top of her head, where her dark hair was hot from the sun. "I'm a man of honor. I keep my word. Just remember—you're not a Blackmar anymore. You're a Cline."

A Cline. Eleanor curled up in the old leather chair and held herself as the tears ran down her face. "I should have known," she said again, but she could still feel his lips touching her head, the joy that had flooded her wrapped in his arms, in his forgiveness. She cried, this time not for her husband, but for her marriage, which had been torn away from her like the most vital piece of her own body.

When her tears stopped coming, she felt very calm. She heard the screen door shut; that would be Adam, she thought, coming in now that there was not enough light out to draw by. She would act very normal, be surprised when John never came home. She imagined herself tearful, in black, saying *He must have fallen into the creek and drowned.* No, that sounded ridiculous. Perhaps she would be able to come up with something better. There would still be talk, she knew, but about John, not her. She would be the model widow, chaste and brave. The whispers would say *How terrible of him to suddenly leave her like that,* and no one would ever know that it was she who had broken the silence and said the wrong thing.

The grandfather clock in the hall chimed six. Six forty-five, thought Eleanor, instantly compensating for the clock, which had been slowly but steadily losing time for fifteen years, ever since the knowledge of how to reset it had died along with the Blackmar name. Supper would be late. On her way to the kitchen, she passed through the living room, where Adam sat with his sketch pad and pencils.

"I'm hungry," he said.

"Your father said he'd be late coming home for supper." She tried a smile, weak, but she had time to practice. She would have to seem surprised when he didn't come home at all.

Adam looked up at her. "Is something wrong?" He frowned slightly, as if his question reflected not concern for her, but a mild discomfort at the thought that everything not be *right.*

For one instant, she wanted to draw him toward her and confess everything, as she had when he was a baby, before John had taken him away along with everyone else. But then he scowled at her with a look so like his father's it made tears well up again. Eleanor laughed hollowly. "No, no. Everything's fine."

The chicken still sat, pink and floured, on the plate where she'd left it not more than an hour ago. It seemed strange that her world had been turned in circles and the chicken was still here, not even spoiled.

She heated oil in the skillet, and when a drop of water flung from her hand sizzled and danced, she began to add the chicken. It crackled as it fried, and its warm cooking aroma filled the kitchen. She hummed to herself as she cooked. She could manage the store, she was sure of that. And Adam was getting old enough—he had grown six inches in the last year and had told her again last week that his shoes were getting tight—soon he would be able to help. It would be lonely in the quiet house with her quiet son, but widows managed, so why shouldn't she?

When the pieces had all turned brown and crispy, she took her tongs and lifted them, one by one, out of the oil to drain on a towel by the sink. A drop of oil spattered as she lifted the last piece out, burning her arm. She sucked air through her teeth, and hurried to put her arm under water. She was not thinking about anything but the sound and the feel of the cool water rushing from the tap over the burned spot. She did not hear the back door open and slam, and when a voice—excited, crazy, drunk—called to her, "Eleanor, come here!" it was so far removed from her plans that she could not place it at first. When she followed the voice into the living room, she was more surprised to see her husband there than the young girl clinging to his arm.

She saw the small wicker suitcase first, and the long, copper-colored hair, but it was not until the yellow cat-eyes raised themselves to look at her that Eleanor recognized the smell that had been on the pillows, the sweet violet-vanilla scent of freedom. Adam stood at the top of the stairs, arms folded, watching the scene. She had to say something. In an instant, she revised her future for the second time that night. The smell of fried chicken wafted in from the kitchen. "I guess we'd better set another place at the table," she said.

There was, of course, talk. In Liberty, gossip breathes with a life of its own, strings itself from house to house by lines—telephone lines now, but back then it was laundry, and if good fences made good neighbors it was because of the alliances made across them on warm and windy afternoons. The Sewing Circle women passed gossip back and forth like borrowed thread, knitted it into sweaters that echoed with the town's whispers long after they were laid to rest among the mothballs and winter coats. The men could feel it, though they did not know what it was that they felt. It was something in the sweaters from Liberty that made clothes from any other place seem wrong, fit tight, or itch in deep, unreachable places under the skin. They called it the wool, but it was the foreign tongue of the whispers, the talk of another town, which the hairs on their arms recognized if they did not. If the men did not trade gossip back and forth, it was because they didn't need to. It was woven and washed into the clothes they wore, cooked and canned into their food. Within a week, men, too, knew to drop their eyes when Eleanor passed.

For a week, Eleanor ignored the whispers, pretended not to notice the very air around her that seemed to form itself into the name Blackmar. The name was knit into the women's talk the way a familiar pattern came automatically to their fingers. Blackmar. Knit one, purl two. Her son's second year of life had shamed the whispers of his first, not into silence, but into a sort of remission, in which the whisperers waited and watched. They would nod their heads as they remembered Evalie, the wild one. Blood will tell, they said; Eleanor could hide behind the name of Mrs. Cline, but she was a Blackmar; scandal was as endemic to her as her long, thin fingers and almost eerily pale, unfreckled skin. And so they heard that a yellow-eyed whore was living in her guest bedroom with a sigh that was almost relief. All was right with the world, and if anyone was shocked, it was only because the news was so deliciously scandalous. The Circle shook their heads and threaded their needles. "Blackmar," they whispered, and Eleanor's blameless life peeled away like an onion skin.

As soon as she stepped outside, Eleanor could feel their coldness, a chill in the hot August air that covered with goosebumps any bare skin she turned toward town. Tears stung her eyes. She would not try to make excuses. What could she say, after all? She could not tell them that she had invited a whore into her house because of the smell not even of her perfume, but of her skin. She could not explain in their language the care she had taken to make the guest bed up with two pillows. Or how, despite this care, late every night, John crept back into Eleanor's bedroom to sleep, just for the delicious torment of separation from the girl. These were things for which the Sewing Circle had no words.

Still, the talk went on until its continuity made it barely perceptible, the way the sound of the rain on the roof had come to be during the twenty-eight days and nights after Henry Blackmar's funeral. And when Eleanor and Natalie met in the halls of the dark, quiet house, they regarded each other with a bewildered and wary silence.

Avoiding the girl proved less difficult than Eleanor had feared. In the first sleepless night as she was hit with the realization of what she had done, Eleanor had worried about mealtimes, about those blatant, questioning cat-yellow eyes facing her across the table. But when Natalie failed to show up for breakfast, and then for lunch, Eleanor understood, and silently cleared her place from the table, relieved, at least, by this small discretion. Natalie ate whatever and whenever she pleased—raw apples and gingerroot for dinner at midnight, garlic cloves on toast in the morning with leftover steak. Sometimes she would eat nothing at all for what seemed like days, then Eleanor would wake to find that an entire jar of pickles had been emptied during the night. Natalie ignored the clock and the sun and slept when she was tired, wherever she happened to be. Eleanor had been startled one afternoon as she hung laundry to dry, to find Natalie lying languidly in the clover, browning in the afternoon sun. After a few days, Eleanor wondered that she had ever questioned the girl's race, unquestionably Negro, though maybe with a little Indian blood. Or perhaps Mexican—she wasn't sure. But then Eleanor would wake in the middle of the night and see her tending the garden, her skin as silver-white as the moonlight.

The garden was, perhaps, the best place for her. It had always kept to its own rhythms, unaffected by season, custom, or propriety. Roses that had spent June withered and brown, resisting all coaxing, would suddenly bloom on a bright December morning, the flowers truly glorious patches of color against the melting snow for the few hours until night fell and they were killed by frost. If Eleanor could have brought herself to speak to the girl smoothing mounds of earth around the base of the honeysuckle, she might have told her not to bother. Though in the distant memory of childhood she could recall summers bright and fragrant with flowers, her adult reality saw July choked with weeds and red dust year after year.

But under Natalie's hands, the garden changed. The honeysuckle grew up so high it grazed the bottom of the bedroom windows, and its overpowering scent steered the direction of everyone's dreams. Flowers came into bloom all at once. No matter what colors they had yielded before, the rosebushes all bloomed in yellow, their blossoms so shamelessly like butterflies that sometimes they would forget their stalks and try to fly away, shaking the entire bush with their effort.

Eleanor had looked out the window at her quivering rosebushes and thought there must be a breeze. If so, she couldn't feel it, hanging the damp clothes out on the line. She looked over at the roses again and felt such a wave of longing that she had to bite down just to keep herself snapping the clothespins into neat rows. It was the smell of the honeysuckle that was doing it to her, that and the humid air, made worse by the long, wet sheets. Summer hadn't smelled this way since her childhood, when she would hide in the long hall of damp cloth made by the parallel clotheslines. She would see shadows passing by, rippling the long dresses, the tablecloths. Sometimes it was Grandmother calling for her, and

Eleanor would crouch down silently, biting her finger to keep from laughing at the delight of being so near, and so invisible.

Sometimes the shadows that passed by were older ones, left like Peter Pan's after their people had gone. They left no footprints in the grass, but if Eleanor peeked through the cracks between pants legs and petticoats, sometimes they would whisper to her.

"I saw Great-grandmama Helena today," she said one afternoon. She was six years old and already looked too much like Evalie the wild one for her own good. "She said to tell Henry there's a crack in the north basement wall, and she won't have her house falling apart at the foundation."

Helena Blackmar had died thirty years before, and her grandmother had slapped her once for telling stories and again for impertinence. But when rain leaked through the north wall and started the bin of potatoes sprouting right up through the floorboards, her grandmother's anger turned to fear.

That girl, that Natalie, she had brought it all back somehow. The very air seemed thick with magic, with possibility. Eleanor sat in the grass. She touched the clothes on the line, and could almost feel her child-hand reaching from the other side, could see in the corners of her eyes the ghosts she had known as a girl. She closed her eyes. The house was humming for Natalie, and it seemed the worst betrayal. First her husband, then her garden, and now her very home had turned from Eleanor to welcome this girl, this stranger.

*I*t was the cool part of the afternoon before Eleanor even thought about starting supper, and as she rummaged through the icebox she cursed herself for giving in to the ridiculous memories of childhood make-believe, the sweet lure of the sleepy afternoon. She was putting frozen chicken pieces in water so they would defrost faster when she heard the sound of the girl's low, butter-smooth voice.

"You need any help?" she said. Eleanor looked up. Natalie's eyes were not the same yellow as her roses, but they seemed so intrinsically and obviously linked that Eleanor decided to give in to the temptation to think of them as the same shade, and so they became bright against the gold tones of her skin. She was standing in the doorway in a faded black shift, a simple sheath of material that covered less than a long underslip. Eleanor had seen her in it before, lying in the sun, slipping quietly in and out of the kitchen, but had never been close enough to recognize the silk brocade from the funeral dresses. It draped lightly over her figure, showing the curve of her braless breasts. Eleanor regarded her carefully.

"Can you peel potatoes?" she said.

Natalie smiled, as if the idea were a quaint, capricious one. "I've never tried," she said. "We always had a cook."

The basement had never been wired for electricity, but a tiny window cast a mottled pillar of golden light through the dust. Eleanor took Natalie's hand and led her down the rickety steps and through the basement to the bin in the corner, and when they lifted up their skirts to fill them with potatoes and onions Eleanor saw that Natalie wore no underwear at all. She watched Natalie's bare thighs brush the hem of her skirt as she climbed the stairs and waited for the shock to hit her, but with no one to tell about it, no eyebrows to raise with the news of the bare skin, it didn't seem that important. She wondered how it would feel to walk about with nothing under her dress, letting the cool air whisk away the sweat that collected under her breasts and at her waist. She wondered if anyone would notice if she tried it.

Watching Natalie roll potatoes out of her skirt onto the kitchen table reminded Eleanor of the cast-iron pot so heavy it had not been lifted since her grandmother had had a maid to cook. It was still there, though, she knew, hidden away in the back of some cabinet. Nothing in the Blackmar house was ever thrown away. And everything, eventually, was used again.

Eleanor knelt down on the kitchen floor and began to open and close the cabinet doors, looking for the pot. When she had found the one she needed, she pulled away the frying pans and mixing bowls, the assorted cabinet debris, and peered into the back.

"Help me here," she said. Natalie knelt down beside her as she reached into the cabinet. The mouth of the cauldron was nearly as wide as the door, and it took both of them to maneuver it into the angles needed to deliver it from the cabinet. They brushed away the dust and cobwebs and lifted it to the sink. Eleanor ran the water over it to wash out the rest of the dirt accumulated from years of living in the recesses of the kitchen, then filled it with water for the stew. They lifted it and, carefully balancing its weight between them, carried it to the stove.

Eleanor leaned against the wall and patted the perspiration from her face as Natalie lit the fire. "Well," she said, "I'm near worn out already, and the water isn't even boiling yet." Natalie didn't seem to be sweating at all, though she accepted with a smile the cool glass of water that Eleanor offered and drank it in one long motion, letting the rivulets of water run down from the corners of her mouth into the hollow of her collarbone.

Eleanor brought four potatoes to the sink and ran water over them, brushing her fingers into their hidden recesses to find the eyes. Natalie watched with interest as Eleanor took a knife and showed her how to remove the eyes and the rotten parts. Natalie pulled the paring knife under her thumb, peeling back the thick, brown skins to reveal the white potato, as naked and smooth in her hands as a newborn baby.

"You blinded them," she said suddenly.

Eleanor looked at her. The silence had just begun to be tense, and she was grateful to the girl for breaking it. "Who?"

Natalie offered as explanation the naked potato. "You gouged out the eyes."

A small smile played at the corners of Eleanor's mouth. "It's just as well. I'd just as soon not eat something that's staring back at me."

Natalie began to laugh, a strange music halfway between a schoolgirl's giggle and the throaty chuckle of a whore. The sound made Eleanor laugh as well and the potato she was peeling slipped out of her hands and slid across the kitchen floor. Natalie reached to pick it up, but was laughing so hard that she dropped her own potato, which rolled under the table. She crawled under the table to retrieve it, and the whole scene was so ridiculous that it set Eleanor off again. She could not remember the last time she had laughed so hard she could not catch her breath, so hard it made the muscles in her stomach ache to go on, but she continued because she simply could not help herself. Her whole head opened to let out its noise.

The kitchen door swung open to let in a silence that muffled their laughter. John stood in the doorway. "What's going on?" he said. He cast his eyes suspiciously from one to the other. Eleanor looked at the knife in her own hand and Natalie, cowering under the table, and almost began laughing again. Instead, she cleared her throat.

"Everything's fine," she said. She wiped the tears from the corners of her eyes and glanced at the clock. Six-thirty already? "We were just . . . making . . . supper." This sent them both into another fit of giggles.

John frowned. "S'late," he growled. He looked at Natalie, who could not speak but offered up the peeled potato as explanation. He took it gingerly from her hand, holding it like something precious and delicate. "Are you all right?"

She smiled as she glanced at Eleanor. "Fine," she said, in perfect imitation. "Just . . . making supper." She took the potato out of his hand and brought it to the sink. He stood watching her, transfixed. "G'wan," she said over her shoulder. "You're in our way."

His eyebrows tilted, and wrinkles appeared on his forehead. He stared at her for a long minute, and she stared back, but said nothing. "Well," he said eventually, "supper. Good." His head humbly dipped forward as the door quietly slipped shut behind him.

Eleanor watched him go. There was an odd lump in her throat, and she wanted to ask Natalie about John—what she had done to him and why, what her intentions were, and did she know the scandal she had caused and did she care that because of her Eleanor had been ostracized from the Sewing Circle, and that it had taken five years of respectable marriage and the death of the Blackmar name before she'd even been invited to join them, the only friends she'd ever had, and now not a single one of them would meet her eye.

She began cutting the potatoes into little white cubes. She

would never ask those questions. She did not even know how to bring up the subject. With any other woman she might have swallowed her pride, hinted that John was acting peculiar, but you couldn't say that to your husband's . . . you just couldn't. And there were no preliminaries, no way to ease the subject into talk of weather or local news. She concentrated on the little clicking noises the knife made on the cutting board.

Natalie took a carrot from the table and began making swift, heavy cuts. "Do you love him?" she asked.

The directness of the question startled her. "What?"

Natalie nodded in the direction of the door. "*Him.* John. Do you love him?" She looked up, and there was no malice in her eyes, nothing but the question, clear and bright and piercing.

The hair at the nape of Eleanor's neck bristled. "What sort of a question is that?"

Natalie shrugged and continued cutting the carrots. "It seems awfully quiet around here, evenings."

"He's my husband," Eleanor said. "We've been married fifteen years." She did not know herself whether this was a yes or a no. She did not know which one, after all, would be the truth. What was love? Love was what one felt for one's husband, wasn't it? A sort of helpless inevitability that sometimes felt like destiny and sometimes like . . . what? "You're going to marry me," he'd said the first time they met. There was no decision to make; from then on, it was as if it had been written indelibly, from the beginning of time.

She gathered the potatoes together in her hand and let them go into the bubbling pot. Natalie added the carrots and their fingers brushed. Natalie was smiling, nodding, waiting for the rest of the answer. Eleanor pulled away. If the girl was going to be blunt, then she could, too. "Do you?" she asked. "Love him, I mean? John." It sounded ridiculous, clumsy in her mouth.

Natalie laughed. "John?" She saw the look on Eleanor's face. "I don't mean it like that. It's just that I don't know what love is. Every man who ever told me he loved me meant something different." She picked up an onion and began to cut it into large pieces. "Do you cry when you cut onions?" she asked. "I never have. My nana used to, all the time. She said that whenever she needed to cry, she'd do it while chopping onions. It keeps you from having to cry twice as many tears later."

"Why did you come here, then?" It was sudden, almost rude, but, Eleanor realized with a little thrill, there was no need to be polite to this girl, or even kind. "If you don't love him, then why?" Love she could understand. She could forgive another woman, perhaps, for loving her husband. But if not love, what had it been? Why would a woman, even a colored girl no one had ever heard of, invite scandal and destroy her reputation?

"Because of you."

"Me?" Eleanor looked at her sharply.

"He said that his wife had told him to bring me here. No one ever said that to me before. I wanted to meet the woman who could say that to her husband, find out who she was."

"He could have been lying."

Natalie nodded. She took a piece of carrot and chewed it thoughtfully. "Was he?"

"No." Eleanor did not look up. "So have you done it yet? Found out who I was?"

"No. I thought that a woman who would say that either loves or hates her husband so much she doesn't care what anybody thinks. But now I'm not sure." Natalie picked up another onion and weighed it in her hand. "That's why I asked you if you loved him. Sometimes a woman will stay with a man she loves, even when she's unhappy. Why do you?"

"Some things you just do." Eleanor took the onion out of her hand. "And I'm not unhappy. You go on now," she said. "I can finish up here." She cut the yellow roots off in one swift motion. "G'wan."

Natalie nodded and wiped her hands on her dress. She paused for a moment at the kitchen door. "You have a beautiful laugh."

As soon as she was gone, Eleanor put down the knife and leaned against the wall, dizzy from the things racing around in her head. She looked at the onion in her hand, turned it over, and peeled away the papery skin. It was golden brown, but split, so the white showed underneath. She reached a fingernail into a seam and pulled back the tough outer shell, then a delicate white layer, transparent and filmy, like her wedding veil. Like the shadows rustling the laundry on the line. The house. The Sewing Circle. Cline. Blackmar. She pulled off another layer. What was in the middle? She transformed each skin into a hollow white globe, a world of its own, always smaller, but never the last, smallest pearl, until the entire front of her dress was wet with tears.

*A*dam was burning. He could feel the heat under his skin, not rising up from it, but trapped just below the surface, and raging, the way the creek moved under the ice in wintertime. He lay on his bed and stared up at the lines of brightness and shadow the sun cast through the window onto the ceiling. They would move, he knew, if he watched long enough and was careful enough about measuring the length of the lines against the cracks and beams of the ceiling. He had spent whole afternoons watching them, content to mark this small proof of the passage of time. But today everything was still. He could swear he had been lying there for hours, but the sun had barely moved. The slowness of it all was maddening. Even his blood felt thick, a warm liquid honey circulating through his veins. It tingled as it ran up his spine.

He heard laughter and women's voices rising from the kitchen below. It was *her*, that girl his father had brought home. His mother had introduced her as their new maid, but Adam wasn't stupid or blind. He knew who she was, how his father went to her room every night, though he came out of his own in the morning. And now she was weaving her way around his mother as well. His mother, who had never in his memory revealed any emotion stronger than mild displeasure, had begun laughing and crying for no reason at all, and his father was touchy and tense, perpetually afraid of something he couldn't quite manage to hold on to. It frightened him, and for days, Adam had watched the girl relentlessly, understanding and not understanding the force that made her so compelling. He didn't know how or why she had done it, but she was the one who made the ordinary world seem unbearable.

When he couldn't stand the stillness any longer, he flew off his bed and threw open the window. The breeze seemed cold against his skin, though for weeks everyone had been wiping their fore-heads and complaining about the heat. Perhaps he was ill. He was breathing hard, but from frustration, not exertion. What was wrong with him? He had never been this way—jittery, impatient, anxious, waiting for something wonderful or terrible that he felt sure was about to happen at any moment now. He had always been proud of his patience, his control, the way he could use it to manipulate time. He could lose hours in a book if he wanted to, or lovingly mark each minute with a piece from one of his model kits, precisely painted and glued into place.

The models filled his room, hanging from wires and lined up on the shelves, each one physical, tangible proof of the hours it took to build. He loved the ships the best—the old ones, with complicated riggings and sails that, if you were precise and pa-tient and the weather was not too humid, could be glued in such a way that it seemed that the wind was actually filling them, carry-ing the ship on some long journey across the sea. As he worked on one, he peopled it with characters from the books he had loved and read so often that, at any moment, he could call up para-graphs and whole chapters in his mind, picturing each book so clearly that he could remember which pages were dog-eared and which words had been smudged beyond legibility by his finger-prints. The people in these books were his closest friends, and deep down he suspected that they were just as real as he was.

He had read of model ships in bottles and he wished there was someone to teach him how to build one. He didn't want to keep it on the shelves with his other models, or even display it so that people could marvel at his defiance of the laws of nature. He just wanted to *build one*, to reach the long thin hooks and wires through the bottle's narrow mouth. He wanted to watch through the glass as he pulled the ship to life, just to prove to himself that such things were possible. It seemed magical somehow, that there were things like ships in bottles, like the sea, things he could dream about without ever having seen.

He had always accepted such things, accepted that there were things like the sea and dragons and flying horses that existed only in books. But now it seemed unbearable that his world was hope-lessly bound by the mundane. Ever since he had read his first fairy tale, he had kept in the back of his mind, almost subconsciously, a list of wishes, so that when his turn came to catch the talking fish or release the genie, he would not be so foolish as the people in those stories, wishing for sausages and such and eventually hav-ing to use up the last wish to undo the first two. Now he realized that it had all been in vain. No one ever actually appeared to grant your wishes, to give you the ability to fly or see the future or run like the wind. It was something he had always known, of course, but now he saw how his whole life in front of him was shaped and bounded by the limits of the possible, of the past. It was suffocat-ing, the thought of a world so small.

*T*he tallest birch on this side of the lake grew up beside a large rock overlooking the water. Boys from town had tied a length of rope around one of the tree's branches, about halfway up the trunk, and on hot days they would swing from the rock, compet-ing to make the biggest splash in the water below. Adam usually came to the rock alone, to think, he said, but usually he just let his mind wander, watching the lake. When evening fell, he could see the lights wink on in the houses on the opposite bank. The brightest was the greenish glow of the whorehouse, and some-times he could just barely hear fragments of music and laughter spilling across the water late into the night.

It was too early to watch the lights, though the sunlight was fading fast. The boys who had spent the day swimming must have just gone; their footprints were distinct in the mud at the bank, and the rope still swung slightly on the branch. Adam climbed up the side of the rock, furious. Did they realize, those boys, all of the things there *weren't* in the universe, all of the things that would never be? Was he the only one smothered by the fact that reality was so much smaller than what could be imagined?

He grabbed for the rope the boys had left, wanting to tear it off the tree, tear away every evidence of the world, but even at the closest point in the arc of its swing, the rope was just beyond his reach. He breathed heavily through clenched teeth as he reached for it, his balance precarious on the edge of the rock. It was useless; he would have to jump to reach it.

The water below him was dark and far away. Boys jumped from this rock every day, he told himself. They could not even imagine being afraid of it. He paused. If he didn't jump, what would he do? Climb down the rock, go back home, wash up for supper. If he couldn't even do this, how dare he think the whole world was too small? He closed his eyes and jumped.

The rope slipped under his sweaty hands and he scrambled for it, legs flailing. He caught the crook of his knee on the large knot that had been tied in the end of the rope to make a swing. He was hanging straight down over the water and the rope made a strained, creaking sound as he swung. There was nothing to do now but climb. His muscles, still twitchy and restless, loved the strain. The tree shook as he pulled himself over the branch and rested, breathing hard, against the trunk.

From here, the rope swing didn't seem so high. The tree stretched out as far above him as below, the crown lost in the tangle of leaves above his head. He lifted himself up onto the branch above him, wondering how long the birch would bear his weight before it bent, or, worse, decided to crack and break. The sun had set, and he was losing light rapidly. He would have to climb quickly if he was to make it to the top. Just to touch the very top of the tree would be enough. He straddled the trunk to balance his weight as he climbed.

The tree was becoming dangerously unsteady. It was just a little bit farther, though. The crown was bent slightly toward the lake. He would need to lean backward to touch it. He stretched for the top. As he reached up, the tree shifted and the trunk gave way. He fell, crying out as the water rushed up to meet him.

There was a sharp jerk as his fall stopped suddenly. Adam opened his eyes. The tree had bent as far as it would go, bowing over the water. He was hanging onto the crown, suspended just a few feet above the lake. It took him a moment to realize he was alive, and when he did, he laughed loudly, triumphantly.

But how to get down from here? He could not climb back the way he came—even if the tree would bear it, his muscles would not. He looked down into the lake. He was not so high that the fall would hurt him, but the water that swirled below still seemed murky and forbidding in the dark. He had no choice. His arms were already starting to tremble, holding his weight. He held his breath, closed his eyes, and let go. He thought he heard someone laughing, then everything was swallowed up in the cold darkness of the lake.

In the water, something brushed against his chest, then grabbed and held tight. The figure that wrapped around him was lithe, female. Was it that girl, the one his father had brought home? Had she followed him? Her naked skin was cold in the water, but he could feel the warmth of her body, of the lips that pressed against his. She breathed into his mouth and he took the air along with her warm, wet tongue. The water surrounded them, moving in all directions; he could not tell if they were rising or falling to the bottom of the lake. His lungs and throat ached. He was suffocating in the kiss, in the water, dizzy. He did not know if the surface was above him or below. Still it continued, her mouth against his, her naked body wrapping around him so that he could not push her away. He needed to breathe, needed it so badly that his entire body was pierced with the ache for oxygen. He panicked, struggling against her, thrashing his arms and legs until he finally tore himself away, drawing in breath just as his face broke the surface of the water.

He coughed, panting, gasping in the air. It hurt his lungs, but his body accepted it greedily. She was gone. The water had gotten in everywhere. It stung his nose, filled up his ears.

"You," he gasped. He heard her laugh, at once ethereal and earthy, floating toward him over the water from far away. It was too dark, though, to see more than a shadow of the lithe figure, skipping like a stone across the bright surface of the lake.

*H*is muscles ached as he peeled off his wet clothing, for once not caring if it landed in a heap on his bedroom floor. He went to the window. Rosemary had grown up tangled in with the honeysuckle against the house, their branches coiling together like sleeping snakes. The roses fluttered as they folded up for the night, and in his room the sails of his model ships flapped in a wind that only they could feel. This was real, he thought, as real as he was. A dam burst open inside him and the joy that crashed out was too big to be held by his body or even his mind. It spilled over, engulfing the town and the sea and the moonlight. Tears ran down his face. He wanted to cry out, to pray. He fell to his knees.

"God?" he said. He hesitated. The word seemed thin and hollow, related to the Reverend Fay and Sunday school, not at all to the freedom pulsing through him to the rest of the world. His knees were beginning to hurt on the hard floor. That wasn't right. God was someone else, belonged to someone else. This, what he was feeling, was his, this was Adam. "Me," he tried, but that was wrong, too—a word anyone could use, and one that changed its meaning depending on who was speaking. This was something that could not be spoken, or even thought in words. Language was too violent for what he felt; naming it would destroy it.

He nodded, as if he had been entrusted with a great secret. "I wish . . . for this," he whispered. "I wish . . . for everything."

They all wanted her. Every pair of eyes that lit on Natalie with disgust or shame or shock left with desire. Women wanted to be her, with the secret, guilty yearnings that no one could ever know, least of all their husbands, but that made them weep unexpectedly for hours, even in the middle of the day. They would snap at their husbands or slap their children for no reason at all, then break down, whispering nerves or fatigue or guilt into their handkerchiefs, but it was desire. Men felt it, too, as Natalie walked by, her body so free and unrestrained under the thin cotton of her dress that it always made one's own clothes feel too tight. They called it lust, and the Reverend Fay preached long sermons against the "whores of Babylon in Liberty," sermons so passionate and explicit that they left the reverend breathing hard and the entire congregation flushed and sweaty, trembling with religious fervor.

At the whorehouse, she was already the stuff of legends, having wandered innocently in one day, asking to rent a room. It was a common enough mistake (a discreet sign reading THE VICTORIA HOTEL was the brothel's only mark), but something about Natalie brought tears to the madam's eyes. Emotional or not, twenty years of business instincts had given her a nose for a good investment, and she offered Natalie a job on the spot. Natalie blushed, stammering in her finishing-school voice that she merely needed a place to stay, and the madam (the girls called her Mother Agnes) offered to rent her one of the upstairs rooms.

Slowly, her lost, frightened air fell away and she wore the wide-eyed look of one whose world has opened suddenly to every possibility. The first time she laughed, the house fell silent, listening to the lovely sound. But Natalie turned out to be bad for business. Every man who saw her wanted her, preferring to wait all night if necessary than take any of the other girls. The girls grew jealous and petulant, and Mother Agnes was run ragged by men who seemed to think that Natalie's unavailability was some sort of bargaining tactic and offered to pay double and triple, in advance.

"You've got to do something," she told Natalie. "Either come to work for me or go. There are eighteen men in the parlor this minute asking for you. I can't get rid of them. They're like barnacles."

Natalie just shrugged. Her room and board were paid in advance, and she had no intention of moving. Eventually Mother Agnes began charging at the door, and men paid just to wait, drinking whiskey and playing checkers as they chatted with the other girls. To make matters worse, Natalie began bringing home men of her own. Sometimes they were random boys from town, but occasionally one from the parlor would catch her eye. She would smile and invite him to come up to her room, and soon their cries of pleasure would drift down into the hall, inflaming the men clustered around the bottom of the staircase and bringing a lump to Mother Agnes's throat.

The men who came out of Natalie's bedroom were never quite the same as they had been when they went in. Afterward, when the cries had faded away and the initial shock of having received what had been so desired was cooling with the sweat on their bodies, a deep disappointment would settle over the men, sinking down into their bones. They would look at Natalie's naked body, glowing golden against the white sheets, and see that possessing her had made no difference; whatever it was that she had and they desired was still hers—they hadn't received it at all. Some of them would propose marriage then, or burst into tears. Others would get angry and refuse to pay, at which Natalie simply laughed, since she never asked any of them for money anyway.

John was one of these men. The girls had been surprised when he was chosen from the parlor, shocked when Natalie announced she was leaving to live with him. He was handsome, sure, but so much older, and he did not joke and talk or bring presents, as many of the young fellows who came in from the mill in Bradford did. Besides, they said, he was married. Natalie just grinned mysteriously and nodded. Then she stepped out the door, leaving everything but the one small suitcase she had been carrying when she came. When the girls could finally bring themselves to clear out her room, they found it full of the presents—perfume and stockings, empty chocolate boxes, kewpie dolls, dime-store jewelry and real gold rings, felt roses, and, in vases crowding together on the bureau and vanity table and in the corners of the room, months' worth of real flowers that had only begun to wilt when she had gone

*T*hey had no business, Eleanor felt, being in town this time of day, especially with supper not even begun. It was not an altogether unpleasant feeling, though. Monday was wash day, to be sure, but the thought of boiling water and running the wringer in this heat was enough to make anyone tired. So when Natalie said, "Let's go into Bradford," Eleanor had hesitated for just a moment too long before shaking her head.

"There's so much to do today. Besides, John couldn't drive us. We would have to take the train."

Natalie shrugged. "So?"

"Besides, what if Adam needs anything?"

Natalie rolled her eyes. Adam usually disappeared outside or to his room and didn't appear until suppertime. "He can get it himself. He doesn't need you here."

Eleanor's resolve was wilting. "It *is* awfully hot today."

"We could get ice cream sodas at the drugstore," Natalie said.

And though Eleanor had not had an ice cream soda in fifteen years, there was suddenly nothing in the world she craved more. Giggling like schoolgirls playing hooky, they held hands as they walked toward the depot. Natalie had loaned Eleanor her ruby-red velvet hat and she was wearing Eleanor's grandmother's opera-length pearls. Before they'd left, she'd even pulled out a tube of lipstick that Eleanor said was much too bright but Natalie insisted went with the hat, and against that logic, Eleanor capitulated.

Avery Mackay was painting his front porch when they walked by. His eyes lit up as they neared, his famous dimples dotting his cheeks, though his hair was beginning to gray as he neared forty. It was a look that Natalie saw every day, but he was looking at Eleanor. "Hello," he called. "Don't you look pretty today! Any occasion?" Two boys ran around the side of the house, alternately screaming and shooting at one another with water pistols.

She smiled. "Just going into Bradford," she said.

"Well, if you're taking the train you better hurry," he said. "Should be coming by any minute." He disappeared after the kids, yelling, "Hey, boys! Your mama better not catch you in her tomatoes!"

"He loves you," Natalie whispered as they stepped onto the train.

"Avery?"

"You can see it in the way he looks at you."

"Naw." Anna Mackay was the only one from the Sewing Circle who even spoke to Eleanor after church now. It would be the basest sort of betrayal, it seemed to Eleanor, to be the object of her husband's affection. "He's just known me all my life. Used to work for my grandfather in the store, when we were just kids."

The conductor was moving through the aisle taking tickets and punching them with a little tool in his hand. When he reached Eleanor and Natalie, he paused, frowning slightly.

"Colored car's one back," he said, nodding his head toward the rear of the train.

Natalie looked up. "I beg your pardon?"

The man hesitated just a moment. Eleanor could read his thoughts in the flush that came to his face—had he made a mistake? No, no, of course not. It was just those crisp round New England vowels, or maybe something in the light, that had made him doubt for an instant what he saw. He cleared his throat. "This car is whites only. Colored car's one back."

A stunned, blank look passed over Natalie's face. "I can't . . . sit here?" she said. Her voice was thin, child-high, and whispery. She looked as if she might cry, her eyes bright as topaz.

The conductor slapped his little punching tool against his hand. "You slow?" he said. "I told you this car's whites only."

Eleanor reached out a hand and laid it on the conductor's arm. "Please," she said. "She's my . . . maid. I can't travel without her." Tears lit on Natalie's eyelashes, but instead of letting them fall she began to laugh. The conductor regarded her warily, then turned back to Eleanor.

"Sorry, ma'am," the conductor said. "I can't change the rules. You can meet up with her at the depot."

Eleanor stood up. "Just a minute," she began. Natalie took her arm. Her head was shaking

"No," she said. "No, it's all right. I should have realized." She wiped her eyes dry and slipped out of her seat.

Eleanor watched her walk toward the door at the back of the car. Natalie's movements were usually so fluid and unselfconscious that it was strange to see her spine so straight and stiff, her chin thrust proudly into the air. Eleanor had been surprised by the tears, but really, Natalie was just a girl, barely more than a child. She watched the trees skimming past the train windows. Just a girl. But could she have said the same thing about herself at that age? When she was twenty-two she'd been married nearly five years and had a son who was no longer even a baby. But what colored girl was so innocent at any age that being told to change cars would affect her so? Even light-skinned as Natalie was.

Still, there were things Natalie saw that she did not. Like what she'd said about Avery. Could it be that he still held some old flame for her? She had to admit the idea was titillating. She might have had a schoolgirl crush on him when she was young. Boys didn't come around—her grandfather's shotgun was famous. There had been a time when every young man in Liberty had lived in mortal fear of it, and the toll of men it had killed grew with every telling of its story. But Avery was different—he had worked in the store with her grandfather, helping out after school, and Eleanor found excuses to drop by the store, hoping to find Avery there. When she was seventeen, she had thought of him every night as she fell asleep. Then Grandfather died and the storm came and everything changed.

The rain went on so hard and heavy and long it made people stare out of their windows and wonder if Henry Blackmar was running Heaven, too. It rained for twenty-eight days and nights, proportions not exactly biblical, but grand enough to pass into their own sort of legend. "It was the ninth day of the rain," someone would say, speaking of the day a cousin came to visit or a child began to teethe. And even years later, harvests both fruitful and scarce were attributed to its enduring effect.

On the fifth day of the rain, Eleanor was sitting in the parlor in her uncomfortable mourning dress, waiting for visitors to come calling to pay their respects. No one would come. No one had come all week, and the sound of the rain on the roof wore at her like grandmother's words.

"We can't afford to think about college now," her grandmother had said that morning. "You should concentrate on getting married. Someone with prospects."

Eleanor thought of Avery, his family struggling to get by with the farm. She thought about college. "I don't know anyone with prospects," she said.

"Well, an old friend of mine is coming to visit this afternoon. He has a son a little older than you." Grandmother pressed a tiny black tube into Eleanor's hand. "Here," she said. "I think you're old enough to wear a little lipstick now."

"But . . ." Perhaps she could win a scholarship, or get a part-time job. But her grandmother had given her a look that said unequivocally the discussion was over.

Eleanor curled her legs up under her on the settee and bowed her head, listening to the sound of the rain, of her grandmother moving around in the kitchen. A tear dropped from her face onto the dark silk of the mourning dress. She thought of the college letters, shut away in her drawer. She could run away, just go. Her grandfather might have helped her, but he was dead now. Another tear landed on her lap. She traced a dark stain on the green velvet of the settee. Why hadn't she noticed it before? A deep sorrow welled up from the stain and Eleanor felt a soft buzzing in her head, like when she had seen ghosts as a child. Someone was there, someone she could just barely see. "Grandfather?" she whispered. Her heart began to pound, louder than the sound of the rain, and under it all, a soft voice murmuring.

Eleanor turned her head sharply, but no one was there. In the corner of her eye, she could just catch the shadow of Evalie's

chestnut curls and a corn-blond boy on top of them. *The wild one.*
If she kept very still, Eleanor could just barely hear the memory,
the sharp pant of their breathing. Evalie would have done what
she wanted. She had chosen passion. She hadn't cared what people thought. But Eleanor was not, could never be, that brave.

"Eleanor!" Her grandmother's voice was sharp. Eleanor's head
jerked up. Evalie and the boy were gone. Instead, her grandmother stood before her with two men, strangers. The older man
was graying, stoutly middle-aged, the younger dark and thin, but
when they turned so that she could see their faces, they seemed
so alike they could have been one person at different ages.

Her grandmother took Eleanor's wrist with a surprisingly firm
grip. "May I present my granddaughter, Eleanor. Eleanor, this is
an old friend, Peter Cline, and his son John." Mr. Cline patted
John on the shoulder and he scowled. He was probably about
thirty, but suddenly looked much younger, adolescent under his
father's hand. Mrs. Blackmar continued.

"I expect the young people would like to be alone." She smiled
conspiratorially at Mr. Cline, leading him into the other room.

Eleanor tried to smile, but she was still shaking. She could still
see Evalie, dabbing uselessly at the stain. She forced herself to
look at John. "It was kind of you to come pay your respects." She
perched on the settee, sitting so that her dress covered the faint
stain.

John glanced back to the living room. "What do you think of
all this?" His eyes passed over her in a way that made her feel not
so much touched as itemized.

"I . . . I don't know, exactly," she said. "My grandmother
would like me to get married, but . . ." She thought of the college
letters in the drawer upstairs. Her thoughts of running away
seemed silly now. Evalie was the wild one, not she. She stroked
the velvet of the settee sadly. "But I haven't chosen a suitor yet,"
she finished.

His eyes, finished with their catalog of Eleanor, roamed past
her to the contents of the parlor. Every ounce of her grandmother's suppressed opulence found its way into the crowded
room. Her family's grand piano, the one she had brought by carriage from Virginia, stood bastionlike in the corner. The walls

were covered with paintings, the tables with small, bright ornaments made out of glass.

Following John Cline's gaze around the room, Eleanor was surprised that she had never realized how colorful it was, how filled with her grandmother's things. On the mantel stood a vase of dried rosebuds and a little porcelain shepherd and shepherdess, with a tiny glass unicorn between them. John's eyes barely brushed against the shotgun on the wall, did not stop on it as they returned to her.

"You'll get married," he said. He smiled and was suddenly handsome. "You're going to marry me."

She wondered for a minute if he was joking, but there was absolute certainty in his eyes. It was that, more than even his words, that shocked her into silence. She was sure that there was some way, flirtatious yet firm, to answer this, some polite response of which Grandmother would approve.

It was not, after all, as if she had her pick of suitors. Her mind touched for an instant on Avery, and she was immediately ashamed of its having done so. She thought of his tousled blond hair and considered it messy. His farm-boy face, his torn overalls curdled like milk in her eyes. In her mind, she put him in the drawer with her college letters, with Evalie, the wild one, with the voices and ghosts of her childhood. She almost heard the click as it snapped shut.

She looked at John Cline carefully for the first time. She hadn't noticed before that he looked like a movie star with his dark hair and eyes. Urbane. Rich, too. His dark gray suit looked new, and his patent-leather shoes were barely scuffed.

Eleanor drew herself up as tall as she could, and tried to sound casual and nonchalant. "Well, Mr. Cline," she said, "we shall see."

He was looking out the window. "Does it always rain here like this?"

*T*he train whistle blew, announcing the Bradford stop. She was still stunned by the memory. That was when it had all turned, the last time she had seen her mother's ghost, the last time any hope, any magic had touched her life. Until Natalie came, at least.

Natalie seemed all right when Eleanor met her in the station, though her eyes were still red-rimmed and her grip on the hand Eleanor offered was less easy than it had been. The crowds seemed to calm her though; Natalie weaved through the people like someone used to moving through cities. Eleanor trailed along behind her, looking up at the buildings two and three stories tall. "Natalie," she said gently. "I've been thinking . . ."

The girl turned to her, smiling. Her face encouraged Eleanor. "It's just that . . . I don't know if you'll be able to go into the soda fountain."

Natalie stopped. "Oh," she said quietly, "I hadn't thought about that." People, men mostly, were turning to look at her as they walked by. She didn't seem to notice. "But . . . I was there just last month. . . ."

"Well . . . let's try, then," Eleanor said. The drugstore was on the street where the white and black business districts met. Perhaps she could get by.

A little bell jingled on the door. Eleanor sighed at the cool air inside. A small sign on the door read WHITES ONLY.

A man in a white apron was wiping the counter with a checked cloth. He shrugged as they chose two seats. "Sorry," he said to Natalie, nodding at the sign. "You can get a Coke yonder, 'cross the street."

Opposite the drugstore was a small reddish-brown building. It was unmarked, but a skinny, tar-black boy, perhaps fourteen or fifteen, was leaning against the wall, smoking a cigarette. A pool cue rested next to him on the wall.

"I'll go," said Natalie. "You can stay here."

"Wait," said Eleanor. "Maybe there's somewhere else . . ." There wasn't, she knew, but it seemed cruel to just . . . abandon her here. "Maybe we could make our own ice cream at home. . . ."

Natalie shrugged and smiled. "I don't mind. I'll meet you back at the depot in time for the train."

Eleanor watched through the window, helpless, as she left. The boy was still leaning against the wall. She could tell the very instant that he noticed Natalie. She had seen at least a shadow of that look on the face of every man they'd passed in town, and this boy was too young to disguise it on general principles or to protect some well-developed sense of pride. A flash of curiosity was overwhelmed by a wave of delighted fear at her very presence, drawing closer to him, smiling. He flung his half-smoked cigarette to the ground and stepped on it while hastily running his fingers through his hair. She approached and spoke to him briefly. He smiled at her words and his body seemed to relax. He nodded, then reached for a pack in his back pocket, handing her a cigarette before taking one for himself. He struck a match and they leaned into it, their faces only inches apart. They drew in breath together and let out matching clouds of smoke. She smiled and spoke again. His eyes widened, and Eleanor could see the blush rising even under his dark skin. Natalie laughed and looped an arm around his waist, and the two of them disappeared down the street.

$\mathcal{B}$y the time they got home, Eleanor's lipstick had worn away except for a greedy-looking ring around her mouth. And the hat looked ridiculous in her mouse-brown hair, especially with that plain navy dress she was wearing. No wonder they'd gotten looks all the way through town—and Natalie, in that dress that was barely a dress and her grandmother's pearls! It was all so stupid, so childish. Eleanor turned away from the hall mirror and pulled the hat from her hair.

"I expect supper will be late, now, too," she said. "What time is it? Five?"

"Not too late." Natalie yawned happily, stretching like a cat. "Sun's still up." When she had met Eleanor in the train station, her clothes were disheveled and her makeup smeared, but Eleanor couldn't bring herself to ask whether Natalie had seduced that boy, that child.

"No time for pie." There were leftovers in the icebox. She could make a casserole. "It's a pity, too, since we have all of those cherries."

"Cherries?" Natalie was suddenly alert. "I didn't know! If we have those, we won't need anything else."

Eleanor smiled. "In the fruit bowl." Natalie bounded ahead into the kitchen and by the time Eleanor reached the door, she was already sitting on the counter, spitting cherry pits into her hand. Eleanor put on her yellow apron and washed her hands at the sink. "Is that really all you want for supper?"

Natalie nodded vigorously. "Joey bought me a hamburger in town," she said.

"Joey? That boy?" She put a pot of water on the stove. "He can't be more than fifteen, you know."

Natalie licked cherry juice off of her fingers. "Romeo was fifteen," she said.

"And I suppose he's as true as Romeo, too."

" 'Bout like them all." Natalie grinned. "As true as Romeo to Rosaline."

Eleanor gave her a look. Natalie was watching from the corner of her eye to see if Eleanor got the joke. They laughed together. Natalie spit a cherry pit, which fell short of Eleanor, landing on the kitchen floor.

"Hey! None of that. I'll never finish supper," Eleanor said, but her eyes were twinkling. She unwrapped the leftover cold ham and began to dice it. "My grandfather had an old bound edition of those plays. It was his mother's. He used to read aloud to me." She smiled, remembering her grandfather's finger moving across the thin, wrinkled page. He did voices for all of the characters, squeaking in falsetto for the ingenues, sighing soulfully for the young lovers, and even now Eleanor could hardly think of the balcony scene without laughing. "I didn't think anyone else in this town read Shakespeare."

Natalie shrugged. "I've been to college."

Eleanor glanced up at her, unsure whether to envy or disbelieve her. "I didn't think most colleges allowed colored girls," she finally said.

Natalie had kicked off her shoes and her white, white feet poked out of the old black dress. She paused for a long moment. "Water's boiling," she said.

Eleanor dropped the noodles into the water and looked at her. "How long have you been passing?" she asked quietly.

Natalie looked up. "Beg pardon?"

"For white," Eleanor said. "How long you been passing for white?"

Natalie was quiet for a long moment. "That what I've been doing?"

"What do you call it?"

"Staying out of the sun."

The grandfather clock chimed five times. Eleanor sighed and stirred the noodles with a wooden spoon. "So how long has it been?"

"All my life," Natalie said. "I didn't even know why myself until a few months ago." She pushed her hair back behind her ears. "And I could have gone on," she said. "I was going to get married this spring, you know. I didn't have to tell him." She looked up at Eleanor. "I could have had your life."

"My life's not so bad," Eleanor said. She certainly wouldn't trade it for Natalie's, would she? Wandering from place to place, from lover to lover. It was a life Evalie might have lived. If she had lived. Eleanor sighed and picked up the celery. She broke off a piece of the stalk and crunched on it as she cut up the rest and mixed it in with the ham. Natalie began throwing cherries into the air, catching them neatly in her mouth. Eleanor watched her, the tautness in the tendons of her neck, the little motion as she caught each cherry in her teeth and neatly spit out the stone.

"You got any Indian in you?" Eleanor asked.

She took a cherry pit out of her mouth and shrugged. "Maybe," she said. "Bit of everything, I guess. Indian, Mexican. Maybe even Chinese. I don't know."

"You don't know?" Eleanor raised an incredulous eyebrow.

Natalie put down the cherries and slid off of the kitchen counter. "You don't know who your daddy was, either. How do you know you're not 'passing' right now?"

Eleanor looked up—was it impertinence? But no, those fierce yellow eyes were asking her to understand. "Your mother didn't tell you who your daddy was?" she asked.

"If you mean the woman who gave birth to me, I asked her. She didn't know," Natalie said.

"She didn't know? What do you mean she didn't . . ."

"He was wearing a sheet." Natalie's voice was flat and cool. The silence fell around them, cold and white, like snow.

"Dear Lord," Eleanor breathed. The air around them was perfectly still, silent.

"Dear Lord," agreed Natalie. She did not smile.

Eleanor put down her knife. She knew that such things happened, it was true. Everyone knew, and no one spoke of it, just as it was not considered polite, in Liberty, to ask how some yellow girl came to be so light. But it was important to ask it, important to look your husband's mistress in the face instead of turning away to hide in the hollow between ignorance and guilt. Tears gathered in Eleanor's eyes. "There's too much that goes on that isn't talked of," she said. Her voice choked on the words. "That's why whatever made me ask John to bring you here did it. I didn't know it myself, I don't even know what it was that made me do it, but that was why."

*D*inner was silent, punctuated by the clink of silverware against china. The sound seemed angrier than usual, the silence more deliberate. "I'm sorry I didn't get a chance to make any pie," Eleanor said again, smoothing her napkin on her lap.

John grunted. The glow that had surrounded him for the first few days of Natalie's stay was gone, and new wrinkles had appeared on his forehead and in the corners of his mouth. He stayed in Natalie's room later and later each night before coming upstairs to sleep with Eleanor, and dark circles were forming under his eyes. Eleanor had considered asking him why he didn't just sleep in Natalie's room, but she wasn't sure whether to be angry or gentle or matter-of-fact about it, so she held her tongue.

"I was reading *Great Expectations* again," Adam said. "But I didn't like the ending, so I was changing it. You can do that, you know. You just have to make up different words."

"Oh." She smiled mildly. "Well, that's good." But he wasn't looking at her—his head was turned toward his father. John grunted again, smiling this time, and patted his son possessively. Eleanor bowed her head.

Something about the day still hung over her, a sense that something terrible was about to happen, something that would be her fault. It had all been her fault. How foolish, to try to bring Natalie to a white soda fountain. She had never noticed the sign before, never thought about it. But of course, Natalie's skin had been growing darker with every day she spent in the sun. When she had first come, Natalie would have had to struggle to pass for black. Six months ago, she had been white. Practically white, at least. Was the difference between them really so slight, something a few weeks of sunlight could change? She looked at Adam, sitting across the table, lost in thought. She shifted his face in her mind, ever so slightly. She gave him Natalie's nose, straight, but slightly wide at the nostrils, and darkened his pale skin a shade. It would still be lighter than the tan white boys, the ones who spent their summers swimming in the creek or playing baseball instead of sketching and putting together model ships. She imagined his hair slightly wavier—just slightly. Natalie's hair was curly, but long, and not at all woolly. She could close her eyes and picture him as Natalie's brother. Or her child. What if Natalie were to have a child, John's child?

John pushed his plate away, belching softly as he wiped his napkin on his face. Eleanor's eyes opened at the sound. John was looking at her almost as if he could read her thoughts. She felt her face reddening in shame—imagining her own son a Negro child! Adam, too, was staring at her. Somehow the food in front of him had disappeared; only the ham was left, a cluster of little pink cubes. "I don't eat meat anymore," he said when Eleanor took the plate.

John reached out and grabbed the plate back from Eleanor, slamming it down in front of Adam. "You'll sit there until that's finished," he said.

Eleanor slipped the plate away again. "It's all right," she said.

John jumped to his feet, knocking his chair to the floor. He took a deep breath. "Where's Natalie?" he said.

"Outside, I think," said Eleanor. John threw down his napkin and slammed the back door. When he was gone, the room was calmer, emptier. Still she walked on eggshells, clearing the plates away. She tried to reach out to comfort her son, but he pulled away, staring at her with his father's narrowed eyes. It was her fault, all of this, his eyes said, and she bowed her head, unable to contradict it.

When she was done washing up, she went upstairs and sat at her vanity table. She took down her hair and began to brush it out. Natalie's words still hung in the air, like the violet-vanilla scent which had permeated the entire house. *You don't know who your daddy was either. How do you know you're not passing?* She examined her face in the mirror, spreading and darkening it, as she had done for Adam's. She imagined her flat, silky hair thick and nappy, and wondered how it would feel against her neck. She thought of her lips, and puckered them to a thick pout.

The eyes were wrong, though, and she could not understand why. They were brown, so she had not thought to change them, but in the picture in her mind the eyes were somehow wrong. They should be flatter, she thought, less alive. Not always, of course—she had seen the colored women doing their washing in the creek, before they had noticed she was there, and saw their sparkle, the quick humor darting from one to the other and back again, but as soon as they turned to her, something was gone, had been flattened by her look. Natalie was the only colored girl she'd ever seen who could stare a white woman in the face and make her look away. That was, Eleanor realized, what made one look at her a minute before realizing that she was black. It was not the light skin or the copper-colored hair. It was the eyes.

Eleanor pulled herself back from her eyes, like pulling away from a window and lowering the shade. It was like what she had done as a child, to make herself invisible to the adults. She lowered her lashes, not coquettishly, but with the vague shame she remembered from childhood, one she had earned before she was born. Yes, those were the eyes of the colored folks who clustered around to the back of the store to be served at the end of the day. She was there, among old women, men, children waiting for Mr. Cline to finish with the white folks and come back to help them. And when he came, she looked into his face and saw the eyes never directed at her before. They were as flat and cold as hers, a pulled shade. They barely touched her, as if the very sight was a contamination in itself. Eleanor opened her eyes and touched the reflection of her white face. The mirror was hard and flat, and an ice-cold fear gripped her between the stomach and the heart.

John appeared in the mirror behind her. "Where's Natalie?" he said. "I can't find her." His voice was sharp, harsh, but his eyes actually touched her, and the recognition was so sweet she almost cried. "What's wrong with you?" he asked.

Eleanor closed her eyes and touched her face, her hair, puckering and unpuckering her lips. John made a sound halfway between a laugh and a hum, and bent over to kiss her lightly on the mouth. It startled her. "There," he said. "Now where is she?"

"I . . . don't know," Eleanor said.

"What do you mean you don't know?" Under the anger, there was fear, a real and terrible fear. To see the weakness in her husband's eyes frightened Eleanor even more than his rage.

Could Natalie have told that boy where to find her later? Perhaps she had run off to meet him. Eleanor bit her lip. "She's not in the yard?"

"I just looked there," snarled John, but he went to the window anyway and leaned out. The scent of honeysuckle immediately impregnated the room. "See? Gone!" He slammed the window shut with such force that Eleanor was afraid he would break the glass. "You shouldn't let her run off like that," he said.

"Well, we don't own her, John. We can't keep her tied up like an animal." A cold fear pricked at Eleanor's throat, settled into a knot in her stomach as if she'd swallowed ice. What if Natalie had gone? Eleanor would not, could never go back to that life before the girl had come, back to the loneliness that once lifted off could not be shouldered again. But when she saw John's fist gripping the whiskey bottle as he paced the floor, rage rippling through his every movement, she suddenly prayed that Natalie was far, far away.

"I pay for her, don't I? This is my house she lives in, my food she eats. She could at least show some gratitude." He cupped his eyes against the window glass to look out again. "I'm going to go find her."

"Wait," Eleanor called, "John . . ." but the sound of his boots was already disappearing down the stairs.

$\mathcal{T}$he birds did not know what to make of the creature perched on their branch. Its yellow eyes glinted, foxlike, as it tilted its head to look at them, but it made no sound.

"Natalie," came the bellowing noise, from below and again "Natalie," and the thing slowed its breathing and faded into the protective invisibility of the tree. The creature closed its eyes and leaned against the trunk, but when the great heavy-footed noise had gone it opened first one yellow eye and then the other, and slipped down the tree and away, silent as the wind.

As she let the back door click softly shut behind her, Natalie's muscles relaxed and she breathed. Adam was hidden in the shadows of the darkened room, waiting for her. He looked like his father, though his presence did not fill a room as John's did. If anything, Adam made it emptier. And yet he looked so much like his father—perhaps that was why her memory kept imagining his face older, his eyes deeper than they were now, looking at her, waiting for her to speak.

"How old are you?" she asked.

He looked surprised. "I'll be fourteen next month," he said. Like her, he was whispering, confessing some great secret.

She grinned. " 'Will be' ain't 'is,' " she said.

"Okay," he said, "I'm thirteen." He smiled and his smile was familiar, somehow, not the way it was now, but how it might become. It reflected off the shimmering edges of a bubble that was forming just above their heads.

Her brow furrowed just slightly. "Have I known you?" she asked. He stood there limply, staring at her with those oddly familiar eyes. She turned away. She had thought he was saying a name, but it wasn't hers, and anyway, when she looked, his lips were still.

*P*rivate. Eleanor felt it immediately. Whatever hung in the air in the look that passed from Adam to Natalie and back again, was as private as a kiss. Standing in the open doorway, cowlike, awkward, Eleanor had broken a circle.

Both faces turned to her in a way that refused to let her in. She felt a twinge of jealousy. What right, what claim did her son have to the secret woman-language, the silent understanding she shared with Natalie? To cast her into the role of a man, of heavy-shoed intruder on their silent conversation, to pull Natalie into his strangeness, it was not fair. She thought of the boy Natalie had seduced, barely older than Adam, and suddenly her son looked like a man, so much like his father she could not look at him. She stepped between them.

"John was asking after you," Eleanor said. "And I could have used some help with the dishes. You should ask me or him before you run off like that." Her voice was harsher than she'd meant it to be.

"I'm going to bed," Adam said, turning away. He would not look at her.

"You go on, too," Eleanor told Natalie.

"Yes, ma'am." Natalie's voice was low, her lashes, too. In the doorway of her room she paused and turned, but Eleanor would not meet her eyes.

*I*n the little pool of light cast by the parlor lamp, Eleanor sat with an open book in her lap and watched the front door. When it began to open, she set the book on the coffee table. *Wuthering Heights*, which she hadn't read since she was a girl. She couldn't imagine what it had been doing in the parlor.

"Oh," John said. "So you're awake." She could smell the whiskey on him even from where she sat, but there was no stumble or sway in his walk. "Did that whore, that two-bit whore, come back?"

"If you mean Natalie, I sent her to bed about an hour ago."

John sat heavily on the settee. "Well, you know what? I ran into the sheriff tonight. And you know what he said to me?"

"John, maybe you'd better get some rest." He grabbed her wrist. "John, you're hurting me," she said. He let go.

"Now listen," he said. "That *sheriff* said that he'd been meaning to stop by the house and have a little talk with me about the legalities of *miscegenation*. Said he'd been *meaning* to, but now he knew it wasn't necessary, because he saw that whore with some nigger boy this afternoon."

"Oh God," Eleanor breathed. She hadn't expected the news to travel this quickly. "So what are you going to do?"

"Do? What am I going to do?" He stood up and kicked the old leather armchair. "That whore!" he yelled.

Eleanor's breathing was shallow, and the sour taste of fear crept into her mouth. "Perhaps you should send her away," she said. "The sheriff's right. It is illegal."

John rushed at her and grabbed her arms, then caught himself and took a deep breath. "I can't," he said. His voice cracked. "A *colored* boy!" He shook his head. "I can't."

"Then what are you going to do?"

The question seemed to calm him. He took the keys out of his pocket, then carefully locked the front door. "What are you doing?" Eleanor asked as he went to the back and locked it as well. Though the doors had bolt locks, they were never kept locked—there was no need in Liberty, and besides, it was so annoying since John had the only key.

"If you can't keep her from running off, I can," he said tightly.

"What's gotten into you? Are you going to keep us all locked up here, then?"

"You don't need to go outside to keep house." He tested the lock to be sure it held, then slipped the key back into his pocket.

"What about laundry? Tomorrow's laundry day." It wasn't—today was supposed to have been—but John never kept track of such things.

"All right," he said. "Tomorrow I'll leave you the key. But she had better be here when I get home. I'm holding you personally responsible."

"Fine," she said, taking his hand. "Now come to bed."

He shook her off and started toward Natalie's room. "You go," he said. "I'll be up soon." She hesitated and he snapped, "*Go!*" in a voice so sharp she had no choice but to obey.

She knew, then, as she slipped into her nightgown, numbly brushed her teeth, splashed water on her face, that she could only wait, and he would come. She would know then; it was no use worrying. She heard her husband's voice, soft and low, then loud, shouting *whore!* and something else she couldn't make out. Natalie's voice, laughing. Laughing? That couldn't be what she heard.

Oh Lord, thought Eleanor, *ohLordohLordohLordohLordohLord*. The words circled in her mind until they lost all sense of prayer and became a rhythm as natural as that of her breathing. She climbed into bed, between her crisp white sheets, and waited. She heard the sharp snap of a slap across the face, then a woman's cry, and the sound of hard flesh meeting soft. She shut her eyes, but the tears fought past her eyelids, the sound crept in through her covered ears.

"Mother?" Her son was a shadow in the soft light cast by the doorway. Eleanor sat up in bed, and Adam came to her side. "Something's wrong," he said. "Why is Natalie crying?" His face was troubled, worried, and in the dim light by the bed his eyes held two pinpricks of light. Eleanor could see the shadow of her face in them.

"It's all right," she said. "Your father is just angry at Natalie."

"Did she do something wrong?" he asked.

Eleanor searched for an answer that a child would understand. "Well," she said, "in a way." Her husband worked hard at the store, provided a comfortable life. He was a good man. Everyone said so, or had until now, when the whispers began to fly. When everyone said that the Blackmar sin had finally come off on him, and what a pity, such a decent man, but what do you expect, marrying someone like Eleanor? And what of Natalie, who thought she could waltz into town, choose to look like whatever race she pleased, do things a white woman would be ashamed of, and a colored one too? Seduce boys who were practically children. Fifteen. Adam wasn't much younger than that, and the memory of the look that had passed between them made Eleanor's breath catch in her throat.

"Yes," Eleanor said. "Natalie did something wrong, and your father is punishing her. But you can go back to sleep now. Everything is all right." She could tell from his look that he did not believe her, but he went back to his room.

When Adam had gone, she lay back in her bed. What had she done wrong? She had been the model wife, hadn't she? Memories of silent days and cold nights flooded back at her. The perfect mother? She recalled her son, quiet and dark, the very picture of John.

She heard the heavy creak of boots climbing the stairs. When John came in, she turned on her bedside lamp and blinked in its brightness.

"Go to sleep," he said.

She shut her eyes and watched the greenish peacock spots inside her eyelids as he undressed in silence. When she felt the heavy sag of his body beside her, she turned out the lamp and stared into the dark.

"What happened?" she said. There was a pause.

"I won't have her making a fool of me."

"Don't you think you've already done that yourself? Getting all worked up over a colored girl half your age?"

"It's not like I have much else to get worked up over, is it?" John's breathing tightened in the way that always accompanied his red-faced anger. Eleanor relaxed. It was when he was calm and angry, she knew, that he was dangerous. Still his words were a slap in the face.

"You know I've never refused you, John," she said. "I've been a good wife to you, as good as you've been a husband."

"Is that so?" She could feel his hand fumbling under the covers, and she realized that he was undoing the drawstring of his pajama pants, then sliding them down to his knees. Her heart began to pound, so loud the sound was almost painful in her chest. He rolled on top of her and grabbed her breast so hard she had to bite her lip to keep from crying out. He kissed her roughly, pushing his tongue into her mouth and leaned his weight into her as he reached up under her nightgown to tug at her underpants. She was crushed, unable to breathe under his body, and she squeezed her eyes shut against his grimace as he moved up and down on top of her. She could hear his breathing, coming hard and fast through his teeth as he moved.

Then she heard something else, so faint she thought at first it must have been a creation of her mind. It was the sound of sobbing, a woman, deep and far away. When John's body was pressed close to her, his breathing obliterated all other sound, but when he pulled back, the crying was there. Back and forth, in and out, he moved over her, the rhythm of the sobs and the breathing, the sobs and the breathing, keeping time to his movements. Eleanor felt far away, as if when she closed her eyes, there would be nothing but the quickening circle of pleasure and pain.

The rhythm of his movements sped until, with a final thrust so deep it made her gasp, John rolled off her. Without his breath in her ears, the sound of the crying was continuous. She slipped deeper and deeper into the sound until she realized that she was herself providing the tears.

John silently pulled the quilt over his shoulders and turned his back to her. Her thighs felt sticky, and, lying there with warm, salty tears rolling down her cheeks into her ears, Eleanor remembered her wedding night, the soft, faraway pleasure and the sharp, sudden pain.

She had worn a corset with her wedding gown, a jabbing reminder of propriety and form every time her spine forgot it was the center of attention. Where the corset had been there were red creases in her skin, a caricature of a woman drawn in on her torso.

John's bare chest had alarmed her, exciting her curiosity and something else, and she was—silently, sheepishly—disappointed when he switched off the bedside lamp before undoing his belt buckle and sliding down his trousers. She breathed in heavily, and the air she took was warm from the closeness of his body, and scented slightly with hair oil and perspiration.

She did not remember much of the act itself. The pain, sudden and sharp, was not so bad after a moment. The pleasure was tenuous, but present. She remembered that his elbow had caught a lock of her hair, pulled at it. She wondered whether to say any-thing. It was distracting, but to pull herself free would certainly break the mood. She closed her eyes and writhed, as if consumed with passion, managing to work her hair free.

Then it was over, and when she was sure he was sleeping, she had sunk into her pillow and cried until her ears were filled with warm, wet salt.

It was so like this night, his back toward her as she lay awake, fifteen years might not have passed. Nothing had changed, nothing had been lost but her innocence. Would she be forced to lose that, again and again? The dull throbbing between her legs tonight, just like the night she had cried herself to sleep, whisper-ing over and over *a Blackmar, a Blackmar.* John was a silent dark mass in the blankets, a rise and fall of breath so soft she could only see the motion when she stopped breathing herself.

The sound of Natalie's sobs had faded, and instead from downstairs she heard a dull rustling noise, the creak of light foot-steps moving through the house. The noise crept to the front door, then paused. Eleanor could almost see her cautiously trying the handle. *Locked,* thought Eleanor, *They're all locked.* The foot-steps were heavier now, less afraid of being overheard as they hur-ried to the back door. Eleanor heard it shake in the door frame, but the lock held. A sharp kick to the door. A low moan of rage. The windows rattled as a hand beat desperately against the win-dowpane, and Eleanor felt sick to her stomach, remembering the little brown bird that had once found its way into the house when she was a girl. Grandmother had gotten a broom and tried to shoo it out the front door, but it kept flying into the windows again and again until it fell to the floor and died in Eleanor's hands.

But Natalie was not a bird. It was just the sound of beating on the glass, but even that had stopped. There was just a quiet that went on and on. Eleanor held quiet, too, listening to the sound of her own breathing until it almost lulled her to sleep. She was half lost in dream when she heard a soft "Eleanor? You awake?" from the mound of blankets on the other side of the bed. She did not answer. Far away, John pulled the quilt up over his head, and for a long time she felt the quiet shake of his deep and ragged sobs.

$\mathcal{E}$leanor's heart was in shadow. Not the moving darkness of her husband above her, blotting out then releasing the moonlight and the silver tears. Not even the purple-black bruise on Natalie's face, a thick crescent curving around her eye like the dark half of a waxing moon. No, the darkness was not that tangible. It did not do her the kindness of showing itself, but lurked in the corners of her eyes, disappearing like a ghost when she looked at it straight on.

It shrouded Natalie, this darkness. Caused Eleanor's eyes to slide off her like she'd been greased. John stared at his eggs, made crumbs of his toast, never noticing or at least never acknowledging the dark figure that moved through the corners of his vision. She had been swallowed up by the air around her, leaving only an anonymous shadow moving in her place.

Adam was the only one who saw her. His gray eyes were the same color as her invisibility, and they followed her as if making up for his parents' distraction. He hated them for not seeing her, the way they never saw him except as their son, a role, not a person, that could be filled by any number of boys. Natalie didn't have a role, so she was invisible to them. He would see her. She moved in and out of her bedroom, paced the perimeter of the house in constant, uneven rotation around his family. He waited for her to lift her yellow eyes, softened somehow by the puffy dark circles around them, the left almost closed.

When breakfast was over, Adam followed her into the kitchen while John laced up his black leather boots. Natalie stacked the dishes in the sink and began to scrub them vigorously. She did not look up at him. Her invisibility had rendered her blind as well, and Adam thought of ostriches, hiding their heads in the sand.

He could hear his father stomping his boot against the ground as he tightened the laces. He knew that it would not be long before John's voice began calling his name, threatening to make him walk the ten miles to school. Another year was beginning, another year of mornings just like this one, days begun in darkness, with his father calling his name. When he did this, it always sent Eleanor into her flurry, combing the scattered miscellany of the house, hoping to find her son among the delicate knickknacks. John always stood still in the living room, as if to draw his son to him by the gravity of his will. It was his way that always worked.

Adam had, he estimated, about three minutes before his father called him to the truck for the drive to school.

"Adam, honey," he heard his mother's voice calling, "you don't want to be late your first day back." He leaned against the wall keeping one eye on the kitchen door. Natalie toweled the water from the full-moon white porcelain plates.

"What did you do?" he asked.

She looked up, but her eyes, still guarded, refused to meet his directly. "Beg pardon?"

"You're hurt," he said. "My father did it." He glued every word into place like the pieces in one of his model kits. He was afraid, though, of what he would have when he put this together.

She put down the plate and knotted up her arms, the dish towel balled in her fist, cradled in the crook of her elbow. She did not say anything, but made a movement that was at once a nod and a shrug.

"Mother said it was punishment. Because of something you did." In the living room, he could hear the second boot stomping. "Is that true?"

Natalie at last met his eyes, and he was disappointed to see that they weren't cat-fierce after all, just yellow-brown, the color of dead grass, like her skin. "She said that?" Her voice seemed to trickle out of her throat.

He wanted to reach out to her, to give something. He felt she expected something, just like yesterday, when she'd held out a hand for him and he'd stood there, helpless, not understanding. *Have I known you?* she'd asked, and he wanted to cry out *Yes! Yes, that is exactly how I've felt, too!* Somewhere in the worlds of fiction and fantasy where he'd spent most of his time for as long as he could remember, he had known her. But she had held out her hand and he hadn't known what to give. She was holding out her eyes now, and still he had nothing for her. He had failed her again. "I . . . I'm sorry," he said quickly. His father was calling through the door, and his gravity pulled Adam into a slow, eternal orbit.

*W*hen Eleanor rotated into the kitchen, arms laden with the rest of the dishes, Natalie was quietly drying her hands with a dish towel. Alone with her, Eleanor could force herself to look at the bruise and bite her lip at the other ways the beating had left its mark—in the curve of her neck, the shadows ringing her eyes. Eleanor had a sudden urge to reach out to her, to lay a tender hand upon her cheek where an untender one had been, and assure her that everything would be all right. But her hands were filled with napkins yellowed with broken egg yolk and crumbs, with John's used coffee cup and the white linen tablecloth stained with its rings. And even if her hands had been free to move, Eleanor was not sure that she, who felt like a stranger touching her own child, was the one to reach across the chasm, to disturb the stillness, distilled into this one long moment.

She could hear the faraway sound of the truck's motor as it turned over and sputtered to a start. The truck pulled down the road, scattering gravel and causing the birds that had settled onto the warm road to shriek in alarm until it passed slowly out of hearing. When the silence had re-enveloped them, Natalie raised her head and met Eleanor with the swollen slits of her eyes.

"I'm leaving," she said. The glitter of betrayal in her eyes was only intensified by their narrowness, the hurt and the pride focused like sunlight through a magnifying glass. A hot thing, like a branding iron, it burned Eleanor, and the darkness ran in again to soothe the wound. She turned away.

"I can't let you," she said. She set the dishes down in the sink. "I gave my word."

"Your word to him?" Natalie said. Her face showed disbelief, betrayal, and Eleanor turned away from it. "Is that what's keeping you here, too?"

Eleanor thrust her hands into the soapsuds and ran the sponge over a plate. "He's my husband." She handed the plate to Natalie in one swift motion. Natalie dried it and set it on the shelf. They worked in silence for a few minutes, falling into the rhythm of passing and exchanging the plates, their movements as precise as a juggling act. The sound of the water against china as Eleanor rinsed a plate kept the beat in its strange kitchen music. "He's my husband," she said again, and this time it was a plea.

Natalie took John's coffee cup and carefully wiped it dry. "He's your husband," she said, "and so you love, honor, and obey."

"I keep my vows."

"And what do you lose? What are you willing to sacrifice for them?" Natalie grabbed her wrist and only then did Eleanor look at the fear in the cracks and corners of the girl's face. Tears sprang up and lit on Eleanor's eyelashes, as heavy as butterflies.

She mutely pushed the soiled cloth at Natalie, who took it, also silently. When Eleanor looked at her again, it was white staring at colored, wife at mistress.

"Put the water on for the laundry and strip the beds," Eleanor said. "When you've finished with that, you can start supper." She pulled her eyebrows into one of her grandmother's expressions.

Natalie refused to hang her head. "Yes, ma'am," she said.

*T*he silence was more terrible than it had been in the awkwardness of their first days together. Natalie took apart the beds while Eleanor did the wash. Natalie cooked while Eleanor hung the clothes out on the line to dry, and try as she might to keep her eyes on her clothespins, Eleanor found herself watching Natalie through the window, and drawing in her breath every time Natalie winced at the sting of salt tears against the bruise of her eye. She hadn't known what to make of the girl at first, hadn't even been sure if she was white or not. Now she watched the dark girl moving in and out of her sight and thought of what her grandmother had said about colored servants. "Protect your privacy and theirs," she had said, whispering, though there was no one to overhear. "Though you have an obligation not to be cruel, it is worse to become too intimate with them." And as a child, Eleanor had nodded, understanding even then the burden of the legacy, never saying "But we don't have any servants." She heard, too, what was left unsaid: though your red baby-mouth suckled at a black breast, and your husband's, in the blindness of night, still does; though your childhood was spent in their domain and cultivation, your parents above as pale and mysterious as ghosts; though your food be grown with their blood and cooked in their sweat, never forget—they are foreigners both to your species and your class. Intimacy is as impossible as understanding, and though their lives be promiscuously entangled with yours, it is best to treat them as shadows, as constant and necessary, but as invisible, as air. But Eleanor had never thought it was supposed to hurt this much.

When afternoon had reached that time that could be called evening if you were watching the clock and day if you looked at the sky, Eleanor came to Natalie, her hands twisting as though she were wringing out a wet dishrag.

"Any sign of John?" she said. Natalie was sitting in the kitchen shelling peas, had been for the last hour. It was true that she would have seen him first, and it was past the hour that he normally came home. But they both knew that John's presence was palpable, that the moment his foot stepped onto the walk, the hairs on the backs of both of their necks would stand, catlike and wary. Her question was as unnecessary as the shake of the head and the low "No" that answered it.

"Adam?" said Eleanor.

"Upstairs."

She nodded slowly, and Natalie kept shelling peas. She had not once looked up to meet Eleanor's eyes, and Eleanor felt the sting, not as sharp as a slap, but like the slap's almost-forgotten memory. Left without further excuse for conversation, Eleanor stood, waiting in perfect silence.

"Let me help you with that," Eleanor said. "We could go sit on the porch. It's cooler there."

With an agonizing slowness, Natalie's head lifted, followed

by her eyes, two orbiting moons, one half-eclipsed by a bruise. They watched Eleanor for a minute, deciding, and she was unsure whether to stand defiant or try to shrink away from their unbroken gaze. But the slap of Natalie's indifference still stung her cheek, and Eleanor plainly, candidly, met her eye. Natalie smiled, not yieldingly or condescendingly, but with a relief that said the coldness had slapped her, too. She nodded, though she looked away when Eleanor had to take the key to unlock the front door.

Eleanor reached into the bowl and munched on a pea pod. "You can leave if you want to," she said. "Just wait—wait until John comes home. You can go in the morning."

Natalie nodded and kept her head bent over the peas. The porch swing creaked under their weight.

"Eleanor?"

She looked up. Her name was so unfamiliar in this girl's voice, she was sure she had never said it before. "Yes?"

"Come with me." Her voice, it seemed, was losing some of its accent, its city sharpness. "You're not happy here, either."

The idea had never even occurred to her. She tried to picture it—running off with Natalie to places unknown, living with her freedom and ease. She smiled at the thought, but it was like reading a book and finding an outrageous character with her name, not like planning for her future. "I can't."

"Why not?"

Eleanor shook her head. "I . . . I just can't. I'm sorry." Perhaps when she was younger she could have done it. She took the bowl of peas from Natalie. "What about Adam?"

"Bring him with us," Natalie said.

Eleanor thought of her son, dark, suspicious. He would be a man soon, and every day he looked more and more like John and his silences grew a little more ominous. Could she save him if she took him away now, keep him from becoming a copy of his father? She shook her head. "It's too late," she said. "He belongs to John, not me." Saying it out loud broke something in her, and she began to cry, her shoulders shaking silently. It was something she had known for a long time, that the wall John had built up between them had her son on the other side. It was enough reason for hate, for rage, but all she could do was cry.

Natalie put an arm around her. "Come with me, then," she said.

Eleanor wiped her eyes on her sleeve and leaned her head on Natalie's shoulder. "Whatever it is you have, you've just got enough for you. That's what John doesn't understand. You either. There's just enough for one inside of you."

"How do you know you don't have it, too? You don't know who you are, who your daddy was."

"I'm a Blackmar." Something was pushing in around her, like a balloon about to burst, like her grandmother's cat, which had scratched incessantly at the door every night though no one let him back in. She pushed it back and searched her pockets for her handkerchief, laughing as much as she could. "But I think you're all the scandal I can handle."

Natalie set down the bowl of peas. "The wash on the line in back should be just 'bout dry," she said.

Eleanor smiled, and sighed. She could still feel the rage and sorrow, a tight knot in her stomach, but if she shallowed her breathing and thought of something else, it didn't hurt so much. "Well, maybe we can get the tablecloth back on the table before John gets home."

The day had been perfect for drying, hot and breezy, but without enough wind to blow dust up to sully the whites. Every woman in the county recognized such a day, and that afternoon the yards had been whiter with clothes than the fields surrounding them had once been with cotton.

Eleanor ran her hands across the clothes, dry and hot from the sun, except for the cool spots where the clothespins had held them to the line. Natalie had stripped every bed in the house, and two whole lines were filled with large white sheets, waving in the breeze like flags waiting to be designed.

The two of them gathered up the underclothes first, shaking the stiffness from silk chemises and cotton drawers. Eleanor had inherited from her grandmother a love of lingerie, and as styles grew simpler, she reacted as they had to her grandfather's imposed austerity, with a lacy and invisible rebellion.

She looked up to see Natalie, waiting with one of the sheets. Wordlessly, they unhooked it from the line, and, holding it between them, shook the wrinkles free.

They folded the sheet lengthwise between them, each bringing her own hands together like closing a book. Then the arms were opened, again, half as wide, and they brought their corners to touch the other's hands. It was like pattycake, Eleanor thought, remembering the girls at school, hands flying almost too quickly to be seen, as their chants rose, as automatic as catechism.

Eleanor had never learned those games, though as she had watched from over her book or under the school yard's shade trees, her fingers had fluttered in silent imitation. She had been too shy herself to approach even the timid girls, and the bold ones had always wrinkled their noses at her, though her dresses were always of finer stuff than theirs.

So their dance, the hands-together-and-apart, stepping close to pass the sheet from one to the other, pulling back to stretch the linen tight, held for Eleanor the feeling of beginning. As they folded sheet after sheet on down the line, it was not the remembering of any memory either of them held, but a dance, the steps to which neither had learned, and which they, together and in turns, both led.

When they reached the last sheet and found it a tablecloth, the basket was full, and the air, too, with its thick, blue-gray almostdarkness. Eleanor took the basket, and Natalie gathered the tablecloth around her shoulders, a makeshift shawl. Laughing, they climbed the back steps to the house, finding them by feel and memory, not sight. The house was dark, except for Adam's room, where a figure, made larger in shadow, sat, nearly still.

They both looked to the clock, and the undisturbed front door. The question hanging in the air had to be taken by one of them, so when Natalie kept her silence, Eleanor claimed it.

"Well," she said, "I wonder what's keeping John."

She didn't, though. She knew that whatever it was, from a new girl to trouble at the store, it was far removed from her world and her control, and, therefore, beyond her interest. He would come home eventually, she knew, set their necks prickling, nerves on edge, interrupt their circle with his desires and demands, then, eventually, leave again. Their lives had been diverted from the path Eleanor had expected, but this had happened long before he failed, one night, to come home at six o'clock. His schedule was as inscrutable as his thoughts.

"It's suppertime," said Eleanor. "Are you hungry?"

Natalie shook her head.

"Neither am I." Still, she brought flatware out to set the table, and found Natalie absently smoothing the tablecloth while she watched the clock's hands go around, their movements nearly imperceptible. Taking the silver, she moved in circles around the table, setting down the forks, the knives, and glancing worriedly at the front door.

At seven-thirty the water ran upstairs, and a few minutes later, Adam's soft steps could be heard as he came down the stairs. He stood behind the chair at his father's place. "I'm hungry," he said.

"There's peas," said Natalie, laughing.

"Why don't we all eat here together for a change," Eleanor said, "since it doesn't look like John will be home for supper."

She brought out bread and jam and a hunk of cheese and some leftover chicken and the rest of the cherries and some fresh peas.

"Like a picnic?" Adam said, his eyebrows raising in delight. Eleanor smiled, searching Adam's face for some sign, a hint that there was some break in the wall that John had built around him. But even John had moments of gentleness, humor, the stray gesture of affection, the tossed-off "thanks" that cast a shadow from another world, from a way things might have been. Adam pushed away the chicken and bit a cherry neatly in half, replacing the seed with a tiny cube of cheese before eating the makeshift sandwich. Eleanor sat at the head of the table, in her husband's place, and the three of them ate with their fingers.

When dinner was over and Adam had hurried back upstairs to finish his book, Natalie moved to clear away the plates. Eleanor stopped her.

"Later," she said. "Plenty of time for that."

Natalie, her hand poised over the bowl of peas, paused. "What should we do?" she asked.

Eleanor shrugged. "Sit," she said. "Maybe see if there's a bit of sunset left to watch."

There wasn't, except for a faint afterthought of periwinkle. But, with the weak competition offered by the waning sliver of a moon, the stars stood out against the sky. It was early enough that they were still coming out, and Eleanor and Natalie took turns pointing out the new ones as they appeared.

Sitting on the porch swing with Natalie, Eleanor opened her mouth. She was going to say something about the stars, about how wonderful and surprising it was that they existed at all, with the darkness pressing heavily against them as it did, but she stopped herself. The quiet was too sweet to break.

She leaned back against the swing, brushing her toe against the porch's wooden slats to set it in a slow, gentle rocking. The faint glow of a lamp left on in the parlor cast soft, regular squares of light through the front windows onto the floor. Their feet moved in and out of the light as they rocked, distorting the squares, then pulling back to reveal them, unchanged and whole again.

A tiny circle, no bigger than a fingertip, shadowed one of the squares, and Eleanor's mind drifted over it for a while before she recognized it as a pea from the pods Natalie had been shelling early that afternoon. She let her toe reach out and brush the pea, and watched it roll across the porch before disappearing over the side, onto the steps. Eleanor sighed, and closed her eyes, listening.

Though she had spent her whole life trapped in a house as silent as a coffin, Eleanor's yearning, strong and bone-deep, for quiet, had not been eased. It was her primal hunger, this quiet (of spirit, not of voice—the house's silence was so weighty it seemed almost loud), and this hunger, as old and deep as her loneliness, was more a part of her, belonged to her more than her own hands or face. To feel both the hunger and the loneliness at once lifted was a pleasure so unfamiliar it seemed disembodied. She put her hand down on the swing's seat to steady herself, and felt along with the weather-smoothed slats of wood, the warm, smooth skin of Natalie's hand. The hand grasped hers, and she felt the young calluses on the fingers wrapped around hers like a child's.

"When you leave here," Eleanor said softly, "where will you go? Back to your family?"

Natalie shook her head. "I can't go back there," she said. "Not looking like this." She held her dark hand in front of her face and chuckled slightly, as if amused by her own skin. "I wonder what Stuart would say if he saw me now." A touch of sadness crept into her voice. "My fiancé."

"They don't know?" Eleanor asked.

"Last time I saw them, I was whiter than you," she said. "Things don't always work out the way you expect."

Eleanor nodded and was silent. She listened to the sounds the quiet made, the soft, rhythmic creak of the porch swing keeping time for the scattered, silvery music of the crickets, breaking through the silence like stars in the dark. When Natalie's song began, a hum, low in her throat, its sweet, mournful sound was the melody for the quiet-song of Eleanor's yearning, a lullaby to the rocking of the swing.

The song continued, and Eleanor thought at times she almost recognized it, as a jazz tune, or an old folk song, or something she had heard a nightingale sing, but then it drifted on to something else. Her mind drifted with it, and it soothed the echoes of the house.

When the grandfather clock in the hall began to chime, Natalie fell silent, and it was more the silencing of the song that woke Eleanor than the soft bells of the clock.

Natalie was still, listening, counting. "Ten," she said when the last chime sounded. Her face was shadowed, but the light ran along its profile, lit on her eyelashes and left her eyes alone.

"Time for bed," said Eleanor. She stood, but Natalie jerked her back as she turned to go.

"Oh, look!" said Natalie. "A falling star!"

"That's good luck." Eleanor yawned. "Did you make a wish?"

Natalie squeezed her hand. "I made one for you," she said. "Since you didn't see it."

Eleanor smiled. She felt sleepy, lulled by the lullaby into a hazy dream state, but not tired. Her body felt light. She was barely aware, as they went into the house, that she still held Natalie's hand. She could not let go of Natalie's hand, risk that she might slip away sometime in the night. To separate would create a hollowness. It seemed the most natural thing in the world that they climb the stairs together, and settle together into the big brass bed, between the crisp linen sheets that still smelled like sunshine.

Through half-opened eyes, Eleanor saw Natalie come awake. In the moon, she saw the shadow of the slight curve of a smile, heard, in the intimacy of their quiet, the high, clear tenor of Natalie's thoughts. There were girls at the Victoria Hotel, who, after all the customers had gone, would climb into each other's beds to find again the pleasure the men had taken from them. What had they done? She could not see the details of Eleanor's face, but she stroked the silky hair spread over the pillow, found the line of the jaw and stroked the hollow of the cheek. Finding Eleanor's lips from touch and shadows, Natalie reached out with her mouth for a kiss.

Eleanor was surprised, but did not pull away. Her mind was still listening to the echo of the song. She smiled but shook her head. "That's not what you need from me." She pulled Natalie into the crook of her arm. "That's what everyone else tries to give you, to take from you. Not me." She drew Natalie toward her, holding her from behind so that their arms, legs, bodies were parallel.

"I love you," Natalie whispered.

Tears formed in Eleanor's eyes. That was it, the tangled feeling pressing on her chest as if it would break the skin from the inside. She wondered if it hurt the ground in springtime to be split apart as the root pushed through. "I love you, too," she said, and tears rolled out of her eyes, watering the cool linen of her pillowcase. She clutched Natalie tighter. "You'll be gone in the morning," she whispered. "Will you come back and visit me some day, see how I'm doing?"

Natalie waited for a moment, then nodded. "All right," she said. "I promise." She shaped her body into Eleanor's, head against her breast, their bodies fitting hollows to curves as they breathed. They settled together and slept.

$\mathcal{E}$ven in sleep, Eleanor could feel it—the wary prickling at the back of her neck, the tightness in her stomach that signaled the presence of his anger. It disturbed her dream, sending her running through the landscapes of her mind from a vague evil before it disturbed her sleep. By the time she woke, the terror was well-established; it was only the detail that was needed by her mind.

She was not surprised to see that John was there, a huge figure standing in the dark at the foot of the bed. Even at that distance, she could smell the alcohol on his breath. But that was the only sign of his drunkenness; his stance was, like his gaze, unwavering.

This was not surprising either. John was not sloppy in anything he did, and alcohol never slurred his words or stumbled his feet. If anything, drink honed his cruelty, focused his anger into complete clarity. She knew he was most dangerous when calm. Standing at the foot of the bed, he was dangerous.

He could not have seen her eyes open in the dark, and Eleanor considered closing them again against whatever his calmness was plotting. But she knew it was useless to feign sleep against a man with whom one has slept for fifteen years. The patterns of breathing were too familiar for lies.

Eleanor sat up, smoothing back her hair. She wondered what time it was—it was still dark outside, but the air had a predawn, early-morning feel. She switched on the lamp at the bedside, knowing that the sudden light would make them equally blind. For a moment, at least, they would not have to meet each other's eyes.

Natalie was still asleep beside Eleanor, was sleeping, in fact, on Eleanor's side of the bed. She was frowning a little, her lips moving slightly like a baby dreaming of suckling, or someone trying to speak without the sound. Eleanor wondered if she felt the prickling, and what sort of nightmares it had given her.

"What is this, Eleanor?" John's voice was soft with fury, low. She had heard that a barking dog was only trying to alert its master; it was the low growl that signaled an attack. She wanted to shrink back in fear, to bury her head in her grandmother's crisp linen sheets, but she forced herself to sit tall and meet his eye.

"Where have you been?" she asked.

He gripped the footboard of the bed until his knuckles turned white with the strain. "This is my bed, Eleanor," he said. "I say who sleeps here."

Natalie stirred and sat up. She looked at John and Eleanor calmly, dispassionately, as if she were watching a film. "I'm leaving in the morning," she said matter-of-factly.

"No." John gripped her shoulders and pulled her out of bed. "Don't even say that."

"Natalie," Eleanor said cautiously, "I think maybe you'd better go back to your own bed."

"Let go of me!" Natalie pulled away from John. "I'm leaving, and Eleanor is going to leave, too." She looked up. "You hear that?" she cried. "She's got to leave."

Eleanor closed her eyes when she saw John's hand move. She felt nothing, did not know even if it was she or Natalie John had hit. It was just a sound, like the snap of a branch breaking. Then silence, a terrible, terrible silence.

"I'm going," Natalie said. John followed her into the hall.

"I love you," he shouted. "I love you." Again and again he shouted it, and each time Eleanor heard his fist striking flesh. She flinched.

"Get away from me," Natalie screamed. Then there was a loud crash, and silence.

Eleanor was trembling. Filled, completely filled with a deep soul-shake that was stronger than any emotion that could have parented it. And no emotion could be named to it, since Eleanor's words had gone. She crouched like an animal on the floor, paralyzed.

She felt the floor bend under heavy steps, then heard the bathroom door creak open, slam shut. In a moment, the shower came on, and she heard the pitch change as the water in the pipes ran from cold to hot. She drew a breath. From the way air hurt her lungs, she guessed that she had not breathed in a long, long time. She quieted, enjoying the luxury of breath.

She had been touched in a place she had thought untouchable, the core of her mind that had always been calm, despite the layers of emotion surrounding it. It was not a thing that came into conscious thought, or cooled her hotheaded reactions in any way. Her mind would be spinning with anger, and the still axis at the center of the spin could not keep the tears from springing to her eyes. But it was always there, waiting, keeping her from breaking too soon. If she'd had to give it a name, it would be *not yet*. Now it was shaken, and she could not hear what it said.

Eleanor pressed her fingers against her eyes until the silver-green pressure filled her head. She waited for the dream to reveal itself, for her eyes to bring the unimaginable into focus, recognize it as something harmless and mundane. But she knew, even as she took the pressure from her eyes and watched her blindness fade into spots, that a nightmare never came when you needed it. The fact that something was unbearable did not mean that it didn't need to be borne.

At the bottom of the stairs, Natalie was just barely moving. Her limbs lifted, untangled themselves in timid jerks, then settled around her body. She seemed like a marionette in the hands of a clumsy puppeteer, her movements awkward, tentative with pain.

Eleanor pulled her stomach into something she could manage and went into the bedroom to find a blanket. She pulled back the wedding quilt, taking it by the wrinkled folds where John had lifted it to pull Natalie from the bed, and began to gather it into a bundle around her.

The quilt, once white, was yellowing with age. It had lain on her bed since before the bed was hers, before she had even been alive. Eleanor had always thought she would die under it as well. She had a sudden urge to pull it around her like a chrysalis and forget the shotgun hanging on the wall and the strange man standing naked in running water a room away. She would cover herself with the heavy smooth cotton and let it dilute the light and sounds of the world down to a manageable consistency.

She held the quilt in front of her like a shield and stepped out again into the hall. In the rectangle of light cast through the door, her shadow stretched out to brush the floor all the way down to the end of the hall. She paused in front of Adam's room and listened. The door was slightly ajar and the room was quiet, so quiet she knew he must be awake. She closed the door.

Natalie shivered at the bottom of the stairs, her breathing shallow, catching on the breathlessness of her tears. Eleanor could not see her clearly in the dark, but she could feel the bare cold skin as she wrapped her in the quilt. She was surprised by Natalie's heaviness; from the top of the stairs she'd appeared little larger than a child. She managed to carry her to the spare bedroom and ease her in the dark onto the bed.

Great drops of sweat were beading on Natalie's forehead, merging together into a slick sheen, tears running like rivers down her already wet face. She was shaking, and Eleanor forced her own body to calm itself to provide some steadiness for the trembling girl.

"Shh, baby," she said, "baby." She tried to keep her voice calm as they rocked together in the darkness. She'd heard that shipwrecked men would cling together, refusing to let go to swim to shore. And though death was the price, they paid it just so they wouldn't have to drown alone. Natalie clung to Eleanor with the same desperate affection.

She had forgotten the sound of the shower upstairs until, with a whistle of slowing water, it stopped. Eleanor tensed and pulled Natalie close. "You'll be all right." She could hear John moving in the bedroom above them, opening and closing dresser drawers. She tried to quiet Natalie, who was struggling out of her arms.

"Oh," Natalie said. "Oh, oh, oh." Her voice raised into a high, hollow call, as eerie and cold as the cry of a loon. The cry prickled Eleanor's skin, each syllable rising in an arc, then fading before the circle rounded again. Eleanor pulled away from the bed, groping in the dark. She pulled the cord and light flooded the room.

Natalie was curled on the bed like a wild animal caught in a steel leg trap. She howled in agony, then Eleanor saw the blood blooming through the white quilt. She pulled back the quilt to find blood covering Natalie's legs. It had soaked the quilt between the joined wedding bands, dark as wine, cream-thick, jelling in clots. But where it bled through to the other side, it erupted into sudden, delicate blooms, like poppies sprung up overnight after summer rains. So much blood. Lord, had she been pregnant? Had John known? A trickle of blood was running out of the corner of the girl's mouth. There was no time for questions, no time to sit down and decide what to do.

Natalie's cry had been a thing of darkness, and the light had silenced it. She turned her knife-sharp eyes to Eleanor with a look that was both question and accusation, both *Why?* and *What happens now?* Eleanor did not look away, but all she could answer Natalie with her eyes was the beat of her heart: *I don't know. I don't know. I don't know.*

They stayed there, staring, the silence circling between them until their helplessness had gathered rhythm, and the questions, silent and impossible, circled with the same beat as their hearts.

When the piano music finally reached them, the notes at first so soft they were more vibration than sound, its cadence so completely matched their own that it seemed to be a thing of their creation. The notes grew louder, joining together into melody, and Eleanor recognized them as Natalie's song, the formless, wild harmony to the crickets' hollow sound.

Leaving Natalie for just a moment, she found John sitting in the darkened parlor, discovering the notes on the keyboard by shadow and touch. He did not notice her until she was close enough to feel the heat radiating from his back. She touched his shoulder, and he jerked his hands from the keys like the piano had become white-hot.

"Where did you hear that song?" Of all the questions in her mind, this was the only one she could force to her lips.

He stood abruptly. "I . . . don't know." She could not stop herself from cringing when he touched her arm. He pulled away, turning his shoulder to her.

"Wait," she said. She forced her voice to calm and laid her hand on his shoulder. "John, wait. I'm sorry." He turned to her. "Please," she said. "Natalie's bleeding. She's hurt."

John pulled away and slumped into the big leather chair, leaning his forehead against his fist. "She'll have to stay here, then," he said. "We'll take care of her until she's well again." He didn't meet her eyes.

A sharp sting of anger grabbed the back of Eleanor's neck. Her stomach churned, furious at him, furious at herself for keeping Natalie in the house, furious at Natalie for having been such a fool as to let herself get involved with this man.

She pushed the anger down and pulled her stomach muscles tight to corset it in. She poised on the settee and modulated her voice into melody, forcing her tightened jaw to form words.

"John," she said. She took in a breath as deep as her tight stomach would allow. The image of poppies of blood blooming on the quilt hit her memory. She felt her hands begin to tremble and folded them, white-knuckled, in her lap. "I think she's really hurt. I think she needs a doctor."

His knuckles were white, too, hands curled into fists. "What white doctor would come all the way out here in the middle of the night for a colored girl?"

"A colored doctor, then." Tears were dropping off of her face into her lap. "John, I think she was pregnant. Maybe someone from the whorehouse . . ."

John stood swiftly and turned his back to Eleanor, propping one hand on the mantel. "So she's gone and gotten herself pregnant," he breathed.

Eleanor's rage frightened her. She pushed it down, something hot and tight in the center of her chest. "Gotten herself?" she said. "I thought it took two." For the first time in years, she noticed her grandfather's shotgun, hanging on the wall above his head. Her heart began to beat faster.

"Do you want the sheriff out here, smirking at me with his little pig face, charging me with miscegenation?"

"I don't know." Eleanor heard her words hiss through her teeth, no longer concerned about keeping her voice gentle. She stood. "Would you rather have him charging you with murder?"

"I didn't hurt her that bad," he shouted. "I didn't!" In one blur of motion his hand darted out. She heard the crash of breaking porcelain before she even saw what the hand had hurled to the floor. She turned and ran from the room.

*N*atalie was sleeping, her breathing shallow and ragged. She barely stirred as Eleanor slipped into bed, slipped her body around the girl's. The blankets were bloody, but Eleanor had no others to give, nothing else to soak up the blood.

"Shh, honey," Eleanor whispered, "shh . . ." though there was no noise to quiet but her breathing. She rocked the girl back and forth, wiped the clammy sweat from her forehead.

Natalie whimpered slightly. Her eyes opened, meeting Eleanor's. "If there's just enough for one, then take it," she said. "It's yours now. Take it. Go."

Eleanor grasped her tighter. She could feel the warm blood seeping onto her hands, her dress. She had a sudden impulse to take the truck and, learning to drive as she went, somehow wrestle it into town to find a doctor, somebody who could help her. Even in fantasy it was a ridiculous sight, and Eleanor shuddered at her own helplessness.

*J*ust before dawn, Eleanor came into the parlor and stood, arms folded across her chest. He was at the piano, not playing, but laying his hands down in automatic patterns on the chords, letting their weight create the sound. Sometimes his fingers would flutter to single notes as he raised his hands from one heavy chord to the next, but there was no melody to be found, just notes as random and lonely as the sound of wind in the aspen leaves.

She stood at his back. His hands fell silent, resting on the keys, as if the weight of her breathing were the last straw, the one unbearable thing that made the air in the room finally too heavy to be resisted. He turned and looked at her, not asking aloud, not asking even with his eyes, only slightly raising his eyebrows, deepening the lines in his face almost imperceptibly.

"She's dead." Eleanor heard the words, far away and in a husky voice that must have been hers. She watched the words hit him, saw the lines on his face congregate in one sudden, momentary flinch, like he had been hit between the eyes by an unexpected drop of rain. He stood and moved toward her haltingly, hesitantly. He laid a hand on her elbow.

He looked up and she could see tears gleaming brightly in his eyes. If he let them fall, she thought, if he only let them fall, hers would fall as well and she could uncross her arms from the tight place between her stomach and her chest and accept his hand on her arm and draw herself toward him and cry.

But he did not let them fall, and she stood clamping her throat and jaw and stomach around the scream that begged for release. His hand left her elbow. It did not reach for his hat but slid tenderly around the bottle of scotch as he slipped out the back door and into the almost-morning night.

Eleanor opened her mouth to scream, but the only sound that her sorrow and rage would voice was a moan, weak and inhuman, like the desperate but meaningless noises made by a mute. Henry Blackmar's shotgun grabbed her eyes. Her heart began to pound loud in her ears, so loud, it seemed, it would have drowned out any noise she could have been able to make. It would be so easy, she realized, so easy to take the gun from the wall and follow John. She could raise it up and aim just as her grandfather had done, and let the gunshot explosion make all the noise she needed. Something was pushing her. She moved forward, toward the mantel, feeling like a river that had finally, finally come to the edge of a cliff and can see for the first time the glory of the waterfall. She need take only one more tiny step to begin the fall she had anticipated all her life.

Her foot brushed against something on the floor. It scattered like a marble and hit the fireplace screen, something small and white. Eleanor picked it up. A small coquettish eye looked at her from part of a milk-white face, a porcelain curl tendriling against a rosy cheek. Eleanor knelt and found on the floor the other half of the shepherdess's face. On the mantel, the shepherd still stood, one hand reaching out for the love whose absence he hadn't yet noticed. She took the pieces of the shepherdess's face and hurried upstairs.

She threw open the lingerie drawer, feeling among slips and silk stockings for the hard, jingling lump in the toe of the stocking worn to runs beyond repair. With shaking hands she undid the knot and cast the money onto the dresser, a cascade of paper and coins. She counted it quickly, twice. Forty-seven dollars and thirty-two cents. A lifetime of pennies skimped, pin money, the price of gingham exaggerated by a nickel a yard. Ten years of darning stockings, going without new. Forty-seven dollars and thirty-two cents. It would not be enough. She remembered the pies, the hundreds of pies she had baked, even on wash days, even days when her fingers were wrinkled and worn so raw it hurt to roll the dough. Every pie a few cents' worth of flour and sugar she could have saved.

She flew to the jewelry box, sifted through the few pieces of costume jewelry her grandmother had left. Rhinestones, bits of colored glass. Nothing of any true value, and any sentimental value they'd had had died along with those who'd remembered when they had last been worn, decades ago. She shut the box and sank onto the bed, defeated.

The chain around Eleanor's neck pinched at her skin, catching her attention. For the first time, she saw the cross as something gold, and therefore salable. Hastily she undid the clasp. Jesus, gazing sadly at his feet, did not meet her eyes. Her wedding ring, she realized, was gold as well. It went, with the chain and the cross and Jesus' eyes, into the stocking of saved change.

The sky was at its uncertain color, half dark night, half morning, when an uncertain but not at all hesitant figure began walking down the long road through town, gripping an old, knotted stocking in one hand. Behind her, a swarm of yellow butterflies rose up over the house, flying as if they had never flown before but had longed for it all their lives. They flew east for a while before disappearing into the rising sun. Eleanor kept her feet moving, watched the sun slowly coming up in front of her. She would not actually do it, she thought. It would be enough just to know that she could. She would walk to the train station and ask the price of a one-way ticket to—New York, for instance. That sounded far away and romantic enough, no realer to her mind than Shangri-la.

She would learn the price of a ticket and count her money to make sure she had enough. Then she would call John from the station and tell him where she was, tell him that if he ever wanted to see her again, he'd better come down and pick her up. She could see his face, angry but afraid, his voice hesitant. She kept walking, setting one foot down in front of the other.

The sun was over the horizon now, and she noticed the blood staining the front of her dress, dried on her hands. She would have to do something about it, she supposed, when she got back home. She fingered the stocking of money again, and felt the lump of the shepherdess face.

She arrived at the station and counted out her money just as the sun was establishing itself in the morning sky. Birds were singing, she supposed, but she didn't hear anything but the stationmaster's voice and the clink of coins. By the time she thought again of the blood on her dress or the look on John's face, or Jesus on his cross, it was well after noon and she was on a train speeding irrevocably toward New York.

$\mathcal{T}$ime passes.

There is a secret about time that the clocks do not know. Clocks move in steady, smooth circles, the second hand passing graceful as a dancer to catch the minute hand and pull it a little farther along, no hour taking an instant more than its share. But memory knows the truth: time moves in starts, sputtering, leaping. Years slide by unnoticed, while a single moment catches like blackberry thorns in the clothes, the hair, refusing to let go at any cost. Time passes in New York, in Liberty.

Each town has its own rhythm. In New York, Eleanor stumbles and nearly falls sometimes; the sidewalks themselves move faster than her feet have learned to walk.

She does not like New York, but it tolerates her, and she returns the favor. A woman can live alone there without a husband or father or past, and, though voices swirl constantly everywhere, nobody *talks*. Noise in the city creeps in like an odor. But it is impersonal noise: traffic sounds, the voices of strangers. It is oddly welcoming to Eleanor, the way, when people avert their eyes and do not say hello, it is a general, not a deliberate, exclusion.

$\mathcal{T}$ime passes. In the spring of 1952, Adam shaves for the first time and Eleanor cuts her finger while slicing tomatoes for lunch. It is not a deep cut, but she cries anyway, tears blurring her eyes as she searches her tiny apartment for a bandage. Not finding one, she cannot stop the tears and she sits on the floor and sobs until the afternoon sun slants onto the redbrick building across the street. Her memory is tenacious that way, and sneaky. It will choose the moment she least expects it to come, when the thought of her husband is silent and still she is silently berating herself for having forgotten her shopping list and searching for what besides milk she needs, when suddenly she smells a woman's perfume, and from the front of the cool dairy case of the A&P, she is transported to a hot, windy day, with Natalie staring at her through her bruises.

Her cat meows from the kitchen. He showed up on the fire escape one day, a bedraggled yellow stray, and she fed him for months before admitting he was hers. By then, it felt odd to give him a name; he doesn't come when she calls him anyway. As she pours out the cat food and sets the dish on the floor, she looks up at the calendar. She's forgotten to turn the page. It's the first of April in New York, in Boston, in Italy and Chicago and France, in places she's never heard of, in tiny towns, in Liberty. As she reaches to turn over the month, she hears a soft rustling, like falling leaves, as thousands of pages on thousands of calendars turn.

*I*ndian summer stretches on in Liberty, 1955 the hottest November on record. In New York, the women in the office where Eleanor types tease her all through lunch for going out without a coat. She laughs and waves away the scarves and hats they thrust at her, patting at the perspiration rising inexplicably on her forehead.

She is typing a letter that afternoon when the cry of *Snow!* bubbles through the office. Suddenly giddy, they gather at the window. It will be rain before it hits the ground but here, ten stories up, the first snowflakes of the season swirl through the air. Darkness comes early; the sky has had an evening cast all afternoon. Eleanor looks at her watch in time to see the minute hand click into place at the top, making a perfect pie slice on the face. Three o'clock.

Down in the street, umbrellas and newspapers emerge to cover heads. The watches all point to three o'clock. Across the city, the bells in clock towers ring out *one . . . two . . . three.*

Down the coast and inland, carved cuckoos emerge three

times from ornately painted doors. The grandfather clock at the Blackmar place, slow now by exactly one hour, chimes twice.

Slumped into a chair, John rouses himself, blinking sleepily. His head hurts, and the whiskey glass next to his chair is empty. "What time is it?" He bellows to the kitchen. He has never learned to compensate for the clock.

"Three." Adam sets a plate beside his father. "Here," he says quietly. "I saved lunch for you."

"Too damn hot to eat," his father says.

*B*efore he leaves for college, Adam opens the clock, and with a few quick twists of a screwdriver, resets it to the correct time for the first time in years. For days, Eleanor is an hour early for every appointment she makes. The man who comes to pick her up for their dinner date finds her waiting impatiently. He cannot understand why—his watch and her own kitchen clock say that he is precisely on time. She does not understand either, but she cannot help but feel, staring across the table at this man, that they come from different worlds. She will tell him that she cannot see him again.

*I*n Liberty, the arrival of someone new changes the town, makes it imperceptibly warmer by the heat of one body, bends the future of the town around one more soul. In New York, too, though the change wrought each moment by a thousand arrivals, departures, births, deaths, decisions of lifetimes and momentary whims fades together into the softly cacophonous hum that the city's people have learned to think of as quiet.

A young man moves into the apartment next to Eleanor's. He wears the same black turtleneck and paint-spattered jeans every day, and his friends arrive nearly every night, shabby and barefoot, for parties that go on until morning.

Eleanor is feeding the cat out on the fire escape when he first speaks to her. He is sitting out on his own fire escape, smoking a cigarette and watching the sunset, and in his worn jeans he looks painfully young, adolescent.

"What's your cat's name?" he says.

She smiles and reaches to scratch the old tom behind the ears. "I don't know," she says. "He hasn't told me."

This surprises him. A slow grin creeps across his face and his eyes crinkle as he looks at her sideways. "You're a pretty cool lady," he says.

His name is Elan, though he admits rather sheepishly one day, his parents spelled it "Alan." He is saving money, he says, to go to Paris to study art. He is a little too thin and drinks a little too much wine, and Eleanor allows a tiny worry to take up residence in a long-dormant corner of her brain. She bakes cookies for Elan and his friends, knits him a black turtleneck sweater for Christmas. He gives her a painting, and when she searches her walls for a bare spot to hang it, she realizes just how long she has been in this place.

When she first arrived at the apartment, its emptiness frightened her. She spent weeks wandering wide-eyed through second-hand stores and furniture showrooms, afraid to make a purchase. But now, her walls are crowded with landscapes, wall hangings, the stuffed doll she won at Coney Island, the charcoal portrait sketched at the street fair. Her shelves are crowded with books and magazines, and she wonders, clearing a space for Elan's painting, how so much *time* has managed to accumulate in just a few years, how more of it settles every day, like dust.

In February, she bakes Elan a birthday cake and joins him in a tiny glass of champagne. She knows that he is twenty-three, but it is not until he mentions offhandedly the year of his birth that she realizes that he is the same age as Adam.

The day Elan leaves for Paris, Eleanor is surprised to find herself dabbing at tears in the corners of her eyes. She should have cried out her lifetime's supply of tears long ago, she thinks, and besides, she is happy, not sad.

Later that afternoon, Adam thinks of his mother as he struggles with his black bow tie. To avoid bad luck, he covers his eyes as he peeks in on his bride, smiling blindly as she ties the bow and plants a delicate kiss on the tip of his nose. Afterward, the wedding ceremony blurs in his memory, but he will remember that kiss for the rest of his life.

*O*n the first day of 1963, Eleanor hangs a new calendar on the kitchen wall. She checks the cat's food. Barely touched. He has been eating less and less in recent weeks. His eyes have grown cloudy, and she does not know if he sees her when she is near or merely feels the heat from her body and knows to purr.

For weeks, she entices him with bits of fish, saucers of cream. She does not scold him for begging but feeds him scraps from her own dinner. He loves mushrooms sautéed with garlic, fried okra, cheese soufflé. She thinks he is gaining a little weight. Perhaps once the weather gets warmer, she thinks, perhaps then his walk will not be so stiff, his breathing so labored. But it has been nearly ten years since he came to her, and he was an old, grumpy tom even then. If he lives until spring, he might survive the summer, but she does not think he will last much longer than that.

In March, there are a few sunny days, and she lets the cat out to sit on the fire escape. One day when she comes home from work, he is gone. There is a chill in the early evening air, and she knows that he has gone away somewhere to die.

She sits by the window anyway. She does not expect him to come back, but she waits. She can feel his tiny weight added to the great burden of her loss. Not even this small grief can she set down into a grave. Her goodbyes have all been unfinished.

In the morning she calls the office and quits her job. She does not give a reason—something has happened, something is about to happen, she does not know. She waits for it. She forgets to wind her watch and time stops, though the light still changes, the sound from the cars in the street waxes by day, wanes in the darkest hours of the night. She does not know what is coming, but she waits. She gets her things in order.

By the time she receives the telegram telling of John's death, her suitcase is already packed, waiting by the door.

Two

*A*bove the tiny whistle-stop station, a bubble of memory waits. It sees the stars are not points but circles and spirals of light, and the seasons wax and wane like stitches of embroidery thread. The sun rises and falls; a woman steps off the train over and over again, and the town parts, always, to make a place for her.

The town of Liberty is more faithful than any lover. It stubbornly clings to the knowledge that someday the woman will learn to return its love. On that day, all the hope it has placed in this brave, timid creature will flower. She is coming home.

The bubble bursts, sending memory spilling everywhere. Memory settles into the dust, seeps into the groundwater, hides in the corners of eyes with the unspilled tears. The woman breathes the early morning air, sweeter here than anywhere else on earth, and for no reason she can fathom she begins to laugh.

Liberty. As soon as she stepped from the train, Eleanor could feel it, the town reaching out to encircle her, eyes brushing like flies against her back, whispers clinging like humid air to the shape of her body. How odd that she noticed it. Maybe that was why she had laughed, recognizing this feeling that had once been as familiar to her as her own heartbeat, or the sound of gravel and leaves crunching under her feet as she walked. That bothered her, too, at first—she had grown used to city walking, where any sound made by your footsteps was masked by the noise of a thousand other feet, of cars honking, the screech of brakes, voices, a woman's scream or maybe laugh, the faint sound of music from an alleyway. Here, even the birds stopped singing as she walked past the trees. By morning, not a soul in Liberty would be unaware of her presence. She clutched the telegram tighter. Her palm was sweating, but she would not loosen her hold though the type blurred under her touch.

She was glad when the road turned away from the main stretch of town and began to pass the farms. Houses were more scattered out here, and tractors moved back and forth in the fields, preparing the earth for the spring seeds. It was a little late in the year for planting, wasn't it? she wondered, and the answer came to her: *long, hard winter, and then the floods.*

She could hear the creek, high still from the heavy spring rains. She clutched the telegram. There was no reason to be afraid. Everything she had ever feared was gone. She turned the corner and the old two-story Victorian appeared. Its paint was peeling and the flowers in the yard had withered into sticks, but otherwise, it seemed unchanged, preserved as in the recesses of her memory. Her breathing shallowed and her stomach grew tight. Perhaps what she truly feared was still here. Perhaps it was not John, but the town itself.

The thought came to Eleanor suddenly, foreignly, and just as she was wondering where it came from, she wondered why she had never realized it before, why on the train all the way from New York, and all along the road through town from the depot, she had clutched the wrinkled telegram in her hand like a passport, a ticket, and it was only now, when she had left the paved road for the dirt path up to the house, that the thought came. *Perhaps it was Liberty all along.*

She could feel the prickling of memory and she was relieved when it arrived that it was not dangerous. It was her grandfather's huge, rough hand taking hers as he looked to the sky. It had been on a cold afternoon—late October, perhaps early November? It was just a few weeks after her sixth birthday, so soon that the novelty of counting her age on two hands had not worn off. Sunday afternoon, watching grandfather as he read to her from the pages of his heavy black Bible. She couldn't understand its odd, old-fashioned language, so different from her children's picture Bible, and her legs, too short to reach the floor, ached with the effort to keep still instead of swinging.

She was looking out the window, watching snow scatter into

little piles outside when she realized that her grandfather's low, melodic voice was no longer reading. She looked up, expecting a reprimand or at least a disapproving look, but saw that he, too, was staring out at the snow.

"Grandfather?" she said, struck with a sudden thought. "What happens to animals when it's winter? I mean, not the deer or the foxes, or the chipmunks or anything that sleep . . ."

"Hibernate," he corrected.

"I mean, hibernate. But what about the fishes or the frogs? When the lake freezes, does God just let them die?" She hesitated, wondering if she should have said "Our Father" or "Our Lord" instead of God. It seemed disrespectful, somehow, like calling a grown-up by his given name.

Grandfather was still staring out the window. Watching, waiting. "Get your coat," he said.

He led her down the dirt path to the frozen pond. The path was slippery with the icy mud, and, though it stretched her child legs to match his stride, she found it easier to put her feet in the huge footprints her grandfather left behind than walk on the untouched path.

Twilight came early this late in the year, and with the sky this dark with clouds it seemed like night. Frozen and dull now, rapidly whitening in the snow, the lake looked dead, and the sight made Eleanor shudder.

Grandfather moved his hand to indicate the frozen pond. "What you see there," he said, "is merely the surface. All of the living things are there, below. You see, almost everything in the world sinks when it gets cold. But not water. Just before it freezes, the warm water will sink down to the bottom of the pond. The ice may look cruel, or dead, but it is protecting the animals in the warmth below." He reached down and took her hand in his. "You see," he said, staring into her eyes, "God protects his innocent creatures."

"Am I supposed to like Him?" she asked. She tried to think of God (someone, despite her imagination's efforts to produce a man with flowing white hair and a beard, ended up, in her mind, with her grandfather's face every time). He squeezed her hand.

"Our Lord is not 'liked' or 'disliked' but feared and adored."

"What does 'adore' mean?" she asked. He smiled.

"Love," he said, "it means love." Grandfather looked up at the dark sky as tears covered his face. His lips moved in silent, rapid prayer as immaculate snowflakes melted on his skin, whitened his hair. Eleanor had watched the lake thinking of the creatures, swimming in their slow circles, waiting for spring in the dark murkiness below. So she was supposed to fear and love the Lord. Like she feared and loved the picture of her mother, Evalie the wild one. Like she feared the wildness within herself. But how do you love someone you fear? she thought.

Oh God. She had not been prepared for this, for how much stronger the memories would be here. For years Eleanor had skipped her thoughts like stones across the surface of her memory but now the memories were flooding over, spilling out in tears. No, she couldn't handle this now. Even the memories she thought were safe held questions she couldn't answer. She brushed away her tears and tried the front door, finding it, as before, unlocked.

The house was silent. In the dining room, the table, the chairs, the centerpiece, all sat untouched and covered with a thin film of dust. She ran her hands over the pattern carved into the backs of the chairs and tears came to her eyes again. Home, she was *home.* She stumbled into a chair and drew her knees to her chest like a little girl, overwhelmed by the little, ordinary things. It was all so much the same that it did not seem odd to hear heavy footsteps on the porch, see a familiar profile shadowed in the doorway. She wiped away her tears. "John?" she breathed.

"The body's already at the church," he said. "I'm not having visitors until after the funeral." She did not move, trying to make sense of his words, and he tugged on the chain of a lamp in the corner. In the shaft of light, his face looked familiar, but she could not place it until he frowned, first in confusion, then in a slow, pained recognition. "Mother?" he said.

It was then that she saw that his eyes were gray, not black. "Adam," she said. Her voice caught in her throat and she stood, reaching for him before she realized what she was doing. He tensed under her touch and she pulled away, embarrassed.

"What are you doing here?" he demanded, his voice low but forceful.

She stared at him, trying to recognize her son in this man with John's body, John's voice. "I . . . have a telegram," she said. She held out the piece of paper and only then did she see that her hand was shaking. He took the telegram from her so sharply she flinched.

He looked at her then. "Jesus," he said more gently, "I'm not going to hurt you."

"Sorry." She looked away while he read the telegram. She could feel her shoulders slumping forward, her chest constricting as she sank back into her Liberty self. She brushed at the dust on the tabletop with her fingers but only made streaks on the wood.

"Who sent this?" he said, his voice tinged with suspicion.

"I thought you had." She reddened. How foolish of her to think he would want her there, to think Liberty would be any less unbearable now than it had ever been. Nothing ever changed; generations copied themselves and began again, and just because a place for her remained didn't mean she wanted to fill it. John was gone, but his son had grown up into another pair of eyes to avoid, another set of accusations to shrink from. A heavy nausea settled over her. "I shouldn't have come," she managed to say.

A young woman appeared behind Adam, framed in the doorway. Standing in sunlight, all bright dark eyes and luminous curls, she seemed to belong to a different world than the heavy, dusty room. "Adam?" she said. She touched his arm and a shadow of that other world softened his face, but only for a moment. He pulled his arm away from her touch, not harshly, but confusion and hurt wrinkled between her eyes, and she questioned him silently.

"It's my mother," he whispered, "Eleanor." The woman raised her eyebrows and a look passed between them of such silent intimacy that Eleanor was embarrassed to witness it. Adam turned to her. "This is Gwen," he said, "my wife."

His wife? It hit her then, exactly how long she had been away. This man, this copy of John was her son, and she had missed more of his life than she had seen. The town had not been preserved by her memory; it had gone on without her, and though the trees looked the same, seasons and seasons of leaves had turned and fallen irreplaceably. Years of time weighed down on er all at once, the layers of air impossibly heavy. She struggled to breathe. "Perhaps I should go."

It was Gwen who caught her arm and led her to a chair before she fell. "Don't be silly," she said. "Of course you can't go now." She turned to Adam for confirmation.

He stood with his arms folded, not looking at either of them. "It's her house, not mine," he said. "Do whatever you want."

"Adam . . ." Gwen reached for him, but he pulled away sharply.

"You two just do whatever the hell you want." His feet were heavy on the wooden floor, and Eleanor was blinded for a moment by the flood of bright sunlight as he opened the back door. It slammed behind him, leaving the women dazed and quiet in the shadowed house.

Gwen went to the window and pulled back the curtain, blinking in the light. She moved, Eleanor thought, rather like a dragonfly, darting quickly from corner to corner. Even her stillness seemed to have an air of hovering. How had Adam discovered this creature, captured her? She thought with a shudder of the boys she had known as a child, the ones who set out to catch things with nets and jars, then left them at suppertime, forgotten, to die in the sun. But that was not the way of the Cline men. They set out webs and waited for their prey, preferring to suck them slowly dry in the comfort of their own homes.

"I'm sorry," Gwen said. "I don't know what's wrong with him. He's not . . ." She took Eleanor's hand. "Please don't go." Her touch was cool and strong and reminded Eleanor of Natalie's. Her eyes brimmed with hurt and confusion as she looked back over her shoulder in the direction Adam had gone. It was a look Eleanor recognized from her own first years of marriage, when John's sudden cruelties still surprised her, in those years before she had stopped expecting a happy life. Gwen brushed at her eyes, laughing a little at the tears that came away on her fingers. "You must be tired," she said. "We'll set up your room."

The bedroom was a little faded, a little mustier, but otherwise just as she'd left it. John's toiletries, his shaving things, still lay out on the dresser. A pair of pants was tossed over a chair. "I'm sorry,"

Gwen said. "We just got here ourselves—I'll clear the things away."

Eleanor shook her head. "No," she said. "No, this is fine." She sat tentatively on the edge of the bed. "I just need some rest, that's all. I didn't sleep at all on the train. I just . . . couldn't."

Gwen nodded slowly. "Sleep, then," she said, and her voice was so soothing and low Eleanor felt she might be able to. It was quiet here, so quiet she could hear the stream and the rustle of the trees. She closed her eyes, listening.

There was still a sag on the other side of the bed, where John had slept. Eleanor moved into it, comforted by the way the mattress reached up around to swaddle her. And it comforted her, too, to know that for all these years, he had still kept to one side of the bed, leaving the other empty, waiting for her.

She thought of Gwen, how the girl insisted even through her tears, even to a stranger, that Adam was not what he appeared to be. Her heart tightened again—what was it that bound them to these men? Even harshness could be a comfort, if it was what one came to expect. She breathed in the smell of the bedclothes. John's scent was there, faint, but undeniably present. She wrapped her arms around the pillow and buried her face in the soft feathers. She fell asleep half-expecting to wake up with her cheek pressed against her husband's back.

$\mathcal{G}$wen knew where to find him. Though she had never been down the path to the lake, she knew it from his stories, whispered in bed as he held her in the dark. He would hold her so close that she could feel the words brush the back of her neck like butter-flies, images perching in her mind like birds.

These spring evenings are still crisp and cold. A figure sitting on the tall, flat rock curls his arms around his knees, but does not leave. In the shadow of the sunset, it is hard to tell whether this slight form is a man or merely a boy, but he watches carefully as one by one, the stars emerge in the clear night sky. Their light is millions of years old and has traveled unimaginably far to come to rest lightly on the surface of this dark lake. And so the water becomes a mirror of the past, of the shards of memory spread out across the sky.

Adam did not look at her as she climbed up beside him, but when she sat down, he leaned into her body, her warmth. They sat in silence for a while, watching the sunset fading, watching the lights come on in the houses across the lake.

"That one's new," Adam said as a light came on in one win-dow. "That house wasn't there when I left Liberty."

Gwen stroked his hair. "The lights look a little like stars com-ing out."

He nodded. "I used to come out here as a kid, after my mother left." Gwen drew breath to ask a question, but Adam kept speak-ing. "I remember when we learned in school that the stars were so far away that the light we see actually left them hundreds or thousands of years ago. And I came out here and looked up and thought, if something wiped out all of the stars, killed them all at once, it would be so many years before we even began to suspect that anything was wrong. One by one the stars would wink out, the closest ones first, then those farther and farther away, but for hundreds of years, maybe, everything would look fine, even though we were all alone."

"Do you want to tell me what's going on? Why you ran out to-day?" She'd meant to ask gently but a waver of something— fear?—crept into her voice and came out sounding like anger. He tensed, and she could feel him close, surely as if he'd pulled down a window shade.

"I went for a walk," he said. "I'm sorry I didn't tell you exactly what I was doing every minute."

"That's not what I meant. You know that." As a child, she had played a game in the school yard with her friends. With eyes closed, two girls would spin in circles then be set to walk ten paces side by side, trusting blindly that their steps would take them in the same direction, to the same place. Then, still dizzy from the spinning and the heat, one would turn and fall back-ward, hoping that the other would be there to catch her. Gwen felt like that again now; every step, she could feel Adam moving away from her, but she was helpless to change direction, unable even to open her eyes to see where he had gone. If she fell, could she trust him? "You told me your mother was dead."

He shrugged. "For all I knew she might have been," he said. "I haven't seen her since I was thirteen."

"Not knowing that someone is alive isn't the same thing as knowing that she is dead," Gwen said. "You said she was dead. Adam, you lied to me."

"No, no." He buried his forehead in the heels of his hands, kneading his thick, dark hair with his fingertips. "Look, she was either alive or dead. I didn't know." His voice was clipped, as if each word were a piece in a precisely crafted puzzle. "I had to be-lieve one or the other. I chose to believe she was dead. It left fewer loose ends." He leaned into Gwen and she put her arm around him, drawing him close. "Please don't be angry."

"I'm not." She wasn't, either. She didn't feel anything at all, except a soft, diffused loneliness. She buried her face in his hair, breathing in his warm, familiar scent. "What else haven't you told me?"

There was a long pause. "Nothing," he said. She could see the lie swirling smoky in the air around him, black and purple, like a bruise. She could feel something drop away between them, her stomach sinking in sudden vertigo. He looked up at her, the expression in his face so desperately, aggressively honest it only confirmed that he was hiding something. She would not give a sign that she knew. She smiled, looking into his eyes without meeting them.

"Come inside," she said. "We could build a fire, and I'll play for you. I tuned the piano today." He shook his head, but when she took his hand, he slipped off the rock beside her in the soft dirt. When they came to the place of the two entwined trees, Adam stopped suddenly. His hand darted into the grass below the tree. Gwen smiled, genuinely this time, and for a moment, everything was familiar, solid.

"Even in this light?" she said. Adam deposited the four-leaf clover in her palm.

"Even in this light." He put his arms around his wife and kissed her, the first real, passionate kiss since they'd come to Liberty. He pulled away and rested his forehead on hers, smiling. "It's not quite dark. Not yet."

He had found his first four-leaf clover the day he met Gwen. It was his first year at Harvard, his first year away from Liberty. It was one of those bright early March mornings that everyone treated like spring just because they were so tired of winter, a sunny morning that could just as easily turn to rain or hail or even snow, if it wanted to.

This particular morning was turning to rain. Adam frowned at the sky and clutched his books to his chest as he hurried across campus. He was late already and he'd been up until just before dawn writing the paper that was shoved casually into one of his books. If it hadn't been for his roommate, Brandon, who had shaken him awake and even pulled the last page of the paper out of the typewriter where Adam had left it, he would have missed class, something he was doing more and more of lately. His life was no longer bound by the borders of Liberty, and the sheer newness of everything gave him vertigo. He had dreams that left him burning and exhausted when he woke, trembling with anticipation and unable to remember anything of the dream but the scent of roses. He was glowing—women looked at him and smiled, seeing their husbands of twenty years ago or their sons of tomorrow in this youth. The old cats who lived behind the dining halls and spit and hissed over the throwaway scraps would roll onto their backs and purr when he passed by, and Brandon, who just had *sense*, had finally asked him when he was going to give in and go mad.

It was certainly very like madness, this exhaustion and frustration and the bright, cold sun. But then, what *wasn't* mad, really? He was passing in front of the statue of John Harvard. His first week at school, Brandon had brought him to it and pointed out that despite what the plaque read, the man in the statue was *not* John Harvard, who at any rate had *not* founded the college, and the date of the college's establishment was wrong by two years. "It's all lies," Brandon had said. "But even so, it's true, because it's written down. Put down in *art*, even. So what's real?" They had laughed at this and finished off Brandon's bottle of red wine and linked arms, fast friends.

He laughed again at the memory, the thought that everything was mad. So it was not too surprising that when he cut across the Yard and saw Gwendolyn Emerson standing knee-high in dandelions, locks of her red hair like snakes in the wind, he was frozen solid where he stood, and when he finally forced himself to breathe, the air was heavy with the scent of roses.

He had seen her before—she was a Radcliffe girl in his philosophy class, the one he was missing right now as a matter of fact. She would sit in the corner of the classroom, quietly listening while Professor Sawyer gave his lectures, then at the very end of class raise her hand to gently ask a question or offer a counterargument that left him speechless. It was a technique that others in the class had tried to copy, and Sawyer had answered them all with his legendary sarcastic rebuttals; Gwendolyn Emerson alone left him without reply.

Standing in the grassy field, wet to his ankles in dew, Adam understood. Her very presence made him mute. He felt a desperate desire for something with which to present her, to make up for the words he had lost. He looked at his feet and found there a four-leaf clover. It was the only thing he could think of to offer, and it had appeared, after all, just as he had called for it.

"Would you like . . .," he began. She met his eyes and he fell silent, dropping the small green token into her palm. When she saw what it was she grinned, and in a flash popped it into her mouth.

"Hey!" Adam did not know what he had expected her to do with the cloverleaf—press it between the pages of a book, he supposed, for luck.

"It wouldn't do any good there," she said. Her voice was strong and musical, the same as when she answered Sawyer's arguments, only colored now by the sunshine and the crisp air. "The luck has to be inside you, a part of you."

Adam smiled then. It seemed no stranger to him that she had read his thoughts than it had to find the clover at the exact moment he had desired it. His restlessness, it seemed, had found a focus; when the last snow of the season came that night, long after anyone had expected the weather to turn, he went to the window again and again, hoping to see her figure moving through the swirling white moonlight, to call out to her, or just to catch a glimpse of the fiery curls escaping in the wind from the hood of her black wool cloak. And though he had never spotted a single four-leaf clover before, from that moment on, he found them wherever he went.

She had brought him to the clover field the third time they made love and he had found a four-leaf clover in the moonlight, poking through the silky curls of her hair. He had been worried, at first, that they would be seen; though it was after midnight, the moon was brighter than daylight, and Harvard Yard was not exactly deserted, even after curfew. The clover patch was a common shortcut for those coming home from the library or sneaking back from some late-night tryst. As it was, the only one who came near was a boy heading for the river, and he was so intent on his stopped pocket watch, he barely glanced up at them as he passed. Gwen brushed her hand through the clover in a circle around them and smiled.

"No one will see us now," she said, and though he laughed, he closed his eyes and buried himself in the recesses of her body, trusting in their invisibility.

He'd married her as quickly as he could, as soon as she would agree to be his, and holding her wrapped tightly in his arms on their wedding night, he'd slept deeply and well for the first time in years. Gwen said it was the lavender she sewed into the pillows, but he knew that it was *her*, her presence, because he would jerk awake from the deepest sleep, his heart pounding, if she got up during the night.

*L*ater, curled together in Adam's narrow childhood bed, Gwen could feel his fear, but not its source. Dinner had been nearly silent, Gwen bookended between two dark figures so quiet they might have been made of stone. Forks clinked against china. Eleanor praised Gwen's eggplant. Gwen thanked her, saying the trick was to salt it before cooking. A lifeless exchange of recipes followed before the conversation died back into full mouths and silence. Adam and his mother were painfully polite to one another, each too stubborn to speak, too shy to look up from the faded tablecloth. When Gwen suggested an early night, both smiled thin half-smiles at her and murmured agreement.

Settling into bed, Gwen tried to ignore the fear and concentrate on the familiarity. She slid a hand under her long hair to pull it back onto the pillow, off of her neck and he, in a well-practiced dance, raised his chin so his forehead settled into the curve of her nape. Adam fit his body into her familiar shape, wrapping an arm around her so that his fingers brushed her collarbone. She shifted against him, her breast slumping cozily into the crook of his elbow. Together they drew deep breaths and sighed, then laughed at their predictability. He kissed the curve where her neck met her clavicle. She smiled and took his hand and he kissed her again, this time grasping with his teeth. She pulled away.

"Like before," she whispered. He brushed his tongue gently against her neck until she turned and met his mouth with her own. He stroked her breast and took a nipple in his fingers. In the dark, warm cocoon of the blanket, everything was all right. She reached for him.

He was hard against her thighs, but when she grasped him he

wilted like a plucked poppy in her hand. His shoulders tensed in frustration.

"Oh God," he whispered.

"Shh." She had been tense, afraid of this, and now that it had happened, it was almost a relief. His arousal had always been fragile, capricious, sensitive to his moods, and ever since they had decided to try to start a family, this had happened every time.

"I want a baby," he said. "Dammit, I really do."

"I know," she said. She kissed him to quiet him. "Shh . . . I know." She regretted ever having asked the question, months ago, the first time this had happened. She just didn't have the energy for another fight, those horrible, nightlong torments, tearing and tearing and tears and, finally, at dawn, capitulation to the inevitability of their love. "It will happen eventually."

"Can I still . . . please you?" he asked. She hesitated, then nodded, guiding his hand.

She waited for the familiar sensations, the prickling pleasure to warm her hands and feet, but when she closed her eyes, she felt the dark mist hovering, swirling with his fear, his lies, the things he still withheld. His long, thin fingers moved faster, tensing, and she worried that her pleasure would not come at all, that the encounter would leave them each alone, separated for the rest of the night by frustration and fear.

She drew into herself, into her memories of a time when he had been able to draw pleasure like music from her, when the tenuous thread of her arousal had tightened and strengthened, sending sharp warmth through her body. She moaned at the memory, making little rhythmic cries. Adam felt very far away, and she pushed even deeper into the past. When she summoned perfectly the memory of the way he had once made her feel, she arched her back, propelling her pelvis into his hand like a ripe, round fruit. She gave a final, shuddering moan and brought herself into the present again.

When her muscles relaxed into the cool, damp pillow, she opened her eyes to find that Adam's were shining. He was covered in sweat, and his breathing was as quick as hers. She looked away, smiling a little as if shyness, not shame, kept her from meeting his eyes. The pleasure was not false, she told herself, just . . . displaced in time. Still, her deception rose from her body like heat, darkening the cloud that hovered over them.

"You're beautiful," he whispered. He settled himself against her body, resting his face between her breasts, which he kissed gently.

"I love you," she said, and he nodded, smiling. He had never, not even proposing, been able to say those words to her. It hadn't mattered to her then—she could see his love playing in his eyes like sunlight on rippling waves, hear its melody running through his dreams at night. But now, his silence weighed on her with a cool, heavy sadness. What was she to do with this child-man? Their love was a strange, fragile creature, something which had been put into her hands, into her care. She had not chosen to love him; perhaps she would have chosen someone else, someone not so shadowed, haunted. But he had been brought to her, was meant to be hers. Even at the beginning, they had spoken like an old married couple, finishing each other's sentences, understanding one another's most obscure references, most subtle jokes. "I love you," she said again, thinking of his brilliance, his intensity, the way he bent with utter concentration over whatever he was doing.

"Forever?" he whispered. She stroked her hands through his hair.

"Forever," she said, pressing him to her breasts so he would not see the tears spilling onto her cheeks.

*D*own the hall, Eleanor lay in the dark, pressing her face into the musty pillow. She had heard the rhythm of the creaking bed, first confused by the noise, then embarrassed. She remembered John's body moving on top of hers, rubbing himself against her, then parting her thighs with his knee. The memory aroused her in spite of herself, in spite of the anger it also brought, and she drew the quilt around her, tucked between her legs.

The men she had dated in New York had wanted to know her past, her history, and she could not find the words. She had never divorced John—divorcing him would mean letting him know where she was—and so she knew she could never marry any of those men. It was easier to stop looking at them at all. She certainly never wondered how the weight of their bodies would feel, or if they would move the way John had . . . though on the hot, sticky nights of New York's summers, she would strip off her nightgown to release the heat of her body, and in the air, thick and palpable on her flesh, she would think of Liberty and Natalie and imagine the caress of a faceless lover.

The thought of Natalie made her clutch the blanket tighter. Would she ever be able to love someone, trust someone again? Natalie had slipped into her heart through cracks and side doors; the men who courted her had tried to waltz in the front gate, only to find the lock had rusted shut.

She realized she had been holding her breath to the memory and released it with a soft sigh. At the same moment, she heard little cries beginning in the next room—not sobs, as she thought for an instant, but a woman's small sounds of pleasure. Eleanor lay still, mesmerized by the building, fluttering voice. She shallowed her own breathing to better hear as the cries rose and quickened. She could feel the house straining to hear, also curious, adding another layer to the peeling wallpaper of its memory. Were these sounds that the house had ever heard?

This stranger who was her son was in that room. She wondered how he moved, what he did with his body, so like John's, to draw out that sweet music. She pictured the two of them, moving to the rhythm of the cries. A shiver traveled down her spine. The rhythm suddenly broke and a tense moment of silence was followed with one long, shuddering moan. Eleanor could hear her heart pounding. She let out a ragged breath.

She felt very warm, and pushed aside the quilt. In the silence, shame settled over her like the cool air. Her cheeks burned, and she remembered the shivers of pleasure Adam's baby mouth had pulled from her nipples while her husband snored, oblivious, in the next room.

The walls of the house watched her, and she pulled the quilt back over herself despite her heat. In her tiny, two-room apartment, she had never felt the sense of claustrophobia this house inspired, the feeling that people could peer right into her shameful thoughts.

Sleep was settling into her now, and her muscles relaxed. What she wanted was someone to touch her, to touch her and to care about how the touch felt on her skin, to speak to her and care what she said in return. Yes, just someone to talk to, laugh with. That would be enough. A tear rolled down her face and settled in her ear. She was lonely, had always been lonely, even in New York, in the crowds and crowds of people. She curled back into the sag on John's side of the bed and wondered if he had been lonely without her. His scent was still there, but lightly, faintly underneath, she could smell Natalie's violet, vanilla odor. It soothed her, and as she fell asleep, she dreamed she felt a hand holding hers in the dark.

*E*vening in Liberty sidles in like smoke, hiding behind each golden speck of dust in the air. Slowly, everything grows heavy. Plants begin to relax and turn their faces from the sun; cats yawn, emerging sleepily from cool barns to seek out warm windowsills. Even the aging shadows stretch out and become soft around the edges. Only the birds find evening fit time to make a fuss, calling and crying, sending whole trees into motion and noise.

Just off the path leading from the Blackmar place into town, two trees grow intertwined. In the summertime, when the leaves cover the branches, it is hard to tell them apart, though in the winter you can see that one is darker and thicker than the other.

The branches are too spindly for climbing, and initials carved into the bark fade away in days, so children leave the trees alone. In the spring, though, flocks of red birds descend for a few days on their migration North. Before the first spring flowers bloom on the ground, the tree swarms with feathers in a living crimson blossom and shakes with a sound like a hundred thousand crickets. For a few days in spring, the tree is as red as autumn; then, like leaves falling strangely into the sky, the birds lift away again, revealing branches now covered in pale green buds.

A single red feather sat on the step in front of the General Store. Eleanor knelt to pick it up as Adam unlocked the door.

Gwen paused behind her. "What kind of bird has feathers like that?"

Eleanor shook her head. "I . . . I don't know. We always just called them the red birds. They come every spring."

"Fall, too." The women looked up at Adam's soft voice. "You just don't notice them so much, because they're the same color as the leaves then."

Eleanor looked up at her son, his pale gray eyes that saw everything. The sun was reflected in them now, turning orange as it began to think about setting. "C'mon," she said gently, "let's see what's in there."

They both drew breath as Adam swung open the door. Everything stood untouched, the shelves in neat rows, the counter up front as always. A thin film of dust had settled onto every flat surface. Gwen sneezed, and the noise was so sudden in the stillness that the three of them laughed. It seemed silly that Eleanor's heart was beating so fast. What had she expected to find there, anyway?

Adam rummaged behind the counter to find a pad of paper and a small stub of pencil. "We'll have to write down everything that's left of the stock," he said. "If we're lucky, we'll be able to sell it all in one lot."

For an instant, Eleanor could see the store standing empty, pale stripes on the floor where the shelves had stood so long, protecting the wood from layers of time and dirt. Her eyes glazed with tears, and when she blinked again, everything in the store was as it had always been. "It seems sad," she said. "I mean . . . the store has been in the family for so long. It's a tradition." Adam gave her a look that said *What do you care about tradition? Or family?* Eleanor looked away. "It just seems a little strange."

"Are you planning on coming back here to run it?" he asked sarcastically. He took the pad of paper to a far shelf and began unstacking cans to see how many rows there were. He glanced down the length of the shelf, closed his eyes for a moment, calculating, and jotted down a number.

"I remember, you were always good at math," Eleanor said. Adam glanced up but did not speak, then moved on to another shelf.

Gwen came and sat on the stool behind the counter, resting

her chin on her hand. "How long has this place been in your family?"

Adam looked up and shrugged. "Years," he said. He made another note on the tablet.

"Generations," Eleanor said. "Since my great-grandmother came to Liberty."

"You can tell," Gwen said. "It *feels* like a place where people have been, a place they came to over and over again." She ran a hand over the surface of the counter, frowning slightly as if trying to recapture a fleeting memory. "Were there ever . . . *jars* here, jars of candy?" She touched the front of the countertop. "Here . . . and here?" Eleanor nodded. Gwen did, too, smiling. "I can picture a little girl in a pink dress reaching into the jars."

Eleanor looked up. *Evalie.* How long did ghosts take to fade? "With long brown hair?" she said. Her voice wavered, and she could barely hear with her heartbeat pounding through her head. "In ribbons?"

Gwen's eyes were alive. "I can smell the candy," she said. "Peppermints were . . . here." She touched the spot where the jar had stood. Eleanor nodded dumbly. Gwen moved her hand about six inches. "And licorice"—she looked up—"makes you sad. Why?"

"Gwen." There was a note of warning, or perhaps fear, in Adam's voice. "I could use some help here."

"I'll help," Eleanor said. She went over to where Adam stood with a bolt of cloth and held the end as he unrolled the bolt to see how much was left. She did not turn to look at Gwen, but instead concentrated on the cloth, a soft blue-gray cotton.

"Is there a tape measure?" Adam said.

"It's four yards," Eleanor said. He raised an eyebrow.

"I used to do a good bit of sewing," she said.

He smiled. "Thanks," he said. She stepped toward him slowly as he rolled up the cloth. He paused to stroke the material before replacing it on the shelf. "You had a dress made of this once."

"When you were a baby," she said. She had loved that dress, sky-colored and soft and loose enough to wear in even the last months of her pregnancy, but it had been worn into rags by the time Adam was three. "You couldn't possibly remember that."

"I remember," he said.

Gwen laughed, a light ripple of laughter that tumbled out like bubbles in the air. "This town is layers thick in memories," she said.

*T*he air was shimmery. Gwen could feel it pressing around her, little warm vibrations against her skin. She could see its ripples in the light like the heat mirages that rose off the road in summertime. Miracle weather, her grandmother, Clarissa, had called it.

They had called her grandmother a witch and so she became one, listening with all her might to the whispering demons that twined their fingers in her hair and learning all she could about the properties of herbs and the phases of the moon. By the time she was eighteen, people were coming to her from all over town to cure their ills, in daylight for matters of digestion or rheumatism, and after the sun set for the pains of love and bitter revenge.

She must have known at least a little about both, because on her twenty-first birthday she appeared, in advanced labor, on the steps of the hospital, screaming that since she was the only woman in town who knew how to midwife, she had no choice but to let some man deliver the child out of her.

They wanted to know which man had put the child into her in the first place. She was unmarried; no one had even known she was pregnant until that morning. But she steadfastly refused to name a man, and when her daughter, Bianca, was born, they had to leave the father's name on the birth certificate blank. She never breathed a word at the speculations, and there was only once that she answered the questions with anything other than a stony silence—when the minister visited, uninvited, to absolve her of her sin, he asked her to give only him the father's name. Clarissa had smiled at him sweetly and answered "God."

Perhaps it was the lack of a father's love that made her daughter, Bianca, Gwen's mother, so hungry for a husband's. From childhood she tried to divine the face of her future love in dreams, or discover his name by crossing out common letters in her name and those of the boys she knew.

She was sixteen when she fell in love with Robert Emerson. He was one of the rich kids at school, part of the laughing, boisterous crowd that brushed past her in the halls without looking twice, or laughed behind her back at her weird, hand-sewn clothes.

Nothing she tried seemed to work—the flower she planted in earth taken from his footprint withered and died despite her diligent care. Candles carved with his name and hers and set to burn in the light of the full moon drowned in their own wax as soon as she turned her back on them or blew out in winds no one felt. Still Robert ignored her, though he was beginning to seem uneasy when he caught her staring at him and she would not look away.

Finally, she turned to the strongest spell she knew. She took scraps of his hair (stolen from the barbershop floor) and burned them in a bonfire with salt and her own blood. It was a curse, really, designed to give the accursed one no peace as her face burned in his thoughts night and day. They would be bound together; only death could free him from her power.

After her own long torture of frustrated yearning, it was a pleasure to watch her torment work on him. He lost weight, and dark circles appeared under his eyes. His parents called it mononucleosis and took him out of school, but within days, he appeared at Bianca's door, declaring what she already knew, that he would have no rest until she was his. They were married that spring.

One night, eleven days after their wedding, he was coming home and his car went over a bridge. He died on impact. Probably never felt a thing, they said; he must have fallen asleep at the wheel—there were no skid marks to indicate that he'd tried to stop, and not even signs that he'd tried to turn away from the cliff that killed him.

Bianca never even cried—she just began slowly to fade away. She would spend her days sitting in a corner, staring off into space. She would eat only when her mother put food in front of her—otherwise, she seemed to have forgotten hunger along with everything else, though her stomach slowly bulged under her dress. When, nine months later, her daughter was born, the milk would not come into Bianca's breasts, and so Gwendolyn's first meals were soups and teas Clarissa heated up, and her first memories were of a grandmother whispering and mixing herbs while her mother wandered dazedly through the house, silent as a ghost.

So before she had learned to spell her own name, Gwen had known that willow bark would treat a headache and that some forms of heartache had no cure. It was a legacy passed down, like linens folded away into a cedar hope chest. But Gwen had never felt this electricity in the air before, and she wondered if madness or sorcery could be monogrammed and passed on.

The sky was dark when she began to sense a buzzing in her head, and by the time they got back to the house, she could feel the shadows brushing against the fine hairs on her skin, pulling at her from the corners of her sight. Before going to sleep she lit a white candle and placed it on the windowsill. The glass reflected the bright flame, the shadowy room, her own body wrapped in the quilt. The flicker of the candle changed the shadows on her face, shifting the expression of her smile from love to regret and back again. Which one was real? She wanted to see it in the light, but a dream was already tickling in the back of her mind, flickering like the candle flame, pulling her eyelids down. She slept.

Music. Somewhere far away, a piano, a soft sprinkling of notes, not quite a song, but somehow familiar. Her breath comes out in a soft hum, catching up with the piano, then running ahead of it. And when she draws breath again, the air is summer-warm, thick with the scent of honeysuckle. *She is sitting on the porch with Eleanor, watching the last wrinkles of sunset in the sky. Eleanor takes her hand. This is love, she thinks.*

But wait—that isn't her hand. The name that comes to mind when she thinks *me* isn't hers. She moves inside, floating.

A man is sitting at the piano. He has Adam's shoulders, Adam's hair, but when he looks at her his eyes are black as lies, his mouth the shape Adam's takes to form cruelties. She can see herself living with this man, sleeping beside him, cringing when he touches her. She thinks—has she ever loved anyone? The man she was going to marry, did she love him?

His face is blurry through her tears. She brushes them away

and sees that he is crying, too, his blond hair falling over his face. Natalie, why didn't you tell me before? he says.

*G*wen woke. The candle had burned down almost to nothing and the window showed the first broken scraps of dawn. A damp chill was in the air. She was shivering, but not from the cold. A man slept beside her, his breathing heavy and regular. She could hear the low murmur of his dreams, but she could not see his face. He was shaped like her husband; he was shaped like the man from the dream. She took the stub of candle from the windowsill and cupped her hand around it, directing the soft glow onto his face. Adam's face. Relaxed, in the soft glow of the candlelight, he did not look at all like that man, the one from her dream. He turned, reaching for her in his sleep. She blew out the candle and pressed against his warm body as much for the soft, ordinary dream as for the warmth. He shifted to wrap himself around her, his face nuzzled into the crook of her neck. His breath was warm, and she pulled the quilt up around her ears, but even then her shaking did not stop.

*L*iberty watches as seasons pass, years spinning faster than the bobbins on the women's sewing machines. To the town, there is no death; children grow and take their parents' places as seamlessly as the frames flickering together on movie screens. The town is old enough that its sight is no longer perfectly clear, and the difference from generation to generation seems no more than a trick of the light.

Death is an invention of mortals. It has an edge to it that age does not, an hour, a minute to point to and say, *Here is where it happened.* Those who can measure their lives in minutes can set one moment under glass, bronzed forever. Telegrams are never sent to say someone is growing old.

And yet, standing there before her husband's coffin, Eleanor was more surprised to find John old than dead. It shouldn't have surprised her—after all, over thirteen years had passed since she had last seen him, more than enough time to etch wrinkles into a face where only character lines had been before, to turn the dark hair that had been only beginning to salt-and-pepper into a uniform steel gray. Still, she had been prepared to see him dead. But no one sent telegrams announcing how the lines had claimed his face, setting his forehead in a perpetual frown. No one's urgent wires had informed her of the appearance of his jowls, or of the paunch that made his dark wool suit too tight.

She didn't pay much attention as the minister—some young fellow she didn't recognize—spoke about John's importance to the town, to his family, and to God. She tried to swallow, but her throat was tight. She felt as if she was suffocating. What was wrong with her? For thirteen years, the tightness had been there—faded, but there, always ready to surface in tears or a sudden, gripping fear that meant she had to force herself out of bed and would spend the day jumping at every sound, her heart pounding in terror. There was always a reason, before, always the possibility that she would turn some corner and John would be there to kill her or drag her back to Liberty (which was, she thought, just about the same thing) or just *be* there, not to say or do anything, just to *know*. John had always been the name she called her fear by, but he was dead now, and she was still afraid. Which meant that she didn't know why she was afraid, which was worse.

She drew a handkerchief out of her bag and patted the sweat from her face. She heard a rustling murmur from the pews behind her, and realized too late that it must have looked like she was wiping away tears. She cringed under the scrutiny. Half the town had turned up, and most of the ladies from the Sewing Circle, and though Eleanor did not know how the news of her return had spread, she could tell by the way that no one looked at her that most of them had come out of other concerns than respect for the deceased. She was the star of this funeral, she realized, and for a moment she regretted that she had not dug up the shocking black silk dress from thirty years ago. She held her head up and forced herself to swallow. For thirteen years she had not grieved for this man, and she would not grieve for him now. If John had been the name she gave to her fear, then Natalie was her grief, and when she woke in tears, she called for Natalie and pushed away all thoughts of her town, her husband, or her son.

She looked over at Adam, sitting at the end of the pew. He did not seem to hear the eulogy, gave no response even when the minister mentioned him, the "proud son" of the deceased. He was staring off into the distance in a way that reminded Eleanor of the remote look he'd had as a child, thinking of his books or model ships. Eleanor could not catch his eye.

He was angry because Gwen had not come. Eleanor had wakened that morning to the sound of their argument. She could not hear the words, just his deep staccato bursts separated by her fluttering protests, like some angry song written for bass drum and flute. Stumbling into her robe, she had met Adam in the hall.

"Gwen's not feeling well," he said. "She's not coming."

Pale in a long white nightgown, Gwen appeared in the doorway. "I'm sorry," she said. She looked as if she had been crying for a long time, her eyes like soft bruises against her face.

Perhaps they *were* bruises, Eleanor thought. She looked over at her son, still sitting, not listening to the minister's voice. She shuddered. She didn't think Adam had hit his wife. *Yet.* Adam's head jerked up, and he met her eyes with a mixture of fear and anger.

Eleanor was stunned. She hadn't spoken aloud, had she? She wasn't entirely sure, now that she considered it. It had been happening to her more and more—she would be walking down the street entirely absorbed in her own thoughts when she would realize that people passing her would stare for a moment before quickly looking away. Only then would she realize that she had been talking to herself. It wasn't merely the small, mundane things, either, the way the women at the grocery store would mutter their shopping lists like rosaries as they searched the aisles. She would feel a memory pricking at her brain, and before she could stop it, it was *there*, a twenty-year-old pain or the embarrassment from this morning, to be relived in full and excruciating detail.

It came, she supposed, from being alone for so long. Memories became impertinent when they had no competition from real life; soon the past started thinking it had as much right to your life as the present and brazenly intruded where it didn't belong. It wasn't right. But especially here in Liberty, the memories would not leave her alone. They pressed in around her, always threatening to appear but never quite settling into conscious thought. Moving into position, waiting to be realized, yet never approaching nearer than the periphery.

She looked up, meeting Adam's eyes again. As they had left that morning, she had seen Gwen take her husband's hand, looking up into his face with the hint of a question, the way Eleanor had once looked for confirmation of John's love. And Adam had brushed Gwen away, the set of his jaw settling into his father's mouth.

*S*omeone had draped dustcloths over the parlor furniture, but nothing could have kept the dust from creeping in, settling into the antique upholstery and covering the glass knickknacks so that they no longer sparkled in the light. Eleanor opened the heavy drapes to let in the early afternoon sun. A ray of light caught in the cranberry glass and cast a reddish beam onto the wall above the piano. The piano had been uncovered and polished so that it gleamed, but the rest of the room stood ghostly and silent. She pulled the dustcloths from the chair and the settee and used them to wipe off the coffee table. The room still smelled musty and unused, but it would have to do. She forced herself to suppress the feeling of guilt creeping up her spine. The housekeeping here was no longer her responsibility, and if anyone dared to raise a disapproving eyebrow over the state of the parlor, well . . . they could just go to hell.

Eleanor grinned and sat on the settee. She wondered if she would have the courage to actually say something like that to Bonnie Fay. It was ridiculous how much the thought cheered her—she had to cover her mouth with her hand to keep from laughing out loud. She had so wanted to be liked by them for so many years. It seemed petty now—none of them had been as true a friend as Natalie, who had broken every rule and raised every eyebrow in town. Well then, Eleanor thought, if her presence in that town was to be scandalous, she would scandalize.

Her hand darted instinctively, nervously to the nape of her neck. When she'd gotten the telegram, only five days ago, she'd gone to the train station. The next train was not leaving for two hours. In the rest room at the station, she looked with intent and curiosity in a mirror for the first time in years, and found staring back at her the same thin, pale face of Eleanor Blackmar. There was a place she'd half noticed across the street. Not a beauty salon—a barbershop. And without a thought, she strode in, let down the neat bun of hair, just beginning to gray, and said, "Cut it off!" She'd emerged ten minutes later, light-headed and surprised to find that her hair, released of its weight, curled around her ears. The first thirty years of her life she'd spent terrified of scandal; now she was almost as afraid to disappoint those scandalous expectations.

She glanced at the grandfather clock. Two-fifteen, and no callers had arrived to pay their respects after the funeral. Had the haircut been too short? She half wished she'd had time to learn to smoke cigarettes as well. But, then, what was she to expect? At Grandfather's funeral, the twenty-eight-day rain had kept everyone away. At Grandmother's, the house had been filled with the sickly sweet scent of flowers and sweet potato pies for weeks, and Eleanor, who had barely finished her wedding thank-you's, found herself writing dozens of notes on black-bordered stationery, looking up at her new husband and feeling very, very alone.

She had just resigned herself to the fact that no one would come when there was a knock, light but firm, on the front door. Anna Mackay stood on the porch, holding a serious-looking white frosted cake. Her hair was pulled back into a careless bun, and little grayish wisps escaped in curls.

Eleanor smiled, trying to remember manners she hadn't needed in years. "How kind of you to come," she said, leading Anna to the parlor. Her voice sounded shaky and very far away.

Anna smiled wryly. "Had to come see the prodigal daughter." She set the cake on the coffee table.

Eleanor blushed. "I'm . . . glad you came. Really."

"Doesn't look like you've had many visitors."

Eleanor shook her head. With anyone else, she might have been embarrassed. But Anna always told the truth and said exactly what she meant. It had frightened Eleanor as a girl, a young wife, trying too hard to do everything *right*, afraid to show any crack of imperfection. But what was a crack now that the role had been shattered? Eleanor met Anna's eye. "I don't know . . . ," she said. "Perhaps they don't want to see me."

"Or maybe some of them didn't care too much for *him*," Anna said. "Most women in the town and some men, too, were surprised you didn't leave before you did. Why, my cousin Andrew would cross the street to avoid saying hello to John Cline." Anna smiled at the look on Eleanor's face. "Are you surprised? Surprised he made his share of enemies? You knew him better than anyone." Anna sipped her lemonade. "Except maybe Adam," she added. "Adam understood him, which was perhaps even harder."

"They're very alike," said Eleanor.

Anna raised an eyebrow. "You think so?"

Eleanor looked up. It wasn't something she had questioned, not in years. "I . . . don't know," she said.

"Perhaps your son isn't who you think he is." Anna looked up and smiled, remembering. "Adam used to come to our house sometimes, for supper, or just to spend the afternoon. Made friends with my oldest boy, Ben. Used to sit around my kitchen table talking about theories and philosophies, and even when I told them to go outside, get some fresh air, get out from underfoot, they would just sit on the front porch and keep chattering away, happy as clams."

The thought of Adam "chattering away" was vaguely unsettling to Eleanor. "I . . . hope he wasn't any trouble."

Anna Mackay shook her head. "No, no. No trouble at all. In fact, he was a great comfort to me when Avery passed on."

Eleanor opened her mouth to say "I'm sorry, I hadn't heard," but something caught in her throat. She was drowning in something, something pressing against her chest from the inside, trying to get out. She choked, and something broke through something inside her that had been blocking it. The sea overflowed in great salty tears, crashing waves of sobs. Avery was dead. Avery was dead, and she had a son who chattered away at other women's dining tables while to her he said so little you would have thought he was mute.

Anna Mackay had a sympathetic but puzzled expression on her face. "It's going on nine years now," she said, almost apologetically. "I still miss him, but I'm not really alone, with the children and now the grandkids." Eleanor began to laugh.

"I'm sorry." The laughter caught in the sobs. Here she was, the woman who had sat stony at her husband's funeral just hours before, sobbing over the death of another man. The laughter won over. "I'm sorry," she said again.

"It's all right," Anna said. She squeezed Eleanor's hand and smiled gently, lowering her voice. "He was in love with you, you know."

Eleanor looked up. Had she heard that? Or were the memories crowding in on her again? She looked up at Anna's face smiling, sad. "Oh God. I'm so sorry. I never did anything . . . I never knew."

"I know, Eleanor, I know." Anna looked away. "You didn't have to do anything. You were always his dream, his ideal. And I'm here to say I'm sorry. When I told you all those years ago about John and the girl, I told everyone, myself even, that it was a kindness, the right thing to do. But really it was meanness, jealousy. It didn't seem fair, your life so perfect, your husband so handsome, so rich, and Avery loved you, too. . . ." Tears welled in Anna's eyes and she blotted them with a handkerchief.

Eleanor drew her arms around her legs, resting her chin on her knees, the way she had as a child when Grandmother wasn't looking. "My life wasn't perfect," she said. Why was that so hard to say? Her voice felt growly, far away, the way it always did when she finally spoke the truth. Was her heart so far away now that what was spoken from it came to her as through a long, dark tunnel? "My life was never perfect," she said. Her heart was pounding rapidly, she spoke rapidly, as if spilling some great secret. "I tried to make it seem so, because otherwise, I would have had to admit . . ." Her throat tightened and she swallowed painfully. "To admit . . . what a terrible mistake I'd made." She moved to the window. The sun touched the tops of the trees, cast shadows over Anna's blue pickup truck, parked by the road. "I was seventeen and foolish and there was nothing, *nothing* I'd ever wanted as much as I wanted John. I loved everything about him that wasn't important—his looks, his clothes, the way he spoke. I did everything I could to win him." She did not look at Anna but kept her eyes focused on the truck, the shadow of a bird flying overhead. "And I won him." A tear loosed itself and slid slowly down her cheek. "And I lost all chance for a happy life."

Anna had come up behind her. She rested her cheek on Eleanor's shoulder. "It's not too late," she said.

When Anna left, waving goodbye from the cab of the pickup truck, Eleanor watched her disappear into the cloud of dust on the road. She felt empty. Lonely, that's what it was, just plain loneliness. Years of being used to being alone could be wiped out by a single hour with a . . . friend? She had known Anna all her life, but could she call her a friend? Someone who might be a friend, at least. The empty room pressed around her again, settling on her with the dust stirred up by the car.

Eleanor ran her finger over the faded velvet of the settee. The rays of late afternoon sunlight on the dust of the parlor gave the air a golden glitter. She walked to the window, trying to rid herself of the prickling tightness at the back of her neck. The frosted white cake Anna had left sat untouched on the table, and amid the dusty knickknacks and old-fashioned furniture of the parlor, it made Eleanor think of Miss Havisham's wedding cake. She smiled. It was a reference Natalie would have appreciated. She could picture the girl hesitating for just a moment, trying to decide whether to let on that she got the joke before allowing a slow, sly smile to steal onto her face. She wondered what Natalie would have thought of Anna's story.

A twinge of pain hit her with the thought. Missing Natalie was harder here somehow, sharper. It was different in New York, where Natalie didn't belong anyway and so her absence was not so . . . so unbearably *present*. Here, a Natalie-shaped shadow seemed to lurk in every room, as if everything she had touched was in a perpetual state of waiting for her return. Her eyes passed over the dried roses on the mantel, the tiny glass figurines poised in mid-movement, as if suddenly and perfectly frozen by the shock of one terrible, beautiful instant. A cloisonné bird, perching to sing, but silent; the almost transparent unicorn raised on his hind feet, rearing back in anger or surprise; the shepherd, reaching out to his blushing shepherdess love.

Eleanor had not thought about the fact that the shepherdess would not be there. Thinking about its absence would mean thinking about why it was absent, something she had never let herself do. She remembered the sound of porcelain shattering on the floor like the echo of something else that had also been broken that night. An early echo, coming before that which it echoed, as if it knew that after whatever was to break had broken there would be no room for any other sound. So she did not remember. But the effort of not remembering that the shepherdess would be gone was so great that the sight of her sitting coyly on the mantel froze Eleanor's blood.

For one overwhelming instant, Eleanor wondered if she was mad, if that night had been a terrible, terribly real nightmare and the horror that sent her flying to New York had been her creation, and not her husband's at all. Then she saw the network of cracks running across the blue porcelain dress, the fine lines crossing the figurine's arms like bizarre wrinkles. Eleanor took the shepherdess in her hand. She was surprisingly light.

"I found that."

Eleanor jumped at the voice. Her son stood in the doorway. His hair was wild, his pants snagged and torn with blackberry thorns.

"The morning you were gone," he continued. "I came down and found that. I tried to put it back together as best I could, but I could never find that one piece."

He took the shepherdess from her hand, turning it so that she could see where part of the face was missing. One rosy cheek. One sparkling eye. Eleanor cleared her throat softly.

"I have it." It was an admission, not a statement. Why had these tones of apology moved into her voice?

"The piece?" A slight twitch of his eyebrow was the only sign of Adam's surprise. She nodded.

"In my little bag." How many times reaching for change had her fingers brushed against the piece of porcelain? So often that the mere touch could no longer spark a memory, trigger the waves of fear as they had at first. It was just another of the things to touch. "You can have it." She opened her purse and found the piece, worn a little smooth and faded from years among her things.

He held out his palm and she dropped the fragment of porcelain in his hand. He cupped it gently, brushed away a speck of dust with his thin, delicate fingers. Eleanor's hands.

Maybe your son isn't who you think he is. The movement loosened Anna's words and they darted around her memory, subtly shifting everything they touched. Eleanor watched as Adam turned the shepherdess face in his hand. She pictured the delicate thirteen-year-old boy kneeling before the fireplace, handling each piece with such gentle care. She had wondered a thousand times about what people said after she'd gone; she had never thought about who had cleaned up the blood.

"It must have been hard for you," she said. "Just to wake up and find me gone . . . no explanations."

"When I woke up her . . . body . . . was gone," he said. "Dr. Breedlove was just leaving—he must have taken her away. And John—Dad—was talking to the sheriff on the porch. They worked out some deal. It was kept quiet." He fit the pieces of the shepherdess together in his hand. "I saw the blood, though. It spilled out of her room, through the house, and down the steps, into the garden. I followed it there, and saw the flowers . . . well, no. I didn't see them—the roses. They were gone. And the honeysuckle, too. All dead." He took a deep breath. "No, that was easy," he said. "The hard part was living the next ten years with John." Their eyes met, and she was almost surprised to find them absent of accusation. There was nothing there but an understanding, laced with sorrow.

"I'm sorry." When she had pictured Adam, it was always as just a smaller, quieter version of his father. Now she saw the way her brows and cheekbones were stranded like foreigners in his face.

"You did what you had to do, I guess," he said. He shrugged, avoiding her eyes. "I escaped as soon as I could, too."

"But . . ." She could have brought him with her, couldn't she? It had been a struggle, arriving all alone and practically penniless in a new and unfriendly city. She had only survived, had only escaped at all because of an inner reserve of total selfishness she hadn't known she'd had. A necessary selfishness, one that kept her alive, kept her from thinking about what had happened that night, what she had lost. No, she thought, even if she'd known who her son was, understood what it meant to leave him behind, she wouldn't have brought him with her. It was something she had to do, could have only done on her own. She looked away. He laid a hand on her arm, and she raised her head. He was holding out the shepherdess. Perhaps Anna Mackay was right. Perhaps it wasn't too late.

"I'll fix it," he said.

*A*dam needed her. Not the way any man he knew needed his wife. Certainly not the way his father had needed his mother (and he had, too, his house and his clothes falling into disarray when she left, his anger, having no fixed outlet, interrupting in unpredictable, whiskey-soaked violence). Not even the way that she needed him, as a lover, a friend. He needed her like he needed air, or the sun. There were nights he would lie awake listening to her breathing, terrified for no reason he could fathom that if he stopped listening, it might suddenly stop. When he slept, he slept wrapped around her, holding her, though whether it was to protect her from harm or keep her from escaping even he did not know. He was afraid of something happening to her, hurting her, but even more afraid that she would leave, or, worse, that he would become something that made her leaving necessary.

When he and Eleanor returned from the funeral, Gwen was gone. Adam swallowed down the panic that immediately rose in his throat, forced himself to breathe normally.

"She must have gone for a walk," he said. Eleanor nodded and did not look at him. "She does that," he added, his voice more defensive than he'd intended. But his heart did not stop pounding until much later, when he brought upstairs the little shepherdess figurine and could not help checking to see that Gwen's suitcase was still there, her clothing folded neatly in the drawer.

Adam reached to touch her heather-gray wool scarf. Her grandmother had knit it for her; she loved that scarf. She would not have left without it. He sat on the bed for a moment, stroking the scratchy-soft wool. Then, instead of folding it and returning it to the shelf, he slipped it into the pocket of his coat. Immediately, he felt calmer, safer.

Gwen had brought him to the ocean on their honeymoon, and he had stood in awe, watching the terrible power of the waves crashing against the black rocks. He had never seen anything so large. He was afraid, but she led him down to the water and they walked along the shore. Crabs, shiny and as black as the wet rocks, scuttled sideways through the salt-crusted tide pools at their feet. Gwen flew along the rocks as surefooted as the crabs, but Adam picked his way from foothold to foothold, glancing warily at the waves sending spray crashing up from below.

They eventually came to a horseshoe-shaped bay where the water was gentler. The mouth where it let out to the ocean was so narrow that the waves broke their patterns and spread out into the bay in great rippling semicircles, leaving bubbles of foam on the pebble beach. They left their clothes on top of the tall rock and climbed down into the water. They treated the swimming as a game, plunging down under the surface to come up again on the other side, splashing each other with salt water. He did not notice the tide coming in, and when a great wave crashed over the protection of the rocks, he was knocked down and pulled under into the sea. He struggled against it, but the water turned him around, so that he did not know where to find the air. He felt the bottom and tried to grab against it, but the sand merely came away in his hand. When his lungs were so desperate for breath he was almost ready to breathe in the sea, he felt himself being thrown roughly against the rocks. He gasped in air and sat up on the beach, scraped and stinging with salt water, but unhurt. He looked around. Gwen was gone.

Again and again he plunged into the water. He kept his eyes open, ignoring the sting of the salt water, but the ocean was murky with sand from the force of the wave. He had to seek her out mostly by touch. He called her name, terrified. Tears ran down his face and fell into the sea.

He was almost delirious with panic when he heard her laughter, echoing and ghostly. It seemed to come from above him, but no one was there. He scrambled up the rock. "Gwen!"

He followed the sound of the laughter to a crack in the rock he hadn't noticed before. He peered through and saw the glitter of water below. "Gwen?"

"Adam!" The voice came up through the rock. "It's hollow!" The laughter again, then: "It's a cave!"

Just below the surface of the water was an opening in the rock. Adam reached under and felt the smooth, waterworn lip of a cave mouth, then through it a pocket of air. He held his breath and pushed through the opening.

The water was waist deep and the color of liquid gold in the thin beam of light from the crack high above. He blinked in the darkness, adjusting his eyes. "Gwen!"

She laughed. She was standing in the beam of light, just bright enough to shadow the curves of her body, light on the soft rosy color of her nipples. In the reflection of the sunlight on the water, her hair glowed golden green, and she seemed like a sea creature, some mermaid luring him deeper into the ocean with her ripples of delighted laughter. He waded through the water toward her and took her in his arms. Her skin was cold, but he could feel the warmth of her body, deep inside. "Thank God," he breathed.

She didn't understand why he had been worried. She never understood why he didn't like it when she disappeared in the middle of the night to go wandering and didn't return until morning. "What if I wasn't there and something happened to you?" he said.

She looked amused. "Do you think if something were going to happen to me you could prevent it by being there?"

"No," he said. "I don't know—maybe. But at least I would know if it did." He could not find the words to explain to her why it terrified him so—even more than the thought of her dead, the thought that he wouldn't know until later. The uncertainty, every time she stepped out of his sight, if he would ever see her again.

She smiled more tenderly then and touched his cheek. "Do you think something could happen to me without you feeling it?" she said. "Of course you'd know—no matter where I was."

He'd nodded, losing himself in her touch, in her acknowledgement of their connection. But her words could not reassure him entirely. It was easy to say that he would know, that if she were torn away from him suddenly, his body would feel her absence, a physical pain. But he could not let himself be sure—what if the strength of their connection was something he merely wanted to believe?

He tried to feel for her now, closed his eyes and let his body call out to hers. But he felt nothing but his own fear, and he touched the scarf in his coat pocket and waited.

*D*own by the lake, Gwen could feel Adam's fear reaching out to her. She pushed it away, pushed away everything but the sound of the wind on the water and in the trees. She could not bear the burden of his fear on top of her own, on top of the sorrows and pain of the entire town.

He had lied to her about his mother, about Natalie. He was pulling farther away from her every day, and now, surrounded by this town that was Adam's home, Gwen felt lost and suddenly very alone.

She picked her way through the weeds and mud in the over-grown path to the house. Eleanor was on her hands and knees in the garden, turning over the dirt with a rusted trowel. She sat up when she saw Gwen and wiped her forehead with the back of her wrist. Gwen sat down on the ground beside her.

"Careful," Eleanor said. "You'll get dirt on your dress."

Gwen shrugged. "It'll wash out," she said. She had pulled a sweater over her old white nightgown, and she fingered the hem, already spattered with mud from the lake.

Eleanor smiled. "Don't be so sure," she said. "Laundry's harder here than in the city." She handed Gwen the trowel. "Here," she said. "I'm trying to sort the herbs from the weeds."

Gwen took up the trowel. Eleanor had plucked a circle in the weeds around a little sprig of sage. Gwen found another and be-gan to work the weeds out from around it. One root was particu-larly deep, and Gwen worked at it with the trowel, frustration building in her shoulders, but when she pulled out the plant, the tiny sage came with it. Tears sprang to her eyes and she wiped them away, embarrassed. She tried to stick the sage plant back into the soil, piling the dirt around the root. "It might be easier just to turn over the whole bed and plant what you want."

"I know," Eleanor said. She uprooted a stem of goosegrass and added it to the growing pile of weeds. "But . . . there was a girl who planted all of these herbs years ago." She paused, as if trying to decide how to explain. "Anything that's still left, that hasn't been choked out, has held on since then."

Gwen looked up. *The garden.* Her breathing shallowed. "Was that . . . Natalie?"

Eleanor nodded. "Adam's told you," she said, her voice low.

"No," Gwen said.

"Then who?"

Gwen brushed the dirt from her hands, staring at her palms. How could she explain? "I think . . . Natalie did," she said.

Eleanor met her eyes. It was the same look they'd exchanged in the store, when the scent of licorice and sorrow had cut through years. Memories didn't fade, the look said, they hid just under the surface of the present, and sometimes they broke through. Eleanor was quiet for a long time. "I understand," she said finally.

They worked in silence for a while, until a bed of herbs began to emerge from the tangled web of leaves and vines. It was a patchwork bed—those things that had survived had grown wild and random, taking root where they could find room. Mint had hidden under the lacy shade of dog fennel, and the rosemary had become a solid waist-high bush, crouching against the house like a squat goblin.

The sun was growing low in the sky, and dusk was creeping in from the east. "It'll be dark soon," Eleanor said. "We should finish up for tonight."

"Where's Adam?" Gwen said.

A light came on in Adam's bedroom. Eleanor looked up, then at Gwen. "Upstairs," they said together.

Gwen laughed, despite the thread of sorrow tightening her chest, drawing her stomach in like a corset. "Is he all right?" she said. "Was the funeral . . . should I have been there?"

"I don't know," Eleanor said. She smiled sadly. "I think I don't know Adam at all."

"I don't know if I do either." Gwen put her hands into the dirt. Natalie had knelt here, had made things grow here, had left her memories for Gwen to find.

"I won't let him hurt you," Eleanor said calmly, her voice matter-of-fact. "I'll take you away before I let him do that."

"He won't," Gwen said. She shook her head. "Please don't think. . . . He won't hurt me. I'm sure of that." She remembered the look in Adam's eye as he'd turned away from her, the dark cloud that separated them growing thicker every day. "Not the way you mean, at least." There were many ways to hurt.

Eleanor pulled a tall shoot of grass threatening the sage. "I understand." She looked up at Gwen. "My husband never raised a hand to me."

Gwen nodded solemnly. As the sun set, the sky was turning violet-gray, and Gwen drew her knees up into her big sweater, the way they'd always told her not to as a child. "Wait," she said as Eleanor reached for a square-stemmed shoot. "Don't pull that—that's heal-all."

Eleanor left the plant. "My grandmother always complained and yanked it up."

Gwen laughed. "Mine grows it in her garden." She looked up, where the moon was rising, pale and speckled in the purple sky, an imperfect circle now. In a few days, it would be full, and hundreds of miles away, Gwen's grandmother would be lighting a candle. Gwen felt a wave of homesickness, but less lonely than before. She helped Eleanor gather up the gardening tools. "Tell me about Natalie," she said.

*B*eginnings are always tentative. In the air of newness, each moment is so jealous for attention that even the most natural motions hesitate. A baby's first steps are such a surprise he falls down; a butterfly stumbles to its feet; uncertain of its wings; and on the edge of Eleanor's property, a small blue pickup truck shudders and dies again.

From the passenger's side, Anna Mackay leaned over and set the gearshift back to neutral. "You have to let it out slowly," she said again.

"I *am*." Eleanor pulled her hands back from the steering wheel and stared at it with suspicion. "I just can't do it."

"You're thinking about it too much," Anna said. "Imagine you're chopping carrots—as soon as you think about where the knife is landing, you cut your finger."

Eleanor turned the key again and tried not to think about the movement of her feet on the pedals. The truck rolled slowly forward. She pressed down on the gas and shifted gears. "I'm driving! I'm driving!" She began to laugh—this was actually giddying, rumbling down a bouncy dirt road at twenty miles an hour. "Where am I going?"

"How about my house?" Anna said. "I'll make you a cup of tea."

"I don't know why I'm shaking," said Eleanor. Fields and trees slid by too quickly to follow. She kept her eyes focused ahead. Anna's house was a yellow dot on a hill far away, then a doll's house small enough for grandmother's figurines, then finally life-size, a place one could actually visit. The truck died as Eleanor eased it into the yard. Anna stepped down onto the grass, scratching the ears of the red dog that came leaping up to greet her.

Anna's house, though clean, was comfortingly cluttered. Books leaned against each other on shelves or sat in casual piles around comfortable chairs. A fluffy orange cat slept curled in a perfect circle, while an old gray tabby tom prowled in the corner, where dolls had been set up around a table for a tea party. Eleanor knelt down and picked up a tiny cup filled with a thimbleful of water.

"My granddaughter Susan came to visit today," Anna said. "And my youngest, Alex, is home from college, so I'm afraid it's a bit of a mess." She handed Eleanor a tall glass of iced tea. "Shall we sit on the porch?"

Clouds were rolling in fast, heading so single-mindedly for Liberty it would be a wonder if any of the neighboring towns were wet at all. "Looks like more rain," Eleanor said. That was spring in Liberty—one rainstorm barely let up before another one started thinking about coming. The orange cat, or perhaps his brother, stalked a bit of windblown fluff across the yard. The wind died and the cat lost interest, leaping instead to the hood of the pickup truck. "I didn't park very well, I'm afraid," Eleanor said.

"Not bad at all for your first day," Anna said. "You should have seen Adam when I taught him. It was over an hour before I could get him to set foot on the gas pedal without flinching."

"You taught Adam to drive? My"—she hesitated—"my Adam?"

Anna nodded. "That very truck, too."

Eleanor fell silent. The air was growing damp, and she felt a chill, though the day was still warm. She sipped her tea. "You've been more of a mother to him than I have," she breathed just loud enough to hear. "No wonder I barely know him."

Anna paused for a long time before responding, picking her words carefully. "I had more of a family to offer," she said. "Despite . . . everything"—her voice hoarsened just a little— "Avery was a wonderful father, and he loved his family, and me, too, maybe more than he ever knew." She looked up at Eleanor, her face shining. "I was lucky, Eleanor. But you wouldn't have done Adam any favors by staying with John."

"I know," Eleanor said. "I know that now. But still . . . it's a little too late to be a mother now."

"But maybe not a family," Anna said. She took Eleanor's hand. "Adam needs you," she said.

Eleanor thought of the pain in Gwen's eyes, so familiar, so like her own. There were many ways for a man to hurt the woman he loved. But Eleanor had not been there to show him the ways not to hurt. Did he really need her? Anna put an arm around Eleanor's shoulder and squeezed.

"He really does."

Eleanor nodded, but her throat was too tight to say *I know*, to say, *I need him, too.*

*T*he music was the key. The rest of the dream had shattered itself on her waking, and the fragments had buried deep inside her spine, the dust settling just under her skin, so that when the wind raised the hair on her arms, its touch was a painful one. It was a tenuous arrangement. Shards of memory would come loose without warning and travel to her brain, bringing with them the sudden image of a face, a green ribbon, a red rose. But the only thing that linked them was the song. Gwen tried to create some sort of understanding out of the images in her head, tried to find why Natalie's memory had come to her. But every time she was overwhelmed by the music. And the fear.

Even the music slipped out of her hands when she tried to grasp it. She had always had excellent musical memory and perfect pitch. Even as a child she could hear a song just once and play it back exactly. But the song that had run through her head for three days, tormenting her like a cat desperate for attention, was gone when she crept into the parlor and laid her hands on the piano keys. Her mind was totally blank. She touched a key tentatively. The note was hollow and flat in the empty parlor. Nothing. A nothing that was so strong that it went beyond the absence of something to become a presence in its own right. Whatever was to be found at the piano was not for her.

Frustrated, she pushed away from the piano and went to the window. It was gray outside, not raining yet, but the air so thick with clouds that it left everything damp anyway. She felt a wave of the homesickness that had followed her for days. She closed her eyes, expecting to see her grandmother's kitchen, with the teakettle on the verge of whistling and one of their eleven cats sleeping in the sun on the windowsill. Instead, the picture that stretched out before her imagination had miles and miles of green fields laid out around a tall white house and a team of brown and white horses pulling a carriage. Gwen opened her eyes and for a moment thought she saw in the window the face of a woman who might have once been beautiful, with a thatch of gray in her jet black hair. But when she looked again, it was only her own reflection in the glass.

"Gwen?" Adam came up behind her and touched her arm. She jumped, startled. Usually, she could feel him come into the room, the warm swirl of his emotions like music in the air, but she had been listening so intently for the song in her head that its silence had muffled everything else. She reached to him and heard, deep in her brain, the soft, constant harmony of his love for her, his hopes, the low, minor chords of his fears. Today, high above it all wavered a tremolo of concern. "I want to talk about what happened yesterday," he said. If she had heard only his voice, she would have thought it was anger, but in his heart she heard the fear.

"I went for a walk," she said.

"All day you went on a walk?" he said. "You weren't feeling well enough to go to my father's funeral, but you went on a walk?" Ever since they'd set foot in this town the softness had melted off of him, the joy blown away. No, it had begun before that, had been happening for a long time. Whenever she asked about their future, about having children, a family, a home, he became a little colder, a little quicker to turn away from her tears.

"I had a . . . dream," she said. She stepped tentatively through the words, hoping for the moment when his face would light in understanding, the way his mother's had. Adam's face remained blank, angry.

"You had a dream?" he said. "All of this for a dream?"

"I had a dream about a woman who lived with a man she didn't love, a man who hurt her." She looked up into his eyes and saw that he'd heard what she hadn't said, that she recognized the feeling, their future. Gwen sat on the settee. "Adam," she said, "you lied to me." She could not look at him, instead stroked the velvet of the settee. She expected to be angry—she *was* angry, but the anger buzzed around the edges of her emotion like a fly trapped by a windowpane. At her very core, a tight, cold spot was growing, drawing all of her emotion, turning in on itself. She closed her eyes. There was nothing to do but say it. "You never told me about Natalie."

The cloud hanging around them parted for a moment, and when it settled again, it was not as dark, lighter by the weight of one lie, at least. She waited for him to grow defensive, to deny. He ran his hands through his hair, sighed, then finally let go and just looked at her. "I'm sorry," he said. Tears glassed his eyes, but even so, she could see Adam, *her* Adam, there. "I didn't want any of this to touch you." He sat beside her and she took his hand. "I don't know how I expected it not to, once my mother showed up."

"It's not your mother," she said. "It's the whole town, it's memories." She touched the window, the mantelpiece, the piano. "This house is so thick with them they've settled into the walls, the furniture." She picked up a figurine from the mantel, a small glass unicorn. She laughed involuntarily as she saw it nestled in wrapping paper, a birthday present to a raven-haired girl so young she thought the horn must be a mistake and cried at the sight of her misshapen horse.

"Memories." The word burst out of him. "Memories, the past, always the past." He sat at the piano bench. "Where does the past end, Gwen? When does *our* life begin?" He pounded his hands on the piano in a sudden cacophony that made Gwen jump. "I'm sorry," he said. He took a deep breath and ran his fingers over the keys, letting his hands, not his ears, pick out the melody. "Do you remember the first time we kissed?" he said. "I had come to watch you at that concert. I remember—you played Tchaikovsky's First Piano Concerto—remember? You were so beautiful, tapping your feet to the music and smiling, even when it wasn't the piano part. And afterward, when the conductor reached to shake your hand, and instead you bounded up and hugged him . . . ? I thought for a minute he might be angry, but then he smiled and kissed you on both cheeks. Remember, Gwen?" His hands moved over the keyboard, drawing out notes that were somehow familiar. His head was bent over the piano, just like in her dream. Gwen drew breath and Adam looked up, his face his own again. "You're not listening, are you?"

"I am." Not to his words, though. Gwen listened to the song in her head played out at his hands. The notes seemed to call the dream out from her spine. "That music . . . that song," she said. "It's"—she listened for a moment—"from the dream. From Natalie's death. Your father was playing it."

"Maybe somehow I remember hearing it then," he said.

"Or maybe it's from your father's memory. Perhaps . . ."

The music suddenly stopped, and the dream faded. "No," he said.

"It's a memory that wants to be saved, Adam." She tried to reach out to him, but he pulled away from the piano. "How can we have a future without understanding . . ."

"I said no!" He turned on her roughly. In one blur of motion his hand darted out. She heard the crash of breaking glass before she even saw what it was that the hand had hurled to the floor.

In the silence, the memory hit them both. Gwen felt tears, warm, then cold, slipping down her cheeks, catching on her lower lip, but she still could not break the silence to breathe.

"Oh God." He was crying, too. He reached out and pulled her toward him and they held each other, gripped each other, their muscles tense and tight. He touched her hair, kissed her suddenly, with passion born of desperation. They kissed, tasting each other's tears, mixed with the saliva on their tongues. They kissed each other's faces, the crying eyes, tasting the cool salt of tears, the spicier one of sweat. He touched her back, her body, warm through the damp dress. He pulled her close, her cheek pressed to his chest.

"Maybe if we don't push it away we can understand," she said. "Forgive him . . ."

"I don't want to understand him," he said. "I want to forget him. I can forgive my mother, but nothing that man did ever caused anything but pain."

Gwen was quiet for a moment, listening to the sound of the rain and the beat of Adam's heart. "He fathered you," she finally said.

Clouds had settled down to cover Liberty when Eleanor left Anna's, and by the time she reached the steps to her own front porch, a light rain was falling. She shook the water from her coat and ran a hand through her short hair. For all the odd looks she got over her hair, bobbed barely longer than her son's, it *was* easier to dry.

The house was dark, but patches of light escaped from rooms into the entryway. From the parlor, soft, hesitant notes from the piano crept out along with a thin, dusty lamplight tinged pink by the tassled shade. The kitchen light was yellower, more robust, and Eleanor could hear water running in the sink, the sound of pots and pans being set on the stove. She hesitated, knocking softly at the kitchen door before easing it open to see if she could help.

Adam stood at the cutting board mincing garlic, his sleeves rolled up to his elbows. If Anna was right and he needed her, he certainly wasn't showing it. She leaned against the door, waiting silently, and finally he put down the knife and looked up, his eyes barely brushing her outline, not seeing her or wanting to. It was the way strangers passed on the street in New York, or white men looked at black men in Liberty. It was the way she'd once looked at Natalie.

"You need any help?" she said.

He shook his head. "I've got it." He went back to the cutting board with quick, even strokes and the same troubled frown he'd worn as a child when his crayon drawings came out anything but perfect. Eleanor waited, silent, and in a minute, he looked up again, resigned. "There's salad makings in the icebox," he said.

Eleanor found a head of lettuce, a tomato, a couple of sturdy carrots. She brought them to the sink and put them under running water, touching the lettuce gingerly with her fingers, feeling under the leaves to see how the head would open. She stole glances at her son as he gathered the garlic together in his hands and emptied it into the skillet. His eyes were a little red, as if he'd been ill. Or perhaps even crying?

He looked up and smiled at her, but not with his eyes. "You're home late." he said. "You were at the Mackays' house?"

Eleanor nodded. "I . . ." She grinned. "I'm learning to drive."

Adam's eyebrows raised in surprise. "You?" She looked at him and they both began to laugh.

"It's crazy, I know," she said. "But Anna said I did really well for my first day. Didn't crash the truck or anything." She patted the lettuce dry.

He chuckled. "That old truck still running?" he said. "*I* learned to drive on that thing." He took a handful of green beans and threw them into the skillet, where they sizzled. "Will you hand me those peppers?" he asked.

She passed him the two red bell peppers sitting on the counter, watching as he cored them expertly, removing the tiny white seeds. Eleanor watched him for a moment, then picked up a carrot, peeling it with her knife as he sliced the peppers. "I didn't know you cooked," she said.

He shrugged. "I learned," he said. "I had to. John certainly wasn't going to."

Eleanor nodded, and continued chopping carrots, bending her head under the familiar weight of guilt.

"But I can cook now," Adam said gently. "If you'd been here, I'd probably never have learned."

"I'd never have thought to teach you," she said. Boys learned enough cooking to make coffee, biscuits, roast hot dogs over a campfire. It was the daughters who learned the recipes by heart, who helped with laundry, who learned to sew. And hopefully sprinkled in with the cups of flour and snips of thread there would be something more passed down, passed on. But what did one pass on to a son?

The soft piano notes had faded so gradually that Eleanor did not notice the silence until it was broken with a loud, discordant chord. They both jumped.

"She's playing," he said. From the parlor, Beethoven crashed and rolled. "She's upset." He splashed a handful of water into the skillet and it hissed and steamed.

Eleanor sliced the tomato and did not look at her son. "She's afraid."

"She has nothing to be afraid of," he said. "The past is past. It can't hurt us."

Eleanor looked up at Adam. "What about the future?" she said.

"The future?" Adam said. He smiled, as if it were some exotic foreign country his mother was proposing that they visit. "Never been there."

Eleanor set down the knife. "I mean it," she said. "Do you think we could be a family again?"

"A family?" Another foreign country. He turned back to the skillet. "Is that what we were?" He dusted the sizzling vegetables with a richly scented gold powder and stirred. "I always thought that families were things created for magazine ads, to sell insurance or baking soda."

Eleanor bowed her head. After her marriage, she had read those magazines, studying the ads for the secrets to their glassy-eyed happiness. "That's my fault," she said. "I never really got to know who you were." She met his eyes. "I'd like to try, though."

The music from the other room stopped abruptly. Adam was silent for a long moment. He turned down the flame under the skillet. "I'm not like John," he said.

"I know that," Eleanor said. She took the tomato over to the salad bowl and tossed it gently into the lettuce.

"I'm *not* like him," Adam said again, as if she had contradicted him, "and I would never hurt Gwen. I just . . . don't know how to show her that. I don't know how to show her . . ." He shook his head and turned back to the stove, checking the rice simmering on the back burner.

"That you love her," Eleanor finished for him.

Adam stirred the vegetables. "My father loved Natalie," he said.

Eleanor nodded. "And so did I," she said. "And so did you."

"My father loved you," he said. "You weren't happy."

Eleanor considered for a moment. "He loved his wife," she said. "I loved my husband." They were flat words, words from a magazine ad. They were pictures, not people. "But we never really knew each other, not the way you and Gwen do." She took his wrist, holding it gently until he met her eyes. "You're very lucky," she said.

Adam was silent. He turned the knob on the stove and the flame died. The kitchen door swung open. Gwen's eyes were still heavy, but the color in her face was better than it had been. "Is everything all right?" she said.

Adam set down the wooden spoon and kissed his wife gently on the forehead. "Dinner's almost ready," he said. A look passed between them, worry and reassurance, sorrow and love.

Eleanor smiled. A memory was passing, but it drew no closer than the tips of her eyelashes, and the tears in her eyes never fell.

*T*he moon was full. That must be it, Adam thought, why he couldn't sleep, why every molecule of air had its own tiny silver shadow and set the hairs on his arms erect in the breeze.

He turned and watched Gwen sleeping beside him, the quilt rising and falling with her breath. If she left him . . . or worse, if she didn't leave, but he lost her anyway, lost whatever it was that burned brightly between them what would he do? He could feel their love becoming a burden, becoming something that tied them joylessly together, and he didn't know what he could do to stop it. Holding tighter just hurt her more. Gwen frowned in her sleep, and he stroked her hair until she turned and smiled again. She had been ill once, desperately ill with a fever that went on and on and would not break. He had tried everything, made soups she could not eat, fluffed pillows that could not make her comfortable. And she'd sipped feebly at glasses of water, tears of pain and frustration rolling down her face while he sat paralyzed and helpless and their cat scratched angrily at fleas. He'd begun to hate her, to hate the tears that demanded of him something he could not give, and Gwen, sensing his hate, had only cried harder. He had run out, run away and gone walking through the moonless night, through the streets where they had so often walked together and past them, to places the two of them had never been. Finally, he had felt free of her. Then he'd looked up to see a shooting star, the brightest one he'd ever seen. He turned from habit to point it out to Gwen and realized then that she was a part of him, that no matter how far he ran, she would be there.

That was over a year ago. Why did the thought that had been such a comfort then seem to mock him now? He sat and watched her sleep, as helpless now before her fear as he had been in the face of her illness. She turned, reaching for him in her sleep and he could almost hear her saying as she had said so many times before, "But the fever did break, eventually, and you came back, and everything was all right. It was hard and we came through it." But it wasn't anything he had done. Perhaps she would have been better off without him there, even. He got out of bed. It was useless to try to sleep.

As he pulled on his coat, he felt in the pocket to make sure Gwen's scarf was still there. He had seen her looking for it earlier, frowning as she pawed through clothes and opened drawers, but she hadn't asked him about it and he had said nothing. He should give it back to her, he knew. He *would* give it back to her. He had thought it out—if she really wanted to leave him, a scarf wouldn't keep her from going. If he became someone she wanted to leave, he wouldn't want her to stay. Morally, logically, he should give the scarf to her. But whenever he thought of letting go of it, he was overwhelmed by a sick feeling that left his heart beating, his breath catching in his throat. She wouldn't leave him, would she? She *especially* wouldn't leave, though, if he had her scarf. He couldn't think about it anymore. He went downstairs.

The parlor was piled with boxes he had brought over from the store, some empty, others tossed casually with some of his father's things—old shoes, papers they would have to sort later, several half-emptied bottles of scotch. They would have to sort through and pack away everything. He picked up a heavy leather boot, feeling its weight in his hand, then tossed it back into the box. He picked up one of the bottles and took a long swallow. It smelled like his father, like anger and sorrow and regret, and it stung as it went down.

He pulled the chain of one of the lamps, but there was only a click, no light. Of course, the bulb had burned out. He didn't want light anyway. He pulled open the drapes and found that the rain had stopped and there was enough moon to see the glass outlines of the knickknacks, the keys of the piano. He knew the tall, dark figures in the corners were boxes piled up, not ghosts. Still, the hair on his arms stood up, and he believed for just a moment that there was someone in the room with him, someone watching him watch the sky. He turned quickly, but he could see no one hiding in the shadows. His hands were shaking, and he rubbed them together, breathed on them for warmth. He sipped some more scotch and sat at the piano bench, letting his fingers pick out a soft melody.

The notes that emerged in the stillness were familiar somehow. His mother had played that song, long ago, hadn't she? He could see her small, plump figure, her red hair piled in curls on her head. The blond roots were showing. She dyed it to please his father, the same shade as his first wife's.

Adam jerked his fingers away from the piano. His mother had never played piano. Where had that memory come from? It wasn't his, and yet there it was in his mind. His father's. "No," he said aloud, but it persisted. *Natalie.* He could still see the coppery hair falling over her shoulders, and when she turned, the moment of shock as he—as his father—had realized that she was black. It was a slap of anger, embarrassment at his desire. He shook his head. It wasn't his desire. This was impossible. It was crazy. But if Gwen was going crazy, then he would follow her in. He closed his eyes. It was his father's memory, not his. As long as he remembered that, he would be all right.

He set his fingers cautiously on the keyboard. Worry washed over him, and with it the feel of rain against his back. He was walking through the rain toward Gwen. She was reaching to him, and he could feel her arms warm around him. But who was he? He took a deep breath and the movement in his body reminded him. Adam, he was Adam. But he was also looking past the girl's black face into her eyes, her yellow eyes. There was a light deep inside them that spoke of freedom. She laughed and the minute the laugh bounced off his ears, he was gone. He knew he would follow her around the world and learn to fly if she took to the stars. Her laugh was air to him, her touch food, her eyes a promise of what he could become if he gave up his future and forgot his past and kept her as his forever. He needed her. He would do anything to keep her. He would do anything, even break her leg if it kept her here long enough for him to explain why she shouldn't run away.

Wait—whose memory was that? *He needed her. He would do anything to keep her.* Adam forced his eyes open, but the memories kept coming, falling one over the other. Gwen's skin, golden in the light of the cave. A cool, lithe body wrapping around his, pulling him down into the water, drowning him with a kiss. Natalie's arms, bruised under hands, his hands, which held her so tight. He couldn't keep them straight in his mind. Through them all ran the fear, the need that could so easily turn desperate, violent. He tried to push away from the piano, but his legs tangled in the bench. When he put out his hand to right himself, he heard the laughter, high and sweet and clear.

She stood in the doorway, her bare skin glowing silver in the moonlight, red hair bursting from her head like the petals of some great carnivorous flower. She laughed again, that laugh that was half madness and half pure freedom. The laugh layered memories in his mind. She was golden against the tousled white sheets, laughing as his teeth pressed into the firm flesh of her shoulder, tearing with a love that was both desire and rage. She was standing naked at the top of the stairs laughing at him, leaving him. He couldn't let her go. He reached out.

Her skin was humid, tropical. He was surrounded by it, suffocating in the softness of her hair, her breasts. Her laugh was dark now, a deep erotic chuckle, so close he could feel her breath, warm and wet against his skin. He was thirteen and falling with her into the water and through it, drowning but still clinging to her, drowning in her. The water was cold, but he could feel the heat, hidden deep inside her body. His lungs ached to be free of her, of the water, of her kiss, but a deeper desire would not let him let go. He needed her. Adam's eyes filled with tears. He didn't know where he was, who he was. Her body was familiar, warm, but where did he know it from? He gave in to desire and let her pull him down into her darkness.

*T*t was midafternoon but impossible to tell the time from the even white light, eerily disconnected from the damp, dusty heat of the attic. Eleanor sat down and leaned against the wall, breathing deeply. Bright spots danced in front of her eyes. Was this what being old was about? She rubbed her temples as her vision cleared. Adam added a wooden crate to a stack in the corner.

They had all slept late. Eleanor blamed the sky, dark with clouds until long after dawn, but that didn't explain the weariness hanging over all of them. Eleanor had tossed for hours before sleeping, turning the pillow to find a new cool side, twisting the bedclothes around her body like vines. But then the dreams had come. Impatient with waiting for her, they pulled her into sleep. They were languid, sensual—her dreams, her body, the whole house. Even the dampness in the air had taken on a tropical feel. It was made worse by the sky, all day waiting to storm, all day holding tense, not letting a single drop of rain touch the ground.

"Well, that's it, then," Adam said, "the last of his things." Six boxes—that was all it had taken to pack away everything of John's. Without even discussing it, they knew to fold double layers of tissue into the suits and pack the shoes tightly with crumpled newspaper. It would be a long, long time before the things saw light again.

"Are you sure you don't want any of the clothes?" Eleanor asked again. For as long as she could remember, they had brought things up to the attic. To give to charity later, they always said, forgetting as soon as the attic door shut on the boxes and dusty crates.

"I tried on the boots," Adam said softly. "This morning." He went to the window and leaned against the wall, looking out, looking for all the world like some painting in the soft gray light, the highlights sharp and shadows soft on his face.

"They didn't fit." She meant it as a question, but the inflection of her voice went flat at the end, smoothing it into a kind of mournful comment. "You could stuff the toes with paper."

He shook his head. "They . . ." He began a laugh, but didn't have enough mirth to carry it through and cleared his throat instead. "They were too—*small.*" He frowned, his eyelashes blinking doubt, then laughed. "The clothes, too. I don't know when I got to be taller than him, but . . ."

"Oh." Adam seemed so slight compared to John. But then, everyone did. John would have had to be eight feet tall with shoulders nearly as broad to have taken up in life the space his shadow cast across her memory.

Adam sighed elaborately and shrugged. "Oh well. I don't even know why we're keeping this stuff, really." He set a hand on the top crate. "But you can't just throw it away."

Eleanor nodded. You couldn't throw it away. She wondered if Adam knew how true that was. You couldn't get rid of them so they'd be really *gone,* whatever you did. Throw them in the lake, sure, but they'd still *be* there and you'd have the largest body of water in your world reminding you besides. Burn them and they'd become a part of the very air you breathed. Even leaving Liberty hadn't helped—everything had been packed away in boxes in her mind, too easily opened the minute she returned. Nothing was ever lost in Liberty. Not even the things you needed to be.

"You can see almost the whole town from here," Adam said. Eleanor went to stand by the window with her son. The fields had come up suddenly green, and though Eleanor knew that most of the plants would be weeds she could not help but be glad at the color against the soft gray sky.

"I love this town." It slipped out before she knew she was saying it; if you'd asked her, she would have said no, she hated the town and everything it represented. But once it was out of her mouth she realized it was true—she loved Liberty, and always had. *Well, how about that?* she thought.

Adam brushed the dust off Evalie Blackmar's dollhouse, examining a tiny, intricately ornate chair. "You're staying, then?"

"I . . . I don't know," Eleanor said. It was too much to deal with. She knelt beside Adam and fingered a doll dressed in an elaborate blue silk gown trimmed with impossibly tiny handmade lace.

"The house is yours," Adam said.

For a moment, Eleanor thought he meant the dollhouse and drew breath to protest that she'd never been allowed to play with it. But he was looking at the walls around them, the sloping ceiling crisscrossed with cobwebs. Eleanor nodded. "I guess so, now that John . . ."

"No," Adam said. "It's yours. It always was. I went over the papers. John had the store in his name, but the house was left to you by the Blackmars. Didn't you know?"

"I guess I never really thought about it," Eleanor said. "It always felt like it belonged to him, like everything else."

Adam looked at the crates. "That was his, everything in there. The rest of it belongs to you." He reached for a large envelope. "And I found this." He handed her a piece of paper. "It was in the safe, with his papers."

The paper had the name of a private investigator at the top, but what caught her eye was an address in the body of the letter. She stared at it for a moment, wondering why it seemed familiar, wondering why her eyes were filling with tears. Her hands were shaking before she realized why the address looked familiar. It was hers, her address in New York. She blinked and tears rolled from her eyes but the letter was clear again. "This . . . is dated 1950," she said.

Adam nodded. "Just a few months after you left. He must have hired someone to find where you were." He took the letter from her shaking fingers. "Are you all right?"

"All that time . . . he knew? He knew where I was?" She took a deep breath and found that it came out in a surprising laugh. "I was so afraid for all those years that he would find me, come after me." She rolled the edge of her sleeve over her fist and dabbed the tears away. She felt light inside and laughed again, at her own disappointment this time. "I wonder why." Why he had tracked her down. Why he hadn't come after her.

"Maybe because he loved you," Adam said softly.

Eleanor looked up. "He had a strange way of showing it," she said.

"Doesn't everyone?" Adam was sitting on the floor, arms wrapped around his knees, the way Eleanor had sat as a child when she wanted to hide. He smiled a wrinkled little sad smile at her. "Or is it just us?"

"I don't know."

He nodded slowly and set the little toy chair back in the doll-house, arranging the doll awkwardly in the seat. He ran a hand through his hair, and when he looked up at her, tears glittered on his eyelashes. "I'm frightened," he said. "I'm frightened for Gwen."

"You're not like John," she said. She was sure of that now. He was silent. She set a hand on his shoulder, awkward, but trying at least to be comforting, motherly.

"I don't know that anymore," he whispered. He was staring at his lap, not looking at her, but he took her hand from his shoulder and held it like a friend, an ally. "I've had one of the . . . dreams, memories, whatever they are."

"John's?"

He nodded. "And there was nothing in him that isn't also in me. The anger, the . . . fear." He brought his hands to his face and closed his eyes. "He didn't mean to hurt Natalie. He needed her as much as I need Gwen. He just . . . *felt* too much, he didn't know what to do about it." His hands were trembling. "I hurt Gwen when I love her too much. I hurt her when I pull away. I just don't know what I can do to keep her safe."

Eleanor looked at her son. You could never be sure, absolutely sure that the people you loved were safe, even from you. There were too many ways to hurt, too many tiny misunderstandings that grew into silent evenings, then vast distances. "What do you want to do?"

"I don't know." Outside, a bird shrieked. Adam went to the window and looked out, then shook his head. "I can't lose her," he said. "But . . . maybe she would be happier . . . maybe I should just go away."

"You mean . . . leave her?" He did not answer. She could see his fear, tangled in the dust of the attic. He looked away. The paint on the windowsill was flaking away, and he peeled a long strip that crumbled in his fingertips. He would do it, too, leave Gwen to keep her from leaving him, to keep on loving her as much as he did. He peeled another flake of paint, and Eleanor saw the entire house coming apart, scratched away little by little in layers thin as an onion skin. She grabbed his hand and he let go of the paint and looked up at her, but still did not meet her eye.

"If you had helped Natalie get away . . ." He didn't finish the sentence.

"That's not fair," she said. Tears filled her eyes. It *wasn't* fair, not when he said it to her now, not when she said it to herself every day of her life. "You can't just run away."

"You did." The sarcasm in his voice was so sharp that she could not help but think of John for just one moment. He pulled his hand from hers.

"I'm sorry." She could not look at him. "I'm *sorry*, dammit. How many times do I have to say I'm sorry?"

"None." He was cold again, quiet. "I told you, I understand. I lived with John, too."

"*I'm not sorry*," she screamed, the woman who never screamed. Her hands were in fists. She released them and bit her lip. "I'm not sorry for leaving him. That's not what I'm sorry for—do you understand?" It was ridiculous, obscene, her yelling while he stood there calmly. She leaned her forehead against the cool windowpane and looked down at the overhang of the porch, cracked and slightly overgrown with moss. "And it didn't solve anything, anyway."

The ladder stairs up to the attic creaked under weight. They both turned to see Gwen, her face wrinkled in worry, poking her head up. "Is everything all right?" she said.

"It's fine," said Adam. He reached out a hand to help her climb up into the attic. His eyes met Eleanor's, saying *Keep this between us*.

"It was just a misunderstanding," Eleanor said.

Adam smiled and reached a hand up to her. "Hold still," he said. He rubbed a thumb against her forehead. "Smudge," he said. "From the window."

Gwen was moving through the boxes and stacks of old things, her eyes wide. "Look at this," she said. The mourning dress stood on the dressmaker's dummy in the corner, swathed in a cocoon of tissue paper. She unraveled the paper to reveal the pleats and ruffles sewn into the black silk. "The waist is so tiny."

"It was my grandmother's," Eleanor said. She followed Gwen's eyes around the room as they lit on years and years of history— John's boxes now, but also Grandfather's suits and the old Bible so fragile it would fall apart if anyone tried to read it, and Grandmother's shocking mourning dress, and Evalie's dollhouse, and even, sitting innocent and shocking in the corner, a small wicker suitcase with a braided handle.

"Dear Lord," Eleanor said.

Gwen had seen it, too, and gone suddenly white. Eleanor reached to steady the girl, though she felt none too steady herself. "That was hers," Gwen said. "Natalie's."

Eleanor nodded and took the suitcase in her arms. Gwen sat down beside her.

"I brought that up here," Adam said. "I didn't know what else to do. . . ."

Eleanor looked up. Of course—who would have brought it up here if not Adam? She tried to picture him sorting through the torn, bloody clothing, deciding what to pack away. Could she have done that at thirteen, fourteen? No, no, but then Adam had been older, somehow, than she was at that age. He seemed older than she was right now, taking her hand gently, easing the suitcase out of her arms. "Do you want to open it?" he asked.

There was a moment as they looked at one another silently. "I do," Gwen said finally. Adam looked to Eleanor for confirmation, and she managed to nod. She wrapped her arms around her knees while he undid the clasp on the suitcase. She was waiting for something to explode, to hit her as the lid lifted, and was surprised to find how easily the suitcase revealed a fold of old velvet, protected somewhat from dust but not unaffected by time. Gwen lifted it gingerly out of the suitcase, catching the small things wrapped in the cloth and setting them carefully on the floor.

"I remember that," Eleanor said. "I sold her that velvet." It felt cool, soft under her touch. How a dress made of that old-fashioned silk velvet would have taken to the heat of one's body, like a constant caress. "I told her it was used for coffins, mostly." The words caught in her throat. Had Natalie even had a coffin?

Gwen picked up an old photograph that had been wrapped in the cloth. Natalie smiled at the camera from the arm of a young blond man. They were dressed in the latest fashions of 1948, and though the photo had yellowed with age, Eleanor could see that the girl smiling proudly in front of the small, neat house was white, or too close to tell any different.

"This is what she looked like when she first came to Liberty," Eleanor said. Only she had looked then like someone who had lost everything. Eleanor looked again, and suddenly the girl in the photograph looked like someone with everything to lose.

"She looks so old," said Gwen. Eleanor nodded. She could see that, too. Though the people in the photograph were clearly young lovers, there was something almost matronly in the corners around Natalie's eyes, something so possessive in the way she held onto the man's arm. That was not the Natalie she knew.

Eleanor could not look at the photograph. She stroked the blood-colored velvet. "I wish she hadn't come here," she said suddenly. "If only . . ." The pulling in her throat, her stomach was too tight to let her speak. She tried to catch her breath.

Gwen put her arm around Eleanor's shoulders. "What happened wasn't your fault," she said.

Eleanor shook her head. "But . . ." She could not speak unless she cried as well, and the tears poured out with the words. "It was, though. Mine as much as anyone's." She clutched the velvet in a ball at her chest. "I could have sent her away, but I was selfish. I didn't want to be lonely again."

Gwen rocked Eleanor. "Shh," she said. "She was lonely, too."

"It was *his* fault," Adam said, "John's. All of this was his fault." He reached into the suitcase and grabbed the black silk shift in his fist. "He was responsible for her death, not you. Why can't you just hate him?"

A yellowed slip of paper fluttered out of the folds of the dress, alighting on the floor near Eleanor's foot. She picked it up and it fit into her hand like the telegram telling of John's death, like any piece of paper had ever fit into the hand of a frightened woman.

"She would never have come here if I hadn't told John to bring her," Eleanor said. "I don't know what made me do it, why something in our blood can't bear to be without scandal, but there it is. He may have been the one who . . . killed her, but I was the one who brought her here."

"Something in her blood, too," Gwen said. She took the paper from Eleanor's hand and read the bold, unhesitating handwriting, the address across the tracks. "An address?"

"The first time I saw her," Eleanor said, "even before . . . when she first came to Liberty. I gave her directions. . . ."

"Who lives there?" Gwen said. "Who is it she came to see?"

Eleanor shook her head. "I don't know," she said.

Gwen considered this for a moment, then stood and offered Eleanor her hand. "Let's go," she said.

"There? Now?" Adam took the address from Gwen. "We don't even know who this is."

"It was someone who knew Natalie," Gwen said. "Maybe we can find out more about her. Maybe even what she wants from us."

Eleanor went slowly to the window. Outside the clouds were dark, thickening. "It looks like rain," she said, but she reached for Adam. Gwen took his other hand.

"It always looks like something," Gwen said.

There is a path in Liberty that no one travels. Winding through the eastern part of town where the colored folks live, it grazes the edge of the river for a while before crossing the train tracks a little south of the depot. On maps it is called Crossing Road, a thin red thread that runs across flat fields spiderwebbed with blue before passing over the railroad's thick black line hatched like the stitches on a crazy quilt. On maps, it is the straightest and strongest road passing through that part of Liberty. In practice, not even cows trample down the weeds enough to keep Crossing Road much more than a part in the grass.

East of the railroad tracks and still in sight of the depot, this slight path meets up with a dirt road that has no name and does not appear on any official map. This is the road everyone uses; it has a gentler slope and a quicker path to town, and if you're in no hurry, you can climb off to the side to the tallest hill in the county and see the town spread out on both sides of the tracks, out to the very edges of what used to be Jean Cardon's thousand acres.

If you follow the road on into town, you will find yourself passing under the railroad tracks, through a riverbed that dried up in the summer of 1872, not long before Helena Blackmar arrived in Liberty. Some said she had caused the creek to dry, since witches could not cross running water even on a train. Others listened and believed, despite the fact that the creek had been dwindling for years and the train tracks passed over rivulets at half a dozen other places in this county alone. So when the road is called anything at all, it is Witch's Pass, with a charm touched or a sign made to ward off evil.

The woman passing through there now reached through decades-old instinct for the cross that had once hung at her throat. It was gone, and instead she felt the heavy swift beat of her heart and reached for her son's hand. His fingers were cold, but he helped her around a branch that had fallen. "Not too far now," he said.

The wind was rising, and framed against the gray sky Adam reminded her of some Romantic poet, intense-eyed and wind-blown in his black overcoat. Gwen, with her long golden hair flying in all directions, pale shawl clutched around her, seemed his perfect complement. Eleanor smiled to herself. Adam noticed her stare and raised an eyebrow with an expression so like her grandfather's that Eleanor almost laughed. She shook her head. "I just can't believe your hair is so long, is all."

"It's the style."

She nodded, and they walked on in silence for a minute. "That wasn't actually why I smiled. You looked a bit like your great-grandfather, just now."

"Henry Blackmar?" Adam looked surprised. "I've never heard that before. Everyone's always said I looked like John."

"Lots of people don't ever really look," Gwen said.

Eleanor did not reply. She had been guilty of that as well, she supposed. Adam had his father's build and dark, wavy hair; she imagined that when they'd stood side by side the resemblance had been striking. But John's presence had always been that way—brought out the obvious, magnified the great sweeping generalities, and dimmed the subtle gesture, the sudden grin, those things that made one unique and not merely a poor copy of previous generations.

They turned onto the main road, where houses gathered in clusters just as on the other side of the tracks. A few people moved around outside the houses, securing windows, bringing in firewood, squinting up at the sky. They eyed Adam and Eleanor suspiciously—white folks in this part of town and with a storm coming, too. Their eyes met, understanding *trouble*. No one came out in weather like this for good news.

"I think it's that one over there," Adam said. A little way apart from the others a house stood. It was small but immaculately clean, bright white even in this light that made everything gray. It reminded Eleanor of the Reverend Fay's house, and she wondered if she really wanted to meet the people who lived inside.

The woman who answered the door was about Eleanor's age, and her dress was so clean and painstakingly pressed there could be no question about who kept the house in its impeccable condition. She gave them a long look, then in a low, graveled voice said, "Can I help you?"

Adam and Eleanor exchanged a look. Gwen stepped forward. "We want to know," she began, ". . . anything, I guess. Anything you can tell us about this girl." Gwen shoved the old photograph at her awkwardly; she did not take it and after a moment, Gwen lowered her hand.

"Nothing," the woman said. "I never knew her." Her hair was braided into a tight bun at the top of her head; the wind was blowing harder now but it did not move.

"Mama?" A voice called. "Who's at the door?" A girl of about fifteen appeared behind the woman. When she saw Eleanor and Adam, she stopped and played nervously with a string of seed pearls, glancing at her mother.

"Never you mind," the woman said to her. "Go on and get your father to bring in more firewood." The girl disappeared, and Eleanor watched her go. Her father must have been rich and black as coal for this woman to have a daughter so well dressed and so dark. The woman herself was light, the color Eleanor had always taken her tea, mere shades darker than Natalie had been after a few weeks in the sun.

Eleanor could see Natalie, too, in the way this woman held her head, in the proud, high cheekbones, the spread of her forehead. Adam started to say something, but Eleanor interrupted. "You're Natalie's mother."

The woman jerked as if she'd been hit. For a long moment, Eleanor thought she would slam the door on them, leave them without any answers at all. Then she looked over her shoulder and stepped out onto the porch, pulling the door shut behind her. When she finally spoke, her voice was low, urgent. "I gave birth to her, if that's what you mean," she said. "I was fourteen years old and she was nothing but pain from the very beginning," she added, her words almost a whisper. She shook her head. "My husband doesn't know, or my girls. I haven't talked about it in over thirteen years. Not since that morning she showed up out of the blue, and before that, not since I sent her away the day she was born. I never nursed her," she said almost proudly.

"But . . ." Adam stepped forward. "Where was she from? Where did you send her?"

"I don't know," she said. "Somewhere up North, some white family." She looked at Adam coldly. "And she come back thinking she can just slip in here, that she was black just 'cause she found out she wasn't white. Maybe you think I sent her away so she could have a better life." She shook her head. "No—I wanted to get rid of her. Same thing I told her. So she left." The woman opened the door and waited, half-shadowed in the door frame. "Same as you all had better do unless you want to get caught in the rain. There's nothing more to tell." She took the picture from Adam and looked again. "What happened to her?" she asked after a long silence.

"She died," Eleanor said quietly. She looked up at Adam; his eyes were pushing her to say more. "My . . . husband killed her."

The woman looked up from the picture and her eyes met Eleanor's for the first time. "He loved her," she said. Eleanor nodded; the woman, too, slowly, sadly. "Well." She handed the picture to Gwen. "It's no concern of mine." When she stepped inside, they could hear the turn of a deadbolt locking the door.

The rain was beginning to fall in heavy, large drops that hit the skin in little sudden shocks of cold and wet. The tears filling Eleanor's eyes were sudden, too, surprisingly hot and, surprisingly, not of sorrow but rage. "Let's go," she said. Gwen hesitated, looking back at the door, and Eleanor began walking swiftly, blindly back toward the road. She could hear them hurrying behind her to catch up, but she did not slow and she did not turn to look. She just walked faster, feeling the cold of the wind and rain but not bothered by it. That *woman!* Her own daughter and she could not even see her blood in Natalie, could see nothing in the girl's face but a faceless father, saw nothing lost in those years and years of silence. She had merely pushed her child away and not looked back, as if the present were not balanced precariously on the past, when Eleanor had been buried under mountains of regret. It wasn't fair.

The rain was coming down hard by the time they finally climbed the hill to the house; their clothes and hair stuck to their skin, plastered there in great sheets that had to be peeled away from the body. They stood in the hallway for a minute and dripped, exhausted by the sudden absence of rain. Gwen began to shiver.

"Go put on some dry things," Adam said. "I'll build a fire."

Sitting in her grandfather's leather chair by the fire, warming her hands, Eleanor calmed a bit. Yes, Natalie's mother had been a fool to turn away from the girl. But had Eleanor really been any different? Her son had always been a mystery, and she had never tried to change that, never reached out to know more—had in fact run away from him as much as from John, the town. She had seen mothers who knew their children only as children and could not see the adults they had become. But here she was, her son a man, and she had never known him as a boy. She was not angry— she was ashamed, racked with a regret so deep it had sunk into her bones, become a part of her body.

Adam came in wearing his father's faded blue sweater, his hair toweled dry. He handed Eleanor a glass. "Here, drink this," he said. "Gwen's upstairs taking a shower."

The liquid tingled and stung her throat. "Scotch?"

"Warm you up," Adam said. "Cheers." She drank with him, finishing off the first glass. He poured another, and the second she sipped more slowly, staring at the fire. She could hear the water come on upstairs, the sound small compared to the heavy pounding of rain on the roof. The sky was dark and the wind was picking up, flinging the raindrops against the windowpanes.

Her son was sitting on the settee, the quilt from his bed wrapped around his legs. "I wish we could have gotten some answers," he said.

"Answers?"

"From that woman." He took the poker and jabbed at the wood. Glowing ashes rose off of the fire. "Natalie's mother. I'd hoped she might . . . I don't know . . . be able to help us."

"She didn't even know who Natalie was," Eleanor said. She

thought of Natalie's mother, her eyes pinched at the corners, the deep lines set into her brow, and she felt only a sorrow for what the woman had not even known she had lost. The anger had faded. The guilt, too. You could push the past down deep and cinch your belt so tight it could never seep its way up again or you could embrace it and wallow in it until you drowned. Adam balanced another log on the fire, precarious, but it held. She leaned in to him. "Why didn't you ever tell me who you were, all those years?"

"Who I was?" He set down the poker and frowned at her. "I don't understand."

"All those years you let me think you were just like your father, never really *there*, never showing your emotions."

"What do you mean, just like my father? John never hid anything." Adam sat on the floor by the fireplace, wrapping his arms around his knees. "You were always the one I couldn't understand. I don't even think I ever heard you laugh until Natalie came."

"I laughed sometimes," Eleanor said, but she wasn't arguing. She'd laughed, true, at the Sewing Circle when someone had told a funny story, or when the others were laughing at something she hadn't quite caught but could tell from the tone was a joke. She'd laughed when it was appropriate to laugh and scolded or flirted or cried when it was appropriate to scold or flirt or cry and kept her feelings to herself. And she had watched her dark, inscrutable son and never realized that he was just like her. A Blackmar, not in name perhaps, but one even so. "Give me your hand," she said. He held out his palm and she saw the Blackmar hands, the long, thin fingers almost unnaturally pale, veins faded but the tendons prominent under the skin.

"Can you read palms?" Gwen stood in the doorway, drying her hair with a thick white towel. She shook her head and her long, damp curls spilled over the floral flannel of her nightgown. "Here, let me."

Eleanor held out her hand and Gwen took it, settling in front of the fire beside Adam on the rug. "You'll have a long life," she said, tracing a finger along Eleanor's palm, "and you have a very strong, deep head line." She grinned. "Just like Adam's. It means you're both stubborn, and you think too much."

"Who, us?" Adam's wry smile peeked over Gwen's shoulder.

Gwen turned over Eleanor's hand. "You don't play the piano?" she asked. Eleanor shook her head. "With these hands, you should. I've been teaching Adam a little. His fingers are even longer than mine, and I had a span of an octave when I was eight years old." Gwen held up her own pale hand, the fingers long and thin. Like Adam's, Eleanor thought, like her own. It was a trait that would be passed down. Eleanor smiled. Red-gold curls would be braided into the Blackmars' thick, dark locks, into the family history, and in a few generations perhaps it would be a family trait as well.

"My great-grandmother played," Eleanor said. "Helena Blackmar. The one they called a witch," she added almost fondly.

"So you have witches in your family as well?" Gwen said. She turned to Adam. "You never told me."

"It's not something anyone really needs to talk about here," Eleanor said. "And then when you leave Liberty, you forget how to pass the stories on."

Adam sat on the settee and Gwen leaned against his knees. "I never really thought about it," he said. "I wasn't born a Blackmar."

"I never really told you about them," Eleanor said. "I'm sorry for that. I tried to be the way I thought I should be. The way I thought a mother should be. I never knew mine."

He nodded. "Evalie," he said, and she nodded with him.

"That was your mother?" Gwen said.

Eleanor nodded. How could one find the words to explain? Everyone knew the story of Evalie, deep down in the tangled web of the town's memory. But wasn't there something wrong in that? They were Evalie's blood—shouldn't they know more than the gossip, the scandal, the sly look, half shock and half titillation that went with the mention of her name?

"They said I looked like her, as a girl," Eleanor said. She had learned to keep quiet, so quiet and still, working on her knitting, playing with her dolls, that she would become invisible and the grown-ups would forget to whisper and say *Little pitchers have big ears*. That was how she had learned all she knew about her mother, piecing together this joke with that careless comment.

But whether she was six or eight or eleven, they had always said that she looked just like Evalie at that age. When had it stopped? A memory was tickling at the back of her brain. Thirteen, that was it, thirteen. "Oh God." She had lost her breath. "I'd forgotten. I'd forgotten."

Gwen leaned forward. "What is it? Are you all right?"

She shook her head. "No. I'd . . . the last time someone said I looked like Evalie . . . I'd forgotten that I chose not to be like her. I *chose* it." Her heart was beating fast, as fast as it had that night. "I've never told anyone about the time I met my father."

"I thought no one knew who your father was," Adam said. It was true; according to the talk, Evalie would lie down for just about anyone and stand up for just about anything.

"I know who he was," said Eleanor. "He came to see me." Her thirteenth birthday had been perhaps a week before, and she could still remember the look on her grandmother's face, disapproving and wary and sad, as if she knew something worse than Judas that made the number bad luck. "He came to see Grandfather that afternoon. I just barely caught a glimpse of him then, but I hid in the corner behind the staircase and I could hear most of what they were saying. He wanted to see me, but Grandfather sent him away." *You stole my daughter's innocence,* Grandfather had hissed. *Why would I let you touch my granddaughter?* And the young man's laughter as he said *Innocence? Her?* had sent shivers down Eleanor's spine, shivers of fear and something else too, new and as ancient as Eden. She could not tell that. Instead she smiled at another thought. "You could hear everything from that closet under the stairs. I'd forgotten that."

Adam smiled with her. "I used to hide there, too," he said. "I suppose every child who's lived in this house has. Once, I even found carved into the wood in the back corner *Henry Blackmar, Aged 12.*" Gwen looked up at him curiously. "My great-grandfather," he said.

Eleanor laughed. "I should have guessed that you hid there too. You forget so much. . . ." There was so much she hadn't thought about, hadn't remembered. The place under the stairs, her grandparents. Even now she was remembering them wrong, she knew, remembering them as they were when they died. They would have been much younger when she was thirteen—her grandmother's hair still raven-black except for one streak at the temple she always brushed at absently as if trying to smooth it away. Grandfather would have been robust, not at all the thin, tired man he became in the last years of his life—but she could not picture them in her mind as she must have seen them then. But the man who stood with them that day in the parlor was still preserved perfectly in her mind, and she could remember the exact shade of his blond hair, not the pale corn-silk color she had always envied on Bonnie Fay, but rich and gold like the ripe corn itself.

"So was that all you saw of your father?" Gwen said. "When you were hiding under the stairs?"

"He came back that night," she said. Her heart was beating fast from the memory and the shock of actually speaking it out loud. But she had begun and she couldn't stop now. It had been— Lord, over thirty years ago now? As she had undressed for bed that night, she had thought about the mysterious man, who would only have been seventeen when she was born. She had caught a glimpse of herself in the reflection of the window, a slim, white figure with the barest hint of curves softening the hips, rounding the calves of her child-leg, and wondered if it was true that she looked like Evalie. Chestnut, they had always called Evalie's hair, which was curly, constantly tousled, as if to match her permanently flushed cheeks. "He came to my window, climbed up, and tapped at the glass."

"And you let him in," Adam said.

Eleanor nodded and sipped her drink. She did not meet Adam's eyes, though there was nothing condemning in his voice, no blame. "I let him in."

"What did he say?"

"Nothing at first. He was breathing hard from the climb. He looked frightened. There was a noise downstairs and he looked for a minute like he was going to jump right out again." There had been a peculiar light in his eyes. The only light in the room had been from the bedside lamp, and she had seen her body cast in shadow against him, the hazy frame of her thin nightgown almost nonexistent. In the shadow, her mousy hair had seemed chestnut, her cheeks flushed in excitement and fear. "I told him to come closer." She drew in her breath, remembering how she had tilted her head so that her hair fell over her cheek, exposing her neck. She had flirted, smiling mysteriously, making that light flash in his eyes. "And he was coming toward me and that's when he said, *You're just like Evalie.*" Eleanor fell silent. Just like Evalie, the wild one. Oh God, what she could have been!

"What did you do?"

She finished off the last swallow of scotch. "I screamed." She set the glass down and stared into the fire. "I screamed and Grandfather came with his shotgun—that very one hanging above the fireplace right now." She could still hear the echo of her scream, the terrified, tortured noise, the long banshee wail and the horror and betrayal in her father's eyes. She had tried to explain, to apologize, but all of her will, her words had been spent in the scream. She did not know if she would even speak again. "My father jumped out the window and was never heard from again." Adam stood and collected the glasses to take to the kitchen. Eleanor was silent, staring at the fire.

"Sounds like the end of a ghost story," Gwen said quietly. " 'And he was never heard from again. . . .' "

Eleanor nodded. She stared into the coals until her eyes could see the bright spots even when she looked away. There was something in the corner of her sight that disappeared when she looked at it straight on, the way the past had appeared to her as a child. She blinked, and the shadowy figures disappeared. "Enough ghost stories," she said.

They could hear Adam moving around in the kitchen, rinsing the glasses in the sink. Eleanor drew the lap blanket around her. The alcohol and the heat from the fire had made her sleepy, and she settled deeper into the chair. The leather was old and discolored but still comforting, and she pulled her feet up under her, settling in like a bird in a well-feathered nest. Gwen yawned and curled up on the settee, wrapping the quilt around her like a great cape.

Adam did not return for a long time, and when he did, he stood and watched them from the doorway before he moved into the circle of light cast by the fire. He kneeled before Gwen as if about to offer a proposal, but instead held out something cupped in his hands, unrolling it into her lap.

"My scarf," she said. "Where did you find it?"

But he merely lay his head in her lap with the scarf. In a moment, she let go of the question and began to stroke his hair. A soft quiet settled over them, rounded by the sound of the rain, the occasional crackle from the fireplace. Eleanor drew the lap blanket around her and settled into the quiet, watching the firelight turn into gold the tears striping Adam's face.

*S*omewhere far away, a cock crowed. Eleanor blinked. The sound of the rain had stopped. The fire, too, had died—not even coals were left glowing. How long had she been asleep? Something had pulled her awake—not the sounds of dawn or the chill in the air, but a fear so strong and sudden it would not let her sleep. The entire house was waiting, tense. *Waiting for what?* Adam and Gwen were gone, and for a moment, that panicked her. She forced herself to calm down. Of course, they had probably gone up to bed long ago. What time was it anyway? She glanced at the grandfather clock, but it was still and silent, had stopped at some two-fifteen long past; but a pale, predawn light edged the windows in silver. She gathered the blanket around her like a robe and made her way to the kitchen for a cup of tea. There were so many things to decide. What was she to do? She remembered Adam kneeling at his wife's feet, defeated, while the memories waited, dancing in the firelight. She didn't believe Adam was really afraid for his wife's safety. Perhaps he wanted Eleanor to take her away just so he could stop dreading the day Gwen would leave on her own. Was it any wonder? Fear fit their family like an old sweater, passed down though it was worn thin at the elbows, unraveling at the seams.

She could take Gwen to New York, to any number of places, really, and teach her to live as Eleanor had lived the past thirteen years. Quiet, nondescript, fearful of being found. A life with few friends and precious little love, being afraid to feel because feeling anything might mean regretting everything. She could not imagine Gwen living that life. Or Natalie either, come to think of it. She thought of what Adam had said, *If you had sent Natalie away* . . . then what? Where would she have gone? Back to her people up North, back to the fiancé who loved her but not the color her skin turned in the sun? Back to the whorehouse, to be found and probably killed by John there, but at least Eleanor wouldn't have had to see it, face the horror in her own house, her own husband. No, there was only one certainty: if she had sent Natalie away, she would never have gone herself. John would not have killed Eleanor—that sort of man only killed what he couldn't live without—but she would have cooked his meals and washed his clothes and had a pie on the windowsill every afternoon for the rest of his life, and maybe by the time he'd finally died, she would have forgotten how to feel anything, even fear. She could not regret what she had done. *I'm sorry, Natalie*, she whispered. The very sound of the running water sounded like Natalie laughing as she tossed cherries up and caught them in her mouth.

She lit the stove and set the heavy kettle down on the burner. She could still hear Natalie's laughter, though, far away. Eleanor went cold. How much had she had to drink the night before? Anything at all was more than she normally had. She sank to the floor and closed her eyes, pulling herself in tight, trying to hold herself together. There were voices arguing at the top of the stairs. She began to tremble, and drew the quilt around her, forcing herself to breathe, breathing the air of thirteen years before.

She could not make out the words but she could hear the woman's voice, angry, frightened. Then the man's, saying *No!* or perhaps *Go!* and then over and over again *I love you. I love you. I love you.* It was not her memory, and it could not be blinked away. The voice sounded like John's, but it was Adam at the top of the stairs. Eleanor shut her eyes and opened the door.

Even with her eyes closed, Eleanor could see them there. She never saw the figures at the top of the staircase all those years ago, but she remembered them anyway, moving in and out of the sliver of light cast through the bedroom door. In her memory, Natalie is light, lighter than a flower, a butterfly. The slightest touch will easily send her flying. She will not fall. Why did she fall, then? She must have jumped. *Whatever it is that you've got, there's just enough for one.* She could not fall, she was too light. She must have flown away. What had she said to Eleanor? *Take it.*

Eleanor opened her eyes. Gwen and Adam were mere shadows at the top of the stairs. "Take it," Gwen said. The freedom, the chance to escape, she held it out before her as a gift, a gift only her pain could give. She could not stay out of the sun; it pulled her too strongly. It was too dear. "Take it," she said again.

"It's not mine," Eleanor whispered from the doorway. "It doesn't belong to me. Do you understand? I need to find my own." Neither of them seemed aware of her at all. The girl laughed that high, clear laugh. Natalie's laugh. Gwen pulled herself from Adam's grip. *No!* he cried. He reached for her wrists, holding them tight. She moved toward the edge of the staircase. Eleanor wanted to call out to stop her, but she didn't know which name to cry; only a strangled animal noise emerged from her throat, half-smothered by a sob. Gwen twisted her wrist free from Adam's grip and they struggled there. He raised a hand to strike her.

"Adam!" called Eleanor. His hand froze, hovering in the air as if frozen there.

"Oh God," he said. He let go of Gwen and covered his face with his hands. "Oh God."

Freed from Adam's grip, Gwen fled. They watched paralyzed as she began to fall. Time slowed, and she hovered in the air a long time, lighter than a feather, lighter than flame. Eleanor froze, her mouth half open in a silent cry. Tears hung on Adam's cheeks. Then the bubble of memory broke, and Gwen fell.

Adam's hands fell away from his face. In an instant, he rose up, reaching for Gwen. He leaped after her, catching her in the air, wrapping himself around her. From where Eleanor stood, the fall seemed to take a long time, the air thick as water with thirteen years of waiting, expecting this. It was Adam's body that hit the edge of the bottom step, his mouth that let out a tiny cry of pain, a tendril of blood trickling from his split lip in the rose-gold light of the sweet early morning. And it was his voice that spoke first, whispering to his wife, who nodded, suddenly awake, suddenly afraid. She clutched her stomach, clutched her husband to her.

Eleanor went to them, sobbing, though not from any emotion she could name, watching the mass of limbs unfolding like tangled marionettes.

"Gwen's all right," Adam said. He was laughing, crying. "I . . . kept her safe." He looked into Gwen's eyes. "I love you," he said. Streaks of sunlight lit over them. Outside, the birds were calling, declaring it morning, shrieking to one another that the storm had gone.

Far away, a forgotten kettle whistled.

$\mathscr{F}$lowers bloomed after the rains; the sun, too, with a boldness that did not rule out any further showers, but still stated unequivocally that Spring Was Here. It was a day that made sorrow impossible; even here in the cemetery, watching Gwen lay flowers on the small, unmarked grave, Eleanor could not cry. She tried, but the body there under the earth seemed disconnected from the soul she had loved. She looked at the solemn granite gravestones, but her attention kept being drawn instead to the dandelions growing between them, to the bees darting in and out of the clover, to the feel of the sun on her face, to life.

Gwen pulled away from the grave and stood by Eleanor, putting an arm around her waist, leaning her head on the older woman's shoulder. She was smiling as well, Eleanor saw. "Do you want to stay?" she asked.

Gwen shook her head. "Adam," she said softly. And though he could not possibly have heard her from where he was standing, he looked up and waved—an awkward gesture with his wrist in the cast. He winced and staggered, exaggeratedly miming the weight of the cast. Gwen laughed and went to him. They spoke for a few minutes, their heads close together, their eyes bright. Gwen touched his cheek with her hand and he turned his face and playfully grabbed her finger in his teeth. They both laughed.

He was lucky to be alive after that fall down the stairs. "You've got your guardian angel earning its keep, son," Dr. Breedlove had said, arriving that morning to set Adam's wrist in a splint. "Those stairs can be murder." The doctor had met Eleanor's eyes then, with a look that was both significant and kindly.

"I just want you to know," he'd said before he left the house,

"I know why you left. I saw what John did to that girl—I was the one who signed the death certificate. And I think you did the right thing, and there are plenty more in this town who feel the same way, though we aren't always the loudest ones speaking." He extended a hand to Eleanor. "You're welcome here."

Eleanor took his hand and met his eyes, clear and pale blue, young under the thatch of silver-gray hair. "Thank you," she said. "But . . . there's so much more about her, about why . . ." She shook her head and he squeezed her hand. "That's not the whole story."

He put on his hat and picked up his bag. "Well, I hope I'll have a chance to hear the whole story sometime," he said. "I'd like that. But I can tell you the end of it, at least." And he'd told her of the unmarked grave in the cemetery where they had buried Natalie's body. It was a bit away from the others, a bit less well maintained. Leaves fell on it in the autumn, and in the summer it was covered in wildflowers. Standing over it now, though, watching the bees in the clover blossoms, Eleanor thought Natalie would have wanted it this way.

Gwen was walking toward her again. "Adam is going to stay a bit," she said. "He says we should go on home." She lowered her voice. "I think he wants to visit his father's grave."

Eleanor nodded. She had come out to John's grave herself three weeks before, the morning after Adam had broken his wrist saving Gwen. She had been planning to yell at the grave in anger, laugh in triumph at his ghost, which hadn't gotten her son after all. But by the time she'd gotten to the cemetery, the rage was gone, and she merely sat there for a long, long time, leaning her head sadly against the lonely stone. It had been enough. She took Gwen's hand. "I understand."

They walked in silence for a while, enjoying the sun, the first truly warm day of the year. Eleanor let Gwen lead her away from the main road and they walked instead through pastures and beside the fields. Some were already planted, long rows of yellow-green seedlings pinstriping the soil. Others had just been plowed, leaving the rich after-rain smell of turned earth in the air. When they reached the edge of the lake, Gwen stopped. "Would you like to take the long way around?" she asked. "It's so beautiful today I don't think I could bear to be indoors."

Eleanor smiled. "Well, Anna McKay is coming at three—she's promised to give me another driving lesson—but I have time for a walk before then."

Gwen sat on a rock and began to unlace her shoes. "Learning to drive. Does that mean you've decided to stay in Liberty?"

"Perhaps," Eleanor said. "For a while. Until I decide there's someplace I'd rather be." She watched as Gwen pulled off her socks and wiggled her toes in the mud at the edge of the water. "That's a good idea," she said, pulling off her own boots, rolling her slacks up to her knees.

They splashed in the shallow water for a while, laughing. It was colder than Eleanor had expected, and slippery along the banks. By the time they scrambled back up into the grass, Eleanor was out of breath and muddier than she'd been since she was a child. She brushed at the dirt on her legs, and Gwen collapsed in the grass beside her, giggling. "Hey, careful," Eleanor said. "I'm an old lady, remember?"

"Not you," laughed Gwen. "Not yet." She gathered up her shoes. "Remember?" She took Eleanor's hand and made an elaborate show of studying its lines "You have a long future, filled with happiness and family . . . and look!" She pointed to a line deep on the left side of Eleanor's palm. "Even love."

"At my age?" Eleanor traced the line with her finger and smiled. "I guess I'm not too old to marry again."

"That doctor likes you," Gwen said. Eleanor raised her eyebrows in surprise and Gwen grinned. "Or is he too old for you?" she teased.

"Andrew Breedlove? Don't let the hair fool you—it's been silver since he was twenty-five. He's actually nearly eight years younger than I am. When I got married, he was still catching frogs in the stream." And imitating their croaks, she remembered. Andy Breedlove had listened, really listened, until he could give any animal call or bird cry in the county.

"Well?" Gwen skipped a little and sing-songed, "He's coming in a couple of weeks to take off Adam's cast."

Eleanor shook her head. Lord, was she even blushing? "Oh no." She was laughing again. "No." She held Gwen's hand and they walked around the perimeter of the lake, arms swinging

202 / MYRLIN A. HERMES

like schoolgirls', their shoes dangling by the laces from their hands.

Walking along, Eleanor watched Gwen from the corner of her eye. How much of Natalie had been left behind in her? Enough to make walking with her, giggling like girls, seem the most natural thing in the world. But she wasn't Natalie. Eleanor felt a thread of grief run through her, like something too cold she had swallowed. Gwen looked up, alarmed, and squeezed her hand, but said nothing.

"I keep thinking," Eleanor said. "When Natalie's . . . presence . . . was there . . . it was frightening, but she was *there*. It was like part of her hadn't died. But it didn't seem like her spirit was at the grave. I couldn't feel her there. . . ." Eleanor shook her head. "I miss her."

"I know." Gwen pushed her hair back from her face and looked at the sky.

Eleanor nodded, and they walked on in silence. They had gone nearly halfway around the lake before she looked up suddenly. "Wait," she said. "We shouldn't go by here."

Ahead in the distance stood the tall plantation house. It had been purple when it had last been painted, long ago. Now its graying paint was peeling badly and morning-glory vines had crawled up the railings so that the entire front porch was hidden in a slither of green leaves and lavender blossoms.

"Why not?" asked Gwen. "It's a beautiful old place. Let's see if we can visit."

Eleanor shook her head, but she found she was laughing, too. She didn't know what to say—she wouldn't have had to tell anyone from Liberty that it was a place nice women didn't go near. But what was she worried about now, her reputation? "Sure," she heard herself say, "why not?"

An old woman was kneeling in the front yard, planting daffodils out of a tray at her side. Her gray hair was still streaked with strawberry-blond, and she'd pulled it into a casual knot at the top of her head. When she saw Gwen and Eleanor approaching, she wiped her hands on her overalls and smiled a smile that made her face nothing but wrinkles, split with a half-moon of bright teeth. They had to smile back, and she waved them closer.

"I know you," she said, waving her trowel at Eleanor. "You're the Blackmar girl. The one Natalie left me for. I should have known you'd be coming by."

"What do you mean?" Gwen pulled away from Eleanor and sat beside the old woman in the grass, drawing her arms around her knees. "You knew Natalie?"

The woman ignored her question. "Ah, what beautiful feet you have, my dear," she said. She patted Gwen's muddy foot with a surprisingly youthful, graceful hand. "There was a time I would have polished those toenails and had fetishists lining up out the door. The hair color is real, yes?"

Gwen nodded. The old woman sighed and pulled Gwen's hair up into a pile on her head. "It's girls like you who make me wish I was still in the business." She stopped suddenly and turned Gwen's head to check her profile, then peered closely at her pupils. She pulled Gwen closer and felt her forehead, then smiled. "Are you pregnant, my dear?"

Gwen blushed and looked at Eleanor, who raised an eyebrow. "Am I?" she said. "I thought it was too soon to tell. I'm only a few days late. . . ."

"Mother Agnes?" A woman appeared through a hole in the mass of vines covering the porch. Her dishwater hair was pulled back into a loose ponytail and a little towheaded boy sat against her hip. "Who's here?"

"Some friends of Natalie's," Mother Agnes called. She turned back to Eleanor and Gwen. "After Natalie left, the business just sort of faded away. A few of the girls stayed on, though, to look after me."

"Natalie?" The woman said. She set the boy down and he ran circles around the yard, flying a little wooden boat through the air. "That's a name I haven't heard in years."

"I told you those roses meant something." Mother Agnes stood slowly and brushed the dirt from her knees. She walked around to the back of the house, motioning for them to follow her. "My roses haven't bloomed in nearly fifteen years," she said. "And then a couple of weeks ago, overnight . . ." She waved her hand at a hedge behind the house. It was covered with huge yellow roses, and more buds peeked through the spaces between the blossoms. "There," she said. "At first I thought it might be a trick my Charlie was playing." She smiled into the distance for a minute, then turned back to Gwen and Eleanor to explain. "My husband, Charlie, passed in 1917, but he still pays me a visit now and again and sometimes he forgets I'm no longer a girl. He always loved to tease. Even more so now."

"But it wasn't . . . Charlie," Eleanor said. Mother Agnes smiled.

"No, dear. It was Natalie. Before she left, she told me she'd find a way to come back some day."

Eleanor slowly reached and touched a sun-yellow rose. It quivered under her hands. "She said the same thing to me," Eleanor whispered. The roses covered the garden with a gentle, hopeful scent. A spring scent.

Mother Agnes nodded. "So you see," she said, "she's coming back."

Eleanor's eyes were filling with tears. "Thank you," she said. She turned away, not wanting to let these strangers see her cry. "We should go." She pulled away and went down to the lake again, where she looked at her own reflection in the water until her eyes were so blurred with the tears running down her cheeks that she couldn't see herself.

Gwen came running down after her. "What happened?" she said, but Eleanor just shook her head and kept smiling through her tears. "Look," Gwen said.

A huge old fish had made its way into the shallow water at the edge of the lake. Half of its body poked above the surface, its scales quicksilver brilliant in the sun. A fire-fish. It flicked its tail and the lake rippled. They stopped at the edge of the water and watched it. Eleanor could feel her tears drying on her cheeks.

"Do you suppose it's stuck there?" she said. It was a huge old fish and the hook scars in its mouth gave it a mean or perhaps amused look. "Maybe we should try to help it."

Gwen took the hem of her skirt in her hand and stepped into the mud. She reached out to push the fish out of the shallow mud. "I touched it," she said. She held up her hand and a drop of silver ran down and swirled into her palm. "Maybe if I can get closer." She took a step forward and reached for the fish again, but seeing her movement it turned and without even a ripple slipped away into the dark water.

*S*ometimes, at night, Gwen can hear the baby dreaming. Sometimes it is a rabbit, sometimes a creature from the sea. Once it decided it was a star and burned so hot and bright inside her belly she could not sleep and lay awake all night, watching the soft glow underneath her skin. Adam is afraid, afraid what happened the night the baby was conceived, afraid of whose soul might be waiting to be born. But she can feel its heart, learning from her own how to beat. It can feel its father come into the room and it knows how to laugh. She looks out the window, at the flowers asleep in the moonlight. She looks to the sky, past the sky, past the stars. She smiles out at them.

*T*hey are in the garden. All three of them are there. It has become one of those fine late June mornings when the summer stretches out before you like the world, all yours, filled with all of the possibilities. Men see flowers sprung up overnight on the side of the road, the suddenness of them catching their eye as much as the petals, yellow and red and purple against the green, green grass. Then, with impulse as sudden as the blossoms, the men tromp through the mud to pull them up and carry them back home to their wives. And the wives lean against doorways and look at the blue, blue sky, and when their husbands come in, the suddenness and the petals are so bright they do not see boots trailing mud on the floor.

A pair of yellow butterflies chase each other in a courting dance. A third joins, struggling to keep up. Eleanor is moving the earth with her hands. She gathers the rich, brown loam into a pile, then makes a place for a seed. She has already planted sage, and Gwen's thyme has come up so strong and full, they'll have more than they ever need. Perhaps she'll take some around to the neighbors the way other women take pies. It would be good to meet the neighbors again, to reestablish the ties, perhaps to talk about starting a new Sewing Circle.

Tomorrow. Today Dr. Breedlove is coming by again, though Adam's wrist has been out of the cast for weeks. Perhaps she'll bake him a pie, if she has time. Right now she is planting tomatoes. She will watch them sprout, set up the little stakes to help them grow. And at the end of the summer, when the fruit has come, the whole garden will be filled with their spicy, sweet aroma. Perhaps she will plant watermelons next. There are no limits. Nothing is impossible. After decades of flowering, the garden will finally bear fruit.

She looks over to the cherry tree. Adam has set up an easel and a chair, and he is painting a picture of the house. He chooses his colors, white and gold for the sunlight reflecting off the windows, green and yellow for the rosebushes. He cannot choose the wildflower colors; they choose him, brighter and more varied than his palette knows. His wrist has healed beautifully, though it still tells him when it's going to rain. It won't rain today. He paints his mother, her purple straw hat casting a shadow over the little mounds of earth. She is smiling at him.

She is smiling because she sees what he does not, that Gwen, her dress still dripping from her swim in the creek, has crept up behind him with water cupped in her hands. When she splashes it on him, he jumps up, and for a moment, he looks as if he is going to be angry, but instead he laughs and begins to chase her around the garden. Her pregnancy has just begun to show, and with the weight of the water in her hair and clothes, she is no match for his speed, but he is not really trying to catch her. They make it an obstacle course, running around trees and hiding behind corners of the house. When they pass by her, Eleanor takes up the chase. Her hat blows off, and she feels the sun on her face. Her hair is growing long again, and somehow curly after all these years; it blows out behind her, loose and free, gray-streaked and all, and she feels young.

When the girls from town come by, shoes slung over shoulders, half-naked in the heat and the anticipation of the cool, sweet water, they see three grown-ups, laughing as if their every wish has come true, crazy in love, chasing circles and circles of joy through a garden, ripe and blooming with everything.